Acclaim for *Same Place, Same Things*

"Strikes notes true and clear.... Robustly local in its settings, speech, and folkways, *Same Place, Same Things* creates a vividly realized milieu."

—Rand Richards Cooper, *Commonweal*

"Simply as great as anything Flannery O'Connor or Anton Chekhov ever wrote about their corners of the world."

—Hope Norman Coulter, *The Arkansas Democrat Gazette*

"Captivating.... [These stories] remind us that it is compassion and grace that make ordinary life bearable."

—Alice Lankford Elmore, *Southern Living*

"A terrific debut collection from a Louisiana writer whose stylish, sympathetic understanding of working-class sensibilities and Cajun culture gives his work a flavor and universality unique among contemporary writers.... Moving and memorable.... The gifted Gautreaux harkens back to the early work of Flannery O'Connor."

—*Kirkus Reviews*

"Memorable.... Gautreaux's empathy for his characters strings a shimmering thread of hope and redemption throughout these dramatic, compelling tales."

—*Publishers Weekly*

"Delightful.... More than any book I've ever read, even more than John Kennedy Toole's masterpiece *A Confederacy of Dunces*, *Same Place, Same Things* captures south Louisiana.... You will be disappointed when you turn the last page, and you will join me in waiting impatiently for the next book by Tim Gautreaux."

—Laurie Parker, *Bookpage*

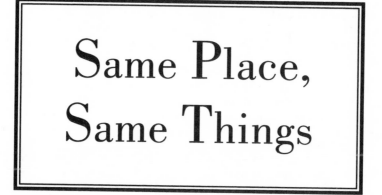

Same Place, Same Things

Tim Gautreaux

Picador USA

New York

Grateful acknowledgment is made to the following publications in which these stories first appeared:
The Atlantic Monthly: "Same Place, Same Things," "Died and Gone to Vegas"; *Story:* "People on the Empty Road," "Waiting for the Evening News"; *Stories:* "The Courtship of Merlin LeBlanc"; *The Standard:* "Navigators of Thought"; *GQ:* "The Bug Man," "Little Frogs in a Ditch"; *The Crescent Review:* "License to Steal"; *The Virginia Quarterly Review:* "Floyd's Girl"; *St. Anthony Messenger:* "Returnings"; *Harper's:* "Deputy Sid's Gift."

Picador® is a U.S. registered trademark and is used by St. Martin's Press under license from Pan Books Limited.

Design by Ellen R. Sasahara

Library of Congress Cataloging-in-Publication Data

Gautreaux, Tim.
    Same place, same things / by Tim Gautreaux.—1st ed.
      p.   cm.
    Contents: Same place, same things—Waiting for the evening news—Died and gone to Vegas—The courtship of Merlin LeBlanc—Navigators of thought—People on the empty road—The bug man—Little frogs in a ditch—License to steal—Floyd's girl—Returnings—Deputy Sid's gift.
    ISBN 0-312-16994-9
    1. Louisiana—Social life and customs—Fiction. 2. Manners and customs—Fiction. I. Title.
  PS3557.A954S26   1996
  813'.54—dc20   96-19622
                                                                   CIP

First Picador USA Edition: September 1997

10 9 8 7 6 5 4 3 2 1

For my wife, Winborne, and our two sons, Robert and Thomas. I would also like to thank the National Endowment for the Arts. I suppose I could have thanked them first, but they haven't ever baked me biscuits.

Contents

Same Place,
Same Things

Same Place, Same Things

T he pump repairman was cautious. He saw the dry rut in the lane and geared the truck down so he could take it through slow. The thin wheels of his ancient Ford bounced heavily, the road ridge scraping the axles. A few blackbirds charged out of the dead brush along the road and wheeled through the sky like a thrown handful of gravel. He wondered how far down the farm lane the woman lived. When she had called him at the tourist court, she had not been confident about giving directions, seeming unsure where her own house was. On both sides of the road, fields of strawberries baked in the sun. It had not rained, the locals told him, for seven weeks.

Leafless branches reached out to snatch away his headlights. Billows of dust flew up behind the truck like a woman's face powder, settling on roadside dewberry bushes that resembled thickened fountains of lava. It was an awful drought.

After a while he arrived at a weatherboard farmhouse set behind a leaning barbed-wire fence. He pulled up and got out. No one came from the house, so he slammed the door of the truck and coughed loudly. He had been in this part of the country long enough to know that the farm people did not want you on their porches unless you were a relative or a neighbor. Now, in the Depression, life was so hard for them they trusted almost nobody. Finally he blew the truck's horn and was rewarded with a movement at one of the windows. In half a minute a woman in a thin cotton housedress came out.

"You the pump man?" she asked.

"Yes, ma'am. Name's Harry Lintel."

She looked him over as though he were a goat she might or might not buy. Walking to the edge of her porch, she looked back toward the field behind the house. "If you walk this trail here for a while, you'll find my husband trying to fix the pump." He did not like the way she made a face when she said "husband." He was uneasy around women who did not like their men. She walked off the porch and through the fifteen feet of thistle and clover that served as a front lawn, moving carefully toward the pump repairman, who regarded her warily. Poor people made him nervous. He was poor himself, at least as far as money goes, but he was not hangdog and spiritless like many of the people he'd met in this part of the state, beaten down and ruined inside by hard times. She looked at his eyes. "How old you think I am?"

She seemed about forty, four years younger than he was, but with farm women you could never tell. He looked at her sandy hair and gray eyes. She was thin, but something about the way she looked at him suggested toughness. "Lady, I've come to fix a pump. What kind do you have and what's wrong with it?"

"My husband, he'll be back in a minute. He'll know what all you need to find out. What I want to know is where you're from. I ain't heard nobody around here talk like you in a while." She had her hair tied back in a loose knot and reached up to touch it delicately. This motion caught his eye. He guessed she might be closer to thirty-five.

Harry Lintel put a hand in his right front pocket and leaned back against the door of his truck. Taking off his straw hat, he threw it over his shoulder into the front seat. "I'm from Missouri," he said, running a hand through a clump of short, brassy hair.

Her expression was still one of intense evaluation. "Ain't there no pump work in Missouri?" she asked. "Or did your woman run you off?"

"My wife died," he said. "As for pump work, when it's dry and the local pump repairmen can't keep up with their work, or there ain't any pump repairmen, I come around and take up the slack."

He looked around her at the peeling house and its broken panes patched with cardboard.

"So why ain't you where you belong, taking up slack?"

He looked at her hard. That last remark showed some wit, something he had not seen in a woman for a while. "Where's your husband, lady? I've got cash jobs waiting for me up Highway Fifty-one."

"Keep your pants on. He'll be here, I said." She folded her arms and came a step closer. "I'm just curious why anyone would come to this part of Louisiana from somewheres else."

"I follow the droughts," he said, straightening up and walking along the fence to where it opened into a rutted drive. The woman followed him, sliding her hands down her hips to smooth her dress. "Last week I was in Texas. Was doing a good trade until an all-night rain came in from Mexico and put me out of business. Wasn't much of a pumping situation after that, and the local repairmen could keep things going." He looked down the path as far as he could see along the field of limp plants. "Month before that I was in north Georgia. Before that I fixed pumps over in Alabama. Those people had a time with their green peppers. Where the devil's your old man?"

"I never see anyone but my husband and two or three buyers that come back in here to deal with him." She began to look at his clothes, and this made him uneasy, because he knew she saw that they were clean and not patched. He wore a khaki shirt and trousers. Perhaps no one she knew wore unpatched clothes. Her housedress looked like it had been made from a faded window curtain. "Texas," she said. "I saw your ad in the paper and I figured you were a traveling man."

"No, ma'am," he said. "I'm a man who travels." He saw she did not understand that there was a difference. She seemed desperate and bored, but many people he met were that way. Very few were curious about where he came from, however. They cared only that he was Harry Lintel, who could fix any irrigation pump or engine ever made.

He walked into the field toward the tree line a quarter mile off, and the woman went quickly to the house. He saw a wire strung from the house into a chinaberry tree, and then through a long file of willows edging a ditch, and figured this led to an electric pump. He was almost disappointed that the woman wasn't following him.

As he walked, he looked around at the farm. It was typical of the worst. He came up on a Titan tractor stilted on wood blocks in the weeds, its head cracked. Behind it was a corroded disk harrow, which could still have been useful had it been taken care of. In the empty field to his right stood two cows suffering from the bloat.

He was sweating through his shirt by the time he reached a thin stand of bramble-infested loblolly edging the field. Two hundred feet down the row of trees, a man hunched over an electric motor, his back to the repairman. Calling out to him, Lintel walked in that direction, but the other man did not respond—he was absorbed in close inspection of a belt drive, the pump repairman guessed. The farmer was sprawled on a steel grid that hung over an open well. Harry walked up and said hello, but the farmer said nothing. He seemed to be asleep, even though he was out in the sun and his undershirt was wet as a dishcloth. Harry stooped down and looked over the pump and the way it was installed. He saw that it was bolted to the grid without insulation. Two stray wires dangled into the well. He watched for the rise and fall of the man's body, but the man was not breathing. Kneeling down, Harry touched the back of his knuckles to the steel grid. There was no shock, so he grabbed the man by his arms and pulled him off the motor, turning him over. He was dead, without a doubt: electrocuted. His fingers were burned, and a dark stain ran down his pants leg. He felt the man's neck for a pulse and, finding none, sat there for a long time, studying the man's broad, slick face, a face angry and stupid even in death. He looked around at the sorry farm as though it were responsible, then got up and walked back to the farmhouse.

The woman was sitting in a rocker on the porch, staring off into a parched, fallow field. She looked at the repairman and smiled, just barely.

Harry Lintel rubbed his chin. "You got a phone?"

"Nope," she said, smoothing her hair down with her right hand. "There's one at the store out on Fifty-one."

He did not want to tell her, feeling that it would be better for someone else to break the news. "You've got a lady friend lives around here?"

She looked at him sharply, her gray eyes round. "What you want to know that for?"

"I've got my reasons," he said. He began to get into his big dusty truck, trying to act as though nothing had happened. He wanted to put some distance between himself and her coming sorrow.

"The first house where you turned in, there's Mary. But she don't have no phone."

"See you in a few minutes," he said, cranking up the truck.

At the highway he found Mary and told her to go back and tell the woman that her husband was dead out by the pump. The old woman simply nodded, went back into her house, and got her son to go with her. Her lack of concern bothered him. Didn't she care about the death of her neighbor?

At the store he called the sheriff and waited. He rode with the deputies back to the farmhouse and told them what he knew. The lawmen stood over the body, looked up at the dry sky, and told the pump repairman to go back to his business, that they would take care of everything.

He and one of the deputies walked out of the field past the farmhouse, and he tried not to look at the porch as he passed, but he could not keep himself from listening. He heard nothing—no crying, no voices heavy with muted passion. The two women were on the porch step, talking calmly, as though they were discussing the price of berries. The widow watched him carefully as he got into the police car. He thought he detected a trace of perfume in the air and looked around inside the gritty sedan for its source.

That day he repaired six engines, saving little farms from turning back to sand. The repairs were hard ones that no one else could manage: broken timing gears, worn-out governors, cracked water jackets. At least one person on each farm asked him if he was the one who had found the dead man, and when he admitted that he was, each sullen farmer backed off and let him work alone. Late in the afternoon he was heating an engine head in his portable forge, watching the hue of the metal so that he could judge whether the temperature was right for brazing. He waited for the right color to rise like the blush on a woman's cheek, and when it did, he sealed a complex crack with a clean streak of molten brass. A wizened Italian farmer watched him like a chicken hawk, his arms folded across a washed-out denim shirt. "It's no gonna work," he said.

But when, near dusk, Harry pulled the flywheel and the engine sprang to life with a heavy, thudding exhaust, turning up a rill of sunset-tinged water into the field, the farmer cracked a faint smile. "If you couldna fixed it, we'da run you out the parish."

Harry began to clean his hands with care. "Why?"

"Stranger find a dead man, that's bad luck."

"It's better I found him than his wife, isn't it?"

The farmer poked a few bills at Harry, turned, and began walking toward his packing shed. "Nothin' surprise that woman," he said.

It was eight-thirty when he got back to the Bell Pepper Tourist Court, a collection of six pink stucco cabins with a large oval window embedded in each. The office, which also contained a small café, was open, but he was too tired to eat. He sat on his jittery bed, staring across the highway to the railroad, where a local passenger train trundled by, its whistle singing for a crossing. Beyond this was yet another truck farm, maybe twelve acres punctuated by a tin-roof shack. He wondered how many other women were stuck back in the woods living without husbands. The widow of the electrocuted man didn't even have children to take her mind off her loneliness. He had that. He had gotten married when he was seventeen and had raised two daughters and a son. He was now forty-four and on his own, his wife having died five years before. The small Missouri town he was raised in couldn't keep him provided with work, so he had struck out, roaming the South and the Southwest, looking for machines that nobody else could repair.

He stared through an oval window at his truck. At least he could move around and meet different people, being either sorry to leave them or glad to get away, depending. He gazed fondly at the Ford, its stake body loaded with blacksmith's tongs, welding tools, a portable forge, and boxes of parts, wrenches, sockets, coal, hardies, gasket material, all covered with a green tarp slung over the wooden sides. It could take him anywhere, and with his tools he could fix anything but the weather.

The next morning at dawn he headed out for the first job of the day, noticing that the early sky was like a piece of sheet metal heated to a blue-gray color. He pulled up to a farmhouse and a small man wearing a ponderous mustache came out from around back, cursing. Harry Lintel threw his hat into the truck and ran his hands through his hair. He had never seen people who disliked strangers so much. The little farmer spat on the Ford's tire and told him to drive into the field behind the farmhouse. "My McCormick won't throw no spark," he said.

Harry turned to get under way, but over the Ford's hood he saw, two hundred yards off, the back of a woman's head moving above the weeds in an idle field. "Who's that?" he asked, pointing two fields over.

The farmer craned his neck but could not recognize the figure, who disappeared behind a brier patch between two farms. "I don't know," the farmer said, scratching his three-day beard, "but a woman what walk around like that with nothing better to do is thinking up trouble." He pointed to Harry. "When a woman thinks too long, look out! Now, get to work, you."

The day turned hot as a furnace and his skin flamed with sweat. By noon he had worked on three machines within a half mile of one another. From little farms up and down Highway 51 he could hear the thud and pop of pump engines. He was in a field of berries finishing up with a balky International, when he saw a woman walking along the railroad embankment with a basket in the crook of her right arm. It was the wife of the dead farmer. He waited until she was several rows away and then looked up at her. She met his gaze head-on, her eyes the color of dull nickel. He admitted to himself then and there that it scared him, the way she looked at him. Harry Lintel could figure out any machine on earth, but with women, he wished for an instruction manual.

She walked up to him and set the basket on top of his wrenches. "You ready to eat?"

He wiped his hands on a kerosene-soaked rag. "Where'd you come from?"

"It's not far from my place," she said. He noticed that she was wearing a new cotton dress, which seemed to have been snagged in a few places by briers. She knelt down and opened the basket, pulling out a baby quilt and sandwiches. He sat on the parched grass next to her in a spot of shade thrown by a willow.

"I'm sorry about your man," he said. "I should have told you myself."

Her hands moved busily in the basket. "That woman and I get along all right. You did as good as you could." They ate in silence for a while. From the distance came the deep music of a big Illinois Central freight engine, its whistle filling the afternoon, swaying up and down a scale of frantic notes. The Crimson Flyer thundered north, trailing a hundred refrigerated cars of berries, the work of an entire year for many local farmers. "That train's off its time," she said. "Seems like everything's off schedule lately." She took a bite of ham sandwich and chewed absently.

"I asked the boys that own this engine about your man. They didn't want to talk about him." He took a bite of sandwich and tried not to make a face. It was dry, and the ham tasted like it had been in the icebox too long. He wondered if she had fed her husband any better.

"He was from New Orleans, not from around here. Nobody liked him much, because of his berries. He tried to ship bad Klondykes once, and the men at the loading dock broke his leg."

The pump man shook his head. "Breaking a farmer's leg's kind of rough treatment."

"He deserved it," she said matter-of-factly. "Shipping bad berries gives the local farmers a bad name." She looked at her sandwich as though she had seen it for the first time, and threw it into the basket. "He was too damned lazy to pick early enough to ship on time."

He was afraid she was going to cry, but her face remained as dry as the gravel road that ran along the track. He began to wonder what she had done about her husband. "What about the services for your old man?"

"Mary's pickers helped me put him in this morning after the coroner came out and give us the okay."

So that's it, he thought. Half your life working in the sun and then your woman plants you in back of the toolshed like a dog. He was tempted to toss his sandwich, but he was hungrier than he had been in weeks, so he bit at it again. The woman put her eyes all over him, and he knew what she was doing. He began to compare himself to her husband. He was bigger. People told him frequently that he had a pleasant face, which he figured was their way of telling him he wasn't outright ugly.

When she stared away at a noisy crow, he stole a long look at her. The dress fit her pretty well, and if she were another woman, one that hadn't just put her husband in the ground, he might have asked her for a date. A row of pale freckles fell across her nose, and today her hair was untied, hanging down over her shoulders. Something in the back of his mind bothered him.

"What's your name?" he asked.

"Ada," she said quickly, as though she had expected the question.

"I thank you for the sandwich, but I've got to get going up the road."

She looked along the railway. "Must be nice to take off whenever you've a mind to. I bet you travel all over."

"A lot travel more'n I do." He bent down and began to pick up box-end wrenches.

"What you in such a hurry for?" she asked, stretching out her long legs into the dead grass. Harry studied them a moment.

"Lady, people around here wonder what the trees are up to when they lean with the breeze. What you think someone that sees us is going to think?"

He walked over to his truck, placed his tools in the proper boxes, row-hopped over to the engine, slung the flywheel with a cast-iron crank, and backed off to hear the exhausts talk to him. The woman watched his moves, all of them. As he was driving out of the field, he felt her eyes on the back of his neck.

That evening after supper in the Bell Pepper Tourist Court Café Harry looked up from his coffee and saw Ada walk in through the screen door. She moved across the hard-scrubbed pine floor as if she came into the place all the time, then sat across from him in a booth and put on the table a bottle of bright red strawberry wine. She had washed her hair and put on a jasmine perfume.

Harry was embarrassed. A couple of farmers watched them and Marie, the owner, lifted her chin when she saw the wine. He was at first grouchy about the visit, not liking to be surprised, but as she asked him questions about his travels, he studied her skin, which was not as rough as he'd first thought, her sandy hair, and those eyes that seemed to drink him in. He wondered how she had passed her life so far, stuck on a mud lane in the most spiritless backwater he'd ever seen. He was as curious about her static world as she was about his wandering one.

Conversation was not his long suit, but the woman had an hour's worth of questions about Arkansas and Georgia, listening to his tales of mountains as though he were telling her of China or the moon. What he wanted to talk about was Missouri and his children, but her questions wouldn't let him. At one point in the conversation she looked over at Marie and said, "There's them around here that say if you hang around me, there's no telling what trouble you'll get into." She put her hands together and placed them in the middle of the green oilcloth.

He looked at them, realizing that she had told him almost nothing about herself. "You said your husband was from New Orleans, but you didn't say where you were from."

She took a swallow of wine from a water glass. "Let's just say I showed up here a few years ago. Nobody knows nothing much about me except I was kept back in that patch and never came in to drink or dance or nothing. Where I'm from's not so important, is it?" She took a sip and smiled at him over the rim of her glass. "You like to dance?" she asked quickly.

"I can glide around some," he said. "But about this afternoon—why'd you follow me with them sandwiches out in the field?"

Ada bit her lower lip and thought a moment. "Maybe I want to move on," she said flatly. Harry looked out the window and whistled.

They took their time finishing off the bottle. She went to the ladies' room and he walked outside, into the dark parking lot. He stood there, stretching the kinks out of his muscles. Ada came out with him, looked up and down 51 for cars, and threw her arms around his waist, giving him a hard kiss. Then she backed off, smiling, and began walking up the dark highway toward her place.

Oh my, he thought. Her mouth had tasted of strawberry wine, hot and sweet. Oh my.

Later that night he lay in his bed with the window open, listening to the pump engines running out in the fields, which stretched away on all sides of the tourist court for miles. They throbbed, as delicate as distant heartbeats. He could tell which type each was by the sound it made. He heard an International hit-and-miss engine fire once and then coast slower and slower through several cycles before firing again. Woven into that sound was a distant Fairbanks Morse with a bad magneto throbbing steadily, then cutting off, slowing, slowing almost to stillness before the spark built up again and the engine boomed back alive. Across the road, a little McCormick muttered in a ditch. In the quiet night the engines fought the drought, popping like the musketry of a losing army. Through the screen of his window drifted the scent of kerosene exhaust.

He thought of the farmer's widow and finally admitted to himself, there in the dark, that she was good-looking. What was she doing right now? he wondered. Reading? For some reason he doubted this. Sewing? What—traveling clothes? Was she planning how to sell the patch and move back, as many women had done, to wherever she had come from? If she had any sense, he thought, she'd be asleep, and he turned over and faced the wall, listening to the springs ring under him. He tried to remember what he had done at night when he was at home, when he was twenty-four and had three children and a wife, but nothing at all came to him. Then, slowly, thoughts of rocking sick babies and helping his wife can sweet corn came to him, and before two minutes had passed, he was asleep.

The next morning the sky was as hard and expressionless as a pawnbroker's face. At eight o'clock the temperature was ninety-one, and the repairman had already welded a piston rod in Amite and was headed south. When he passed the woman's lane, he forced himself not to look down its rutted surface. He had dreamed of her last night, and that was enough, he thought. Times were so hard he could afford only his dreams. A half mile down the road he began working at pouring new babbitt bearings for an old Dan Patch engine. The owners of the farm left him alone so they could oversee a group of inexperienced pickers, and at nine-thirty, while he was turning the blower for the forge, she came out of the brush to the north, carrying a clear glass jug of lemonade.

"I'll bet you're dry," she said, giving him the jug and a tin cup.

"You're an awful friendly lady," he said, pouring himself a drink and looking at her slim waist, her long hair.

"I can be friendly when I want to be." She rested her hand on his damp shoulder a moment and let it slide off slowly.

They talked while he worked the forge. He tried to tell her about his children, but she seemed not to be interested. She wanted to know where he had been and where he was going. She wanted to know how it was to live on the road, what people were like in different places. "Do you stay in tourist courts every night?" she asked, wide-eyed.

By the time he had finished his repair, she had told him that she had just buried her third husband, that she had never been a hundred miles from the spot they were standing in, and that she didn't care if she never saw another strawberry for the rest of her days. "Sometimes I think it's staying in the same place, doing the same things, day in, day out, that gets me down. Get up in the morning and look out the window and see that same rusty fence. Look out another window and see that same willow tree. Out another and see that field. Same place, same things, all my life." She heard a distant train whistle and looked off toward it, caught up in the haunting sound.

Harry Lintel was at a loss in dealing with unhappy people. He remembered that putting his big arms around his young wife years ago would stop her from crying, but he had no notion why this worked. Looking at the delicate hollow of Ada's cheek, he felt sorry he didn't know what to do for her. He wondered if she would take up with him in his truck if he asked her, would just go off with him up the highway to Tennessee or Georgia, wherever the next drought was needing him to fix engines or windmills. Would this heal what was wrong?

After a local freight train racketed by, three men in overalls drove across the track, got out of their pickup, and began telling him about a big engine in a dry field six miles west, and how nobody could get it to run all week. The men ignored the woman, and as the repairman packed his tools and dumped the forge, he watched her walk off. She went south, away from her place, along the dirt lane that sidled up to the railroad, keeping her thin brown shoes out of the heaped-up dust ridge. After he loaded the truck, he cranked it and headed not west, along the route given him by the three men, but north. Turning into her lane, he bumped down along the ruts to her farmhouse. He walked to the back of the property and noticed her berries blanched by the sun as if they'd had kettles of boiling water poured over them. Returning to the house, he opened the fuse box nailed to the rear outside wall and discovered that one fuse was blown, even though it was a special heavy-duty type. He used his pocketknife to pry off the faceplate and saw where a switch wire cut into the circuit and ran from the bottom of the box through a hole into the house.

He found the front door unlocked. Walking through the house, he noticed there was little furniture: only a set of dark varnished chairs, two small, rough tables, and a rickety, curled-up sofa. The windows were dirty. In the kitchen he found the wall switch that activated the pump, and, peering close, he saw that it had been turned on. He was sure that many farms with electric pumps also had inside switches. But surely the man would have killed the circuit before he went out to work on the thing. And then he remembered that he hadn't seen any switch out in the field.

He sat down at the oilcloth-covered kitchen table and squinted out the front window. He saw a rusty fence. Looking out a side window, he saw a willow tree. My God, he thought. He turned to look through the rear window, into a field. Near the broken tractor was a freshly dug mound of dirt. He put his face down into his hands and shook like a man who had just missed being in a terrible accident.

During the next ten days he worked the whole parish. Wild animals came out of the woods looking for water. Bottoms of drainage ditches cracked open and buckled. He saw pickers brought out of the field with heatstroke. The woman found him only twice, and he was polite, listening to her tell him about her nights and what she saw through her windows. She wore the same dress but kept it clean and ironed. Once, she asked him to come over for supper, but he said he had work to do past dark.

At the tourist court he avoided the café and went to bed early, putting himself to sleep by thinking of his wife, painfully, deliberately. He remembered the kindness of her meals in their kitchen and the fondness of her touch, which was on him still, teaching him.

On a Thursday morning, before dawn, he was awakened by a drumming sound to the northwest. At first he thought it was someone at the door, but when the sound rolled down on the parish again, he knew it was thunder. By first light the rain had started in earnest, and at eight o'clock he was still in his room, staring out at sheets of wind-tortured spray welling up in puddles along the highway—three inches at least, and more to come, by the looks of the sky. It was time to move on.

In the café, for the first time Marie had no repair calls for him. He paid up, gave her a hug, and headed out north in his groaning truck, rainwater spilling off the taut new tarp covering the back.

The highway followed the railroad up through a series of small towns, and he made good time despite a traffic of small truckloads of produce and an occasional horse-drawn farm wagon. He felt light-hearted for the first time in days, and whistled as he steered around slower vehicles navigating the rainy road. There was something good about getting out of this section of the country, he felt, something good about pointing his headlights toward Jackson or Memphis, where he would hole up in a boardinghouse and read a big-city paper until the weather reports would tell him where he'd find lots of dust, heat, worn-out pumps, and busted windmills.

About noon he pulled over at a café south of McComb. Walking to the back of the truck, he saw that one of the tarp ropes had come undone. When he raised the cloth to check inside, he saw the woman lift her face toward him, her eyes rusty and dark. "When I heard the rain start on my roof, I knew you'd be pulling out," she said. "You can go somewheres. I can't."

He stared at her for a long time, trying to figure what to say. He looked up and down the red-dirt highway lined with spindly telephone poles and then at the café, which was closed, he realized, the front door padlocked. Finally, he climbed in and sat on a toolbox lid next to her in the oily dark. "You can't come along with me."

"Don't say that," she said, putting her arms loosely around his neck. "You're the only person I ever met can go where he wants to go." She said this not in a pleading voice but as a statement of fact. "I can go with you. I'll be good to you, Mr. Lintel."

He looked at her eyes and guessed that she was desperate for his freedom of movement but not for him. The eyes seemed already to be looking ahead, looking at a whole world passing by a truck window. "Where you want to go," he said at last, "I can't take you."

She pulled her arms away quickly. "What you mean by that? You just going to toss me off on the side of the road like a wore-out machine? There's something in me what needs to get away with you."

Harry Lintel leaned toward her and took her hands, trying to remember the ways he had once brought solace to his wife. "If I could help you, I'd bring you along for the ride," he said. "But I can't do a thing for you." He half-expected her to cry when he said that, but she only shook her head.

"You've got a heart like a rock," she told him.

"No, ma'am," he said. "I loved a good woman once, and I could love another. You can't come with me because you killed your old man."

Her eyes seemed to pulse, and what softness lingered around the corners of her mouth disappeared into a flinty expression of fear and desperation.

He reached for his wallet. "I'm going to buy a ticket and put you on the southbound. You can walk home from the station."

She grabbed a bill from him before he offered it, then straightened up, throwing an arm in back of her as if she was searching for the handle of her cardboard suitcase. Harry stared at his empty hand for a moment and turned to climb out into the drizzle. He heard the music of a tempered wrench being picked up, and then a bomb went off in his head, and he was down on the floorboards, rolling in cinders and wire, his arms and legs uncontrolled, his eyes letting in a broken vision of the woman standing over him, looking down the way someone might examine a stunned fish. "I've never met a man I could put up with for long," she told him. "I'm glad I got shut of all of mine."

His head roared like a forge, and he tried to rise, his eyes flickering, his arms pushing him toward the woman's upraised fist, where his biggest box-end wrench glimmered like a thunderbolt. The blow was a star-giving ball of pain, and he felt the tailgate in the small of his back, the world going over like a flywheel, his face in collision with gravel and clay, a coppery rill coursing through his nose and mouth. The only thing in his head was the silver ring of a tool, and then the exhaust of a four-cylinder engine pulling away, fading into a clash of gears at the top of a hill, and then, for the longest time, nothing. Somewhere a cow bellowed, or a car passed without stopping, or wind blew through the grass around him like knowledge through an ear.

Near dusk he woke to a dove singing on the phone wires. He wondered where she would sell the truck, to what town she would ride on the train. It didn't matter. She was a woman who would never get where she wanted to go. He was always where he was going.

One eye began to work, and he watched clouds, the broken pieces of the world hanging above like tomorrow's big repair job, waiting.

Waiting for the Evening News

Jesse McNeil was running a locomotive while he was drunk, and he was doing a fine job of it, charging up the main line at fifty with the chemical train, rattling through the hot Louisiana night like a thunderstorm. He watched the headlight brighten the rails to mile-long silver spears sailing through the sandy pine wastelands of the parish. Another nameless hamlet was rolling up in the distance, one in a row of asbestos-siding-and-tin communities strung along the railroad like ticks on a dog's backbone. He had roared through it a thousand times with a hundred cars of propane and vinyl chloride and had never so much as touched the air brake, had only to blow a signal for the one crossing, and then was gone like a gas pain in the bowel, discomfort and noise for a moment, soon forgotten by the few hundred folks who lived in wherever-it-was, Louisiana. He reached for the whistle lever in the dark cab and missed it, remembering the half-pint of whiskey he had gulped behind the engine house thirty minutes earlier. He was fifty years old today, and he wanted to do something wild and woolly, like get half-lit and pull the chemical train, known by enginemen as the "rolling bomb," up to the Mississippi line on time for a change. He could make this run in his sleep. After he got the train stretched out and up to the speed limit, all he had to do was blow the damned whistle. The train was on tracks and couldn't get lost or wander off among somebody's cows.

Jesse looked over at his brakeman, who was watching for automobiles on his side of the train. A highway followed along the tracks and at least once every trip a noodlehead with the windows rolled up and the radio blasting would turn in front of the engine at a crossing, notice the train, maybe mess in his britches, and then shoot on across to safety. Jesse reached again for the whistle lever and pulled it, sending a five-chime-whistle note crashing off all the tin and asbestos for a mile around. The gravel crossing winked in the moonlight and was gone, the train invaded the town, and Jesse looked out his window at the black air, listening to the hollow thunder in his head and laughing at how free he felt, how nobody cared what he was doing, how lost he was in the universe. He was the anonymous taxi driver of ethylene oxide and caustic soda, chlorine and ethyl antiknock compound, a man known intimately only by his menopausal wife and the finance company.

Then with a jolt, loose wrenches and lunch boxes flew forward in a convulsion of iron, and Jesse was knocked from his seat, his thermos flying over his head and sailing out into the thundering darkness. The locomotive lurched as though a giant hand had grabbed it from behind and wiggled it like a toy. Leaning out the window and looking back along the mile-long trail of tankers, he saw a whirlwind of sparks thirty cars back, and his heart divided in two and hid up under his shoulder blades. Somewhere an air hose parted, and the brakes jammed on with a squeal. He remembered to shut off the throttle, and as the engines bucked and ground rails for a quarter mile, he saw a white tanker turn sideways in the distance. Then he knew the train was breaking apart, the rear section running in like an accordion, and here he was in the dark woods at the edge of town, more than half-drunk, witnessing a catastrophe that would have happened even if he had been stone-sober and riding the rails with a Bible in his back pocket.

The black locomotives trembled to a stop, jumping as derailing cars smacked into those tankers still on the tracks. The brakeman and conductor hit the ground, running toward all the thunder. Jesse McNeil climbed down the engine steps carefully and put his hands in his pockets, wondering what he would do, what he would tell everybody. Then the first chemical tanker exploded, pinwheeling up into the night sky, slinging its wheels and coming down into a roadside 7-Eleven, the building disappearing in an unholy orange fireball. The strange pounding Jesse heard was the sound of his own feet running north along the railroad, scattering rocks and dust until he reached a spot where he could get down to the highway and lope along the blacktop. He ran until he had no wind and his heart pounded like a fist. Then he turned and saw the sky lit up a smoky yellow. He began to stumble backward through an unnameable fear, and when an old pickup pulled out of a side road and drove north toward him, he stuck out his thumb.

Jesse hitched to the next jerkwater town up the line, and even there he could see a poisonous glow on the horizon. A log-truck driver gave him a lift to the interstate, and he was faced with the choice of going north, farther into the trash-woods sand hills where he was raised, the land of clapboard fundamentalist churches and mildewed trailers, or south toward the alien swamps and that Sodom of all Sodoms, New Orleans. He crossed the median to the southbound lane. No one would look for him in New Orleans.

After a while, a black sedan approached, and he stuck up his thumb, thinking that if he could get away long enough for his system to clear of bourbon, maybe he could tell the company officials that he'd had an attack of amnesia, or anxiety, or stupidity, and had run off like a fool to sort things out for a day. What could they do to him for being stupid? Fire him? He didn't need much money anyway. His frame house was paid for, and the only reason he worked at all was to spend time away from Lurleen, his prune-skin wife, who was always after him to paint or fix something. But if they had found him stumbling around by the engine, drunk, maybe the law would get involved. Maybe it would mean a great big fine, and if he ever did want to work for a railroad again, they wouldn't hire him to run a windup locomotive around a Christmas tree.

To his surprise the black sedan stopped, and soon he was cruising south in the company of an old Catholic priest, a Father Lambrusco, semiretired, who was filling in for a vacationing assistant pastor at St. Louis Cathedral.

"You out of work?" the priest asked, speeding past a gravel truck.

"Yeah," Jesse said, studying the eastern sky through the windshield. "I'm a carpenter."

"Ah. Joseph was a carpenter."

"Joseph who?"

The priest checked his rearview. "Joseph, the father of Jesus."

Jesse frowned at himself. A priest talks about Joseph the carpenter, and Jesse thinks at first that maybe he's talking about Joseph Wiggins from McComb, Mississippi. "Oh yeah, that Joseph," Jesse said.

"You go to church?"

"Well, some. I'm sort of a fundamentalist."

"Isn't going to church fundamental? No, never mind. I didn't pick you up to preach. To tell the truth, I was falling asleep at the wheel." He turned his bald head toward Jesse and smiled, keeping his mouth closed, as though he had bad teeth. "Tell me, Mr. Carpenter, do you believe Catholics worship statues?"

Jesse assured him he did not, that one friend he had made in the service had been a Catholic chaplain.

"Were you baptized by total immersion in your church?" the priest asked.

"All the way under. We got our own special tank."

"Was your life changed?" The priest swung around a Volkswagen.

Jesse pursed his lips and looked far down the road, as if he might see his life changing up ahead. "The minister said it might take some time in my case."

He and the priest talked for an hour and a half about snake-handler preachers and why nuns didn't have any spare time.

At two in the morning Jesse checked into the Night O' Delight Motel on Airline Highway in New Orleans. The desk clerk, a young Asian man, asked him if he wanted a fifteen-dollar room or a sixty-dollar room with a bed warmer. "What fool would pay sixty dollars just to sleep in a room?" he told him. He gave the man three fives, plus the tax, thankful that he had just cashed his paycheck and held back a few hundred to pay Lurleen's cousin to come over and paint the house. When he got to the room he turned on the television to check for news, flipping through channels until he reached the last station on the dial, which was showing a vividly pornographic scene.

Jesse mashed the off switch and drew back his finger as though it had been burned.

He looked around at the warped paneling and the window unit, which labored without a grille in its hole near the ceiling. Tomorrow he would call in his story. Things would go fairly rough with him for running off, but he would worry about that the next day. He pulled off his coveralls and climbed into the bed, which jittered and rang, sagging badly in the middle.

The next morning his bladder woke him in time for the eight o'clock news, and as he fumbled with the dials, he wondered if the wreck would even be mentioned. The fire probably had been put out by now. The railroad would have to buy somebody's 7-Eleven, but they could have the line clear by late afternoon.

However, on Channel 4 was a helicopter view of Satan's living room, fifty tank cars crashed together and burning. Black-and-green smoke rose a mile into the air, and on both sides of the track, seed elevators, storehouses, and shops flamed in fierce amber heaps. Jesse stepped back and cupped a hand to his forehead. He tried to say something like "What in God's name?" but he couldn't make a sound. The voice narrating the video told that the town had been evacuated and that fire-fighting teams were driven back by a mix of a dozen chemicals spilled from ruptured tankers, that the town's ditches were running with vinyl chloride and paint stripper. Then the voice told the world that Jesse P. McNeil, the train's engineer, had disappeared from the scene and it was thought that he had run off into the woods east of the derailment, where parish posse members were searching for him with teams of dogs.

When he heard his name fly out of the television, Jesse sat down hard on the creaking bed. Hardly forty people knew he existed, and now his name had sailed out into the region like parts of his exploded train. Why, he wondered, was it important to name him at all? And sheriff's officers were in the woods searching for him like he was a criminal. When the news report ended, he turned off the television and wondered if his blood would now test free of alcohol. He decided to eat a big breakfast. Stepping out of his room, he walked over to a run-down strip of glass and blond-colored brick businesses across the highway, entered a smoky café, and sat at the counter. On a shelf over the coffee urn, a grease-stained television blinked and buzzed. A local channel was showing the wreck from ground level. A handsome announcer listed twenty evil-sounding names of chemicals that were burning, spilling, or threatening to explode. He also mentioned that the engineer was a man of average build, with red hair combed straight back, last seen hitching a ride north of the wreck site. The waitresses were absorbed in the broadcast and didn't see Jesse slowly turn away from the counter and head for the door. Outside, he stood on the curb and felt light-headed, anxious that the next person to lay eyes on him might recognize who he was. He looked up and down the neon-infested highway for escape. Next to the café was a cubbyhole-sized barbershop, and he sidled over to its door and backed inside. Jesse found an Italian-looking gentleman stropping his razor and watching a TV mounted on a rack in the corner. The engineer sat in the chair and wondered how he could ask for his hair to be combed in some new way, maybe with a part on the side, anything different from the straight-back crimson mane he sported at the moment. The barber smiled and clicked his scissors in the air twice.

"Hey, what you think of the train wreck? Some mess, right?" He ran a comb through Jesse's hair slowly, as though admiring it.

Jesse looked at him warily. He hated the big-city accent of New Orleans folks. They sounded like New Yorkers to his piney woods ear. "I ain't heard of a wreck," Jesse said.

The barber bobbed his head. "Aw yeah. You just come in from the forest, hey? You from Mississippi, right? Hay-baling time and all that shit."

Jesse found himself nodding, glad to be given some kind of identity. Just then the television screen flashed a stern company photograph of his face. "Look here," he said, grabbing the barber's arm and pulling his attention away from the TV, "can't you give me kind of a modern look? Something maybe a little younger?"

The barber sucked in his cheeks and studied Jesse's head the way an expensive artist might. "Yeah, man. I could wash all that oil out, shorten everything up, and kinda spike it." He clicked his scissors once. "But your friends back in the woods gonna think you a Communist rock star or somethin'."

Jesse took in a deep breath and watched the white-hot center of the chemical train pulse over the barber's shoulder. "Do it to me," he said.

After his haircut, he spent the entire morning in the café next door, reading the newspapers. The noon TV news devoted a full five minutes to the train wreck. At that point he decided he would not call in for a while, that he would wait a few days until this was past and everyone would begin to forget, that he would lie low along Airline Highway in the Night O' Delight Motel until everyone and everything cooled off and the poisonous fumes of his train wreck had blown clear of the unlucky town. It took him a good while to decide this, because out-of-the-ordinary decisions seldom came up in his life. The engineer had been running the same routes with the same trains for so many years that lately he found it hard to pay attention to the usual telegraph poles and sweet-gum trees sailing past his cab window. In the same way, the stunted pines along the road to his house, and the little house itself, had become unseeable. Sometimes he imagined himself an unseen part of this faded, repetitive background.

The sense of being invisible made Jesse think he could not be taken seriously, which was why he never voted, hardly ever renewed his driver's license, and paid attention in church only once a year at revival time. He thought of the plywood church at the end of the dirt lane and wondered what Father Lambrusco would think of it.

During the afternoon he watched soap operas, amazed at all the little things the characters could get upset about. He laughed as he thought of Lurleen watching the same shows, a cup of coffee in her lap, a cigarette mashed in the saucer. He began to feel some of the gloom brought on by the noon newscast evaporate, and he looked forward to the five o'clock news because he knew it would tell that the crisis was over, people were returning to their homes, and the railroad would be repaired in a day or so. Waiting for the evening news, Jesse pondered life's good points, how most injuries healed up, most people changed for the better, and whatever was big news today was small potatoes on page thirty tomorrow. He lay back on his bed and studied the rain-stained ceiling and the mismatched paneling on the walls. Even this room would be remodeled someday and no one would suspect how ugly it had been. Things would improve.

But when the local news theme began to play over his scratched motel television, his face froze in a disbelieving stare. A black sky coiled and spread for miles above a crossroads town, and an evil-looking copper blaze flashed at the heart of a mountain of wreckage. The announcer stated that the train's brakeman had accused the engineer of being intoxicated at the time of the accident. Jesse balled up a fist. "Son of a bitch," he shouted at the television, "that hophead smokes weed day and night." The announcer went on to say that the parish sheriff's department had a warrant out for the engineer's arrest and that railroad officials were hiring private investigators to locate the runaway employee. Meanwhile, firefighters were having to let the wreck burn because of an overheated propane tanker and the danger that two cars of chemicals would rupture and mix, producing mustard gas. Jesse's mouth fell open at this last awful announcement, and he began to fear that somehow everything was being blamed on him. He watched aerial shots of the fire spreading into the town, and as he did, another propane tanker went off like the end of the world, skyborne rills of fire torching a poor neighborhood of wooden houses to the east of the tracks. He sat on the floor, gathering fistfuls of cheap shag carpet, holding on, anchoring himself against the TV's revelations.

At the end of the report, he was shaking, so he snapped off the set. His name was on the air again, broadcast all over two states. And why did they want to arrest *him*? The train had come apart on its own. A wheel rim had cracked off, or a rail broke. He hadn't been speeding. Nobody knew what went wrong. Billy Graham could have been at the throttle of that locomotive and the same thing would have happened. He left the room, crossed the highway, and bought a deck of cards, returning to the little table by the window and dealing a hand of solitaire. He hoped the game would take his mind off the wreck, but after a while he began placing red eights on red nines, and he wished for his wife's face over his shoulder, telling him where he'd missed a play.

The next day he woke up and glared at the dark set a long time before deciding to shave. He refused to watch the news. Each broadcast injured his notion of who he was, and he would have no more of that. He caught a bus to the French Quarter and in Jackson Square sat on a wrought-iron bench, amazed that no one looked like his friends from his shriveled-up hometown. Jesse missed the red clay ditches and the boiled turpentine smell of Gumwood, Louisiana. He had never seen so many weak-looking men dressed in baggy, strange clothes, but he envied their anonymity, for at the moment he felt as obvious as the soaring statue of Andrew Jackson that rose before him, splattered by pigeons.

He spent all day in the Quarter, poking his sharp face into the doors of antique shops and bars, hankering for a hot charge of supermarket whiskey but holding back. Whenever he passed a newspaper vending machine, he saw a smoky photograph on the front page and felt a twinge of remorse. He wondered if he should turn himself in.

At the motel, he avoided the local news, deciding to turn the set on only for the national stuff, where, he was thinking, he would see the really important events, nothing about some local train burning a pissant town off the map. But as the CBS evening news played its intro theme over a film snippet of the main story, Jesse let out a pained yelp.

There on the screen was his wife, Lurleen, shaking her rat-gray hair and telling a reporter, "I don't know where he run off to leaving a blowed-up train behind like that." She sniffed and pointed a finger toward the camera. "But it don't surprise me one bit," she said to the world. "No sir, not one thing that man would do would surprise a jumpy cat." Jesse interlaced his fingers and placed his hands on top of his brushy head. On the screen, Lurleen looked powerful and almost attractive, in a dirt road kind of way. The program cut to an anchorman, and Jesse was thankful, for he half-expected Lurleen to start telling about him not paying her nephew for painting the house, and then everyone in red-white-and-blue America would know he was too lazy to paint his own damned living room. The announcer, low-voiced and serious in a blue sport coat, told how a white cloud of escaped chemical had rolled over a chicken farm and killed ten thousand hens, how three firemen were seriously injured when the wind shifted and they were overtaken by a toxic blanket.

"But the real mystery," the announcer continued, "is Jesse McNeil, the fifty-year-old engineer from Gumwood, Louisiana, who ran away from the scene of the accident. There are many speculations about his disappearance. Fellow workers suggest that McNeil was depressed because of his fiftieth birthday and was having marital and family problems. Whatever the reasons, he left behind a growing scene of destruction and pollution perhaps unequaled in American railroad history. Our live coverage continues from southeast Louisiana." And there it was. Jesse's eyes widened as a camera did a slow pan of his home on Loblolly Road, and he watched his partially bald yard, his house, which from this angle looked like a masonite-covered shoe box, and his carport, which seemed wobbly and anemic under its load of pine straw. He imagined voices all over America saying, "Is that the best he could do after fifty years?" And there was Lurleen, sitting on the sofa in front of the big picture of the ocean surf, talking to the reporter about her husband. What could be worse than this, Jesse wondered, to be introduced to the English-speaking world by Lurleen McNeil, a chain-smoking canasta dragon whose biggest ambition in life was to have everything they owned painted sea-foam green by a dopehead nephew who never got out of the sixth grade? He listened as Lurleen told the world about him.

She leaned back on the couch and he saw her checkered shirt tighten at the shoulders. She looked thoughtful and not as dowdy as usual; he had never seen her like this. "Sometimes he's a little out of it," Lurleen said, blowing a stream of smoke from the side of her mouth and looking off in the opposite direction. "I don't mean to say he's a bad man, but whenever he gets upset he tends to drink a little too much, if you know what I mean."

Jesse jumped up straight as a rail. "And who the hell wouldn't take a drink if they was married to a slave-driving snapping turtle?"

Lurleen looked into the camera as though she had heard the remark. "I just wish he could put all this mess behind him and come home to help paint the living room."

"The living room," Jesse yelled, jerking his fists out from his sides. "My name is on national TV and all you can think about is hiding that cheap paneling you put up last year."

Lurleen gave the camera a wry smile and she was off; more footage of the wreck followed, more details of chemicals, casualties, government inspection teams. Agents from the Environmental Protection Agency were now looking for Jesse McNeil. The president of the local Sierra Club, a fashionably dressed thirtyish woman, stated flatly that Jesse should be hunted down like a dangerous criminal.

"What have I done to you?" he yelled, holding his outstretched palms toward the screen. "You don't even know me. I'm nobody important."

After the news report, Jesse went into the bathroom to splash water on his face, a face framed in the mirror by a spiked crown of hair shaped like a thistle bloom. He should have stayed at the site of the wreck, he told himself. He would have been fired and fined, but there would have been nothing like the publicity he was generating.

In his absence, what he had done was growing like a thunderstorm feeding on hot air and invisible moisture, or bigger, like a tropical storm, spinning out of control, created by TV people just because it was good business. He could not for the life of him imagine how drinking a half-pint of whiskey could generate such a hurricane of interest in who he was, or why the people of the United States had been brought into his unpainted living room to find out about him. He went back to the bed, sat down, and put his head in his hands. "No more news for me," he said aloud. "Not for a while."

For four days he avoided the newspapers and television. He rode the bus downtown, watching the faces of his fellow riders for any trace of recognition, for now he felt as famous as Johnny Carson, guilty as Hitler, and half-expected the next old lady he saw to throw up her arms and exclaim, "It's him. It's the train wrecker." He slouched on a bench in Jackson Square, across from the cathedral, again wondering at all the tourists, worried that even some Korean or German might recognize him. He wondered once more why a man's mistake grows with importance according to how many people know about it.

He was so deep in thought, he didn't notice when an old priest sat next to him and unfurled a fresh copy of the *Times-Picayune.* The priest, a bald man with a silver ring of hair above the ears, was on Jesse's right, so the engineer had a good view of the open front page, which carried a photo of a blazing boxcar. The priest looked over the page at Jesse. "Are you still out of work?" It was Father Lambrusco.

"Uh, yeah. Sort of," Jesse growled.

"Would you like a section?" he asked, shaking the paper at him.

"Uh, naw. I was just reading about the train wreck."

The priest folded the paper half-size in his lap, studying the photograph. "That's a big mess. I hope they get the fellow who did it."

The phrase "the fellow who did it" gave Jesse a brief chill. He felt obligated to mount a defense. "The engineer was just in the cab when it happened. He might not've had anything to do with why the train came apart."

The priest turned to him then, his dewlap flowing over his Roman collar. "He'd been drinking and he ran away. You've got to admit that looks bad."

Jesse scowled and kicked at a pigeon wandering too close to his shoe. "Maybe the newspeople are blowing this thing up too much. You know, the more they yak about it, the worse it gets."

The priest sucked a tooth and thought a moment. "You mean, if someone does something wrong, and no one finds out, then it's not really all that wrong?"

Jesse sat back on the bench as though the priest had touched him in a sore spot. "I didn't say that, exactly."

"Secrecy is not innocence," the priest said. "If the engineer is not responsible, the facts should be brought out to that effect. But he's gone into hiding somewhere locally. . . ."

Jesse lurched forward, sending two pigeons fluttering off toward General Jackson's statue. "Does the paper say that?"

"The police think he's been sighted in New Orleans," the priest said, picking up the paper and opening it again.

Jesse stood up then, pretending to dust off his pants, casually looking around. "I've got to get going. So long."

"So long," the priest said, turning a page. "You had lunch yet?"

"No," he said, walking backward a couple steps. "I've got to go."

"Well, if you come around this time of day and I'm here, I'll buy you lunch." The priest raised up the front page and began reading an article on the back of it.

Another day dragged by. Jesse was seated in the grim motel room, rubbing his hands together, staring at the dead television. The statement "Secrecy is not innocence" kept running through his head, and he now wondered whether the newspeople were right in exposing his drunkenness, whether he might have noticed something wrong with his train had he been completely sober. Jesse McNeil looked back over his whole life much as a newscaster would do in a thumbnail sketch, and he shuddered to think that he had been guilty of many mistakes. He craved the television set, but he would not let himself touch the knobs that would bring him more bad news to feed his growing guilt. He pulled his wallet and saw that he was nearly out of money. He guessed it would not be long before they would find him.

Then he called his wife in Gumwood, figuring that she would tear into his shortcomings like a tent preacher. But she didn't. She was worried about him.

"Jesse," she whispered, "they're all around here in the woods waiting for you to come home. I know you messed up big, but please don't come back here. If you turn yourself in, find a single policeman somewhere and do it. Baby, these people think you're something

awful, and I'm worried they might hurt you." She told him what it
had been like for the past few days, and he listened, moved by her
care for him. For a moment he thought he had the wrong number,
and then with a pang he realized that there might be more to Lurleen
than he'd noticed. While she pleaded with him to be careful, he worried that she had become one of the details of his life that he no longer
saw, like a telegraph pole flying by his engine window for the thou-
sandth time. A series of clicks sounded in the background, and his
wife cried for him to hang up because the line might be tapped. He
slammed down the receiver and thought of her voice wavering on
the wire. It took a lot to shake his wife's confidence, and it scared
him to think of what she had been told.

He got off a bus at midday and found the old priest reading *The
Catholic Commentator* on a bench in front of the cathedral. They had
lunch in a café facing the square. Jesse marveled at the hamburger
he was served, a domed giant with pickle spears on the side, nothing like the flat, bland burgers he bought at the Gumwood Café. The
priest made him taste one of his french fries, which was as big as a
spike. "Go on," he said, "have another. I love it when they leave the
skin on." He and Father Lambrusco talked vaguely about the
weather and then the priest spoke about guilt, as though the two were
somehow related. Eventually, Jesse twisted the conversation like a
stiff wire back to the train wreck. "Now take that poor engineer we
were talking about the other day," he told the priest. "What he did
might have been bad, all right, but the press blew the dang thing up
so much, he seems like some sort of public enemy number one."

Father Lambrusco took a sip of wine and looked off toward the
square. He suddenly laughed. "I once saw a cartoon in which someone had installed loudspeakers on top of a church and a microphone
in the confessional, and all over town these sins were being broadcast."

"Good Lord," Jesse said, wincing.

The priest put down his glass, a strange small grin on his lips.
"Now that I think of it, I wonder what the newspapers would do with
some of the things I hear in the confessional. What would the

sinner's employers do, his neighbors?" He gave Jesse a piercing look with his dark, earnest eyes. "What would you think of me if you knew what was in my heart? Would you even talk to me?"

Jesse put down his hamburger. It was so big it took away his appetite. "I'm the one wrecked the train," he said in a low voice, glancing quickly at the diners at a small table near them.

"The train in the paper? The burning train?"

"Yes."

The priest sat back and sucked his lower lip. "What are you going to do?"

Jesse wagged his head. "I thought the longer I stayed put, the more people would forget. But it's the other way around. If I stay out one more week, I'll be right up there with Charlie Manson."

The priest sniffed and looked again toward the square. "You know, one of our missions burned to the ground in that little village."

"I didn't carry a torch to it," Jesse whined.

Father Lambrusco closed his eyes. "When you throw a rock in a pond, you make ripples."

Now Jesse stared off toward the cathedral, where he noticed a white pigeon perched on a gatepost. According to the priest, he was directly responsible for every poisoned and burned board in the ruined crossroads. "What can I do?" he asked.

"Nothing," the priest said. "It can't be undone. Just turn yourself in. Ask forgiveness."

Jesse scratched his jaw. Forgiveness from whom? he thought. The railroad? The crossroads town? The millions and millions who followed his mistake on television? For some reason he thought of Judas and wondered if he realized as he climbed the limbs of the fig tree, the hanging rope slung over his shoulder, how many people would come to know about him down through the years, how many would grow to hate his name. "Do me a favor, Father. About news time tonight, ten o'clock, call somebody and turn me in." He explained where he was staying and the priest bobbed his head, closed his eyes, and tasted a french fry. Jesse walked out onto the sidewalk and blended with the tourists. He wandered, distracted and haunted by a need for a drink, until he found a liquor store near Canal Street, where he purchased a fifth of Old Overholt rye. He told himself he needed one stiff shot to calm his nerves.

By news time that night, he was staggering drunk. He found the Gideon Bible next to the telephone and started reading Genesis for some clue to how everybody's troubles began. At news time he swayed from the bed and turned on the local station. The first story showed the train wreck. Additional cars had become involved, one new leak in a tanker of chlorine was keeping fire crews away still, and the little town was now a smudge on the map, a garden of chimneys and iron pipe rising from plots of ash. The screen showed a man in a lab coat standing a mile from the wreck, the smoke plume blossoming over his shoulder. He announced that such a deadly stew of chemicals had been spilled that the town could never be inhabited again, that all the soil for one square mile would have to be removed down to six feet, treated, and hauled off to a toxic-waste pit at a cost of tens of millions. The numbers spun slowly in Jesse's head.

There was a loud knock at the door, but he ignored it, turning the volume up high. The anchorman came back on with a somber comment: "Rumor has it he was spotted in New Orleans, but so far he has eluded the many agencies seeking his arrest. But what kind of person is Jesse McNeil, a man who would father such devastation and disappear?" Following the question was Jesse's biography, starting with a bucktoothed photograph from his grammar school yearbook and ending, after a one-minute narrative of the main events of his life, with a photo of him seated on a bar stool, a detached, ordinary smile given to the world at large.

He stood and slammed his palm against the side of the television, which bobbled toward the door on its wheeled rack.

"Everybody knows me," he roared, waving his fists toward the ceiling. "Everybody knows who I am or what happened." He lurched to the scratched metal door of his room and pulled it open. "You know me," he shouted into the parking lot. Two policemen were standing a few feet away, cradling shotguns. Jesse held out his hands to them. "I read in the Bible where Noah got drunk in his tent, yet he was the one they let run the ark." Five men wearing suits walked in briskly from the highway. Behind Jesse, the announcer told of an upcoming live scene in a late-breaking story.

"The Lord trusted him to save our bacon," he told them all. To the left Jesse saw men in military garb or SWAT uniforms trotting out of sight behind a building. More policemen walked stiff-legged out of the darkness. Above him, on the roof, was the sound of boots stirring gravel. He heard a helicopter somewhere and soon a spotlight lit up the parking lot, casting Jesse's hair in a bristly glow. What do they all know? he wondered. They think I'm the most dangerous man alive.

Another brutal light fired up in the parking lot and a news camera poked between two worried-looking sheriff's deputies. No one said anything and no one touched him. They seemed to be looking past him into the motel room, and he turned to see on the television most of the law officers and a pitiful figure in the center, staggering in wilted coveralls and a botched haircut like the most worthless old drunk imaginable. Everyone was frozen, watching the screen to see what would happen next. Could he say something to the world? He shook his head. Everyone knew it all, or nobody knew the first thing.

The announcer's voice was underlined with the adventure of the capture: "Jesse McNeil has been surrounded by local, state, and federal agents at the Night O' Delight Motel on Airline Highway in New Orleans. He appears intoxicated and unable to speak now at the end of a nationwide search for the man who is at the heart of one of the largest ecological and industrial disasters the country has ever known." For all the policemen, the truth was in the bright eye of the television. Only Jesse turned away, ashamed of the drunk on the set, yet able to stare defiantly at the crowd of officers around him. He wavered in the peeling doorway, feeling as empty-handed and innocent as every man on earth.

The cop nearest him finally touched his arm. "Are you Jesse McNeil?" he asked.

"I feel like I'm two different people," Jesse said feebly.

The cop began to close handcuffs around his wrists. "Well, bud, we'll just have to put both of you in jail." A mean-spirited crackle of laughter ringed the parking lot, and a dozen more camera lights flooded on. Jesse was pulled through the fierce blaze until he felt a policeman's moist hand on the top of his head, shoving him under the river of light and into the backseat of a cruiser, which at once moved onto the highway, bathed by strobes and headlights and stares, locked in inescapable beams.

Died and Gone to Vegas

R aynelle Bullfinch told the young oiler that the only sense of mystery in her life was provided by a deck of cards. As she set up the card table in the engine room of the *Leo B. Canterbury,* a government steam dredge anchored in a pass at the mouth of the Mississippi River, she lectured him. "Nick, you're just a college boy laying out a bit until you get money to go back to school, but for me, this is it." She pulled a coppery braid from under her overalls strap, looked around at the steam chests and piping, and sniffed at the smell of heatproof red enamel. In the glass of a steam gauge she checked her round, bright cheeks for grease and ran a white finger over the blue arcs of her eyebrows. She was the cook on the big boat, which was idle for a couple days because of high winter winds. "My big adventure is cards. One day I'll save up enough to play with the skill boys in Vegas. Set up those folding chairs," she told him. "Seven in all."

"I don't know how to play bourrée, ma'am." Nick Montalbano ran a hand through long hair shiny with dressing. "I only had one semester of college." He looked sideways at the power straining the bronze buckles of the tall woman's bib and avoided her green eyes, which were deep set and full of intense judgment.

"Bullshit. A pet rat can play bourrée. Sit down." She pointed to a metal chair and the oiler, a thin boy wearing an untucked plaid flannel shirt and a baseball cap, obeyed. "Pay attention, here. I deal out five cards to everybody, and I turn up the last card. Whatever suit it is, that's trumps. Then you discard all your nontrumps and draw replacements. Remember, trumps beat all other suits; high trumps beat low trumps. Whatever card is led, you follow suit." She ducked her head under the bill of his cap, looking for his eyes. "This ain't too hard for you, is it? Ain't college stuff more complicated than this?"

"Sure, sure. I understand, but what if you can't follow suit?"

"If nontrumps is led, put a trump on it. If you ain't got no more trumps, just throw your lowest card. Trust me, you'll catch on quick."

"How do you win?" The oiler turned his cap around.

"Every hand has five tricks to take. If you take three tricks, you win the pot. Only on this boat, we got a special rule. If only two decide to play that hand after the draw, then it takes four tricks to win. If you got any questions, ask Sydney, there."

Sydney, the chief engineer, a little fireplug of a man who would wear a white T-shirt in a blizzard, sat down heavily with a whistle. "Oh boy. Fresh meat." He squeezed the oiler's neck.

The steel door next to the starboard triple-expansion engine opened, letting in a wash of frigid air around the day fireman, pilot, deckhand, and welder who came into the big room cursing and clapping the cold out of their clothes. Through the door the angry whitecaps of Southwest Pass raced down the Mississippi, bucking into the tarnished Gulf sky.

"Close that damned pneumonia hole," Raynelle cried, sailing cards precisely before the seven chairs. "Sit down, worms. Usual game, dollar ante, five-dollar rip if you don't take a trick." After the rattle of halves and dollars came discards, more dealing, and then a flurry of cards, ending with a diminishing snowstorm of curses as no one took three tricks and the pot rolled over to the next hand. Three players took no tricks and put up the five-dollar rip.

The engineer unrolled a pack of Camels from his T-shirt sleeve and cursed loudest. "I heard of a bourrée game on a offshore rig where the pot didn't clear for eighty-three passes. By the time somebody won that bitch, it had seventeen hundred dollars in it. The next day the genius what took it got a wrench upside the head in a Morgan City bar and woke up with his pockets inside out and the name Conchita tattooed around his left nipple."

Pig, the day fireman, put up his ante and collected the next hand. "That ain't nothin'." He touched three discards to the top of his bald head and threw them down. "A ol' boy down at the dock told me the other day that he heard about a fellow got hit in the head over in Orange, Texas, and didn't know who he was when he looked at his driver's license. Had amnesia. That sorry-ass seaman's hospital sent him home to his scuzzbag wife, and he didn't know her from Adam's house cat."

"That mighta been a blessing," Raynelle said, turning the last card of the deal to see what trumps was. "Spades." She rolled left on her ample bottom.

"No, it wasn't," the day fireman said, unzipping his heavy green field jacket. "That gal told him she was his sister, gave him a remote control and a color TV, and he was happy as a fly on a pie. She started bringing her boyfriends in at night and that fool waved them into the house. Fixed 'em drinks. Figured any old dude good enough for Sis was good enough for him. The neighbors got to lookin' at her like they was smelling something dead, so she and her old man moved to a better trailer park where nobody knew he'd lost his memory. She started into cocaine and hookin' for fun on the side. Her husband's settlement money he got from the company what dropped a thirty-six-inch Stillson on his hard hat began to shrink up a bit, but that old boy just sat there dizzy on some cheap pills she told him was a prescription. He'd channel surf all day, greet the johns like one of those old dried-up coots at Wal-Mart, and was the happiest son of a bitch in Orange, Texas." The day fireman spread wide his arms. "Was he glad to see Sis come home every day. He was proud she had more friends than a postman with a bagful of welfare checks. And then his memory came back."

"Ho, ho, the *merde* hit the blower," the engineer said, slamming a queen down and raking in a trick.

"Nope. That poor bastard remembered every giggle in the rear bedroom and started feeling lower than a snake's nuts. He tried to get his old woman straight, but the dyed-over tramp just laughed in his face and moved out on him. He got so sorry he went to a shrink, but that just cost him more bucks. Finally, you know what that old dude wound up doin'? He looked for someone would hit him in the head again. You know, so he could get back the way he was. He offered a hundred dollars a pop, and in them Orange bars most people will whack on you for free, so you can imagine what kind of service he bought hisself. After nearly getting killed four or five times, he give up and spent the rest of his settlement money on a hospital stay for a concussion. After that he held up a Pac-a-Bag for enough money to get himself hypmotized back to like he was after he got hit the first time. Wound up in the pen doin' twenty hard ones."

They played three hands of cards while the day fireman finished the story, and then the deckhand in the game, a thick blond man in a black cotton sweater, threw back his head and laughed—*ha-ha*—as if he was only pretending. "If that wadn' so funny, it'd be sad. It reminds me of this dumb-ass peckerwood kid lived next to me in Kentucky, built like a string bean. He was a few thimbles shy of a quart, but he sort of knew he won't no nuclear power plant repairman and got along with everybody. Then he started hanging with these badass kids—you know, the kind that carry spray paint, wear their hats backward, and pack your mailbox full of live rats. Well, they told the poor bastard he was some kind of Jesse James and got him into stealing hubcaps and electric drills. He started strutting around the neighborhood like he was bad shit, and soon the local deputies had him in the backseat for running off with a lawn mower. Dummy stole it in December."

"What's wrong with that?" the day fireman asked, pitching in a dollar.

"Who's gonna buy a used mower in winter, you moron? Anyway, the judge had pity on him—gave him a pissant fine and sent him to bed with a sugar tit. Said he was a good boy who ought to be satisfied to be simple and honest. But String Bean hung out on the street corner crowing. He was proud now. A real gangster, happy as Al Capone, his head pumped full of swamp gas by these losers he's hanging around with. Finally, one night he breaks into a house of a gun collector. Showing how smart he is, he chooses only one gun to take from the rack, an engraved Purdy double-barrel, mint condition, with gold and ivory inlays all over, a twenty-thousand-dollar gun. String Bean took it home and with a two-dollar hacksaw cut the stock off and then most of the barrel. He went out and held up a taco joint and got sixteen dollars and thirteen cents. Was arrested when he walked out the door. This time, a hard-nut judge sent him up on a multiple bill and he got two hundred and ninety-seven years in Bisley."

"All right," Raynelle sang. "Better than death."

"He did ten years before the weepy-ass parole board noticed the sentence and pulled him in for review. Asked him did he get rehabilitated and would he go straight if he got out, and he spit on their mahogany table. He told them he won't no dummy and would be the richest bank robber in Kentucky if he got half a chance." The deckhand laughed—*ha-ha.* "That give everybody a icicle up the ass, and the meetin' came to a vote right quick. Even the American Civil Liberties lesbo lawyers on the parole board wanted to weld the door shut on him. It was somethin'."

The pilot, a tall man dressed in a pea jacket and a sock cap, raised a new hand to his sharp blue eyes and winced, keeping one trump and asking for four cards. "Gentlemen, that reminds me of a girl in Kentucky I knew at one time."

"Why, did she get sent up two hundred and ninety-seven years in Bisley?" the deckhand asked.

"No, she was from Kentucky, like that crazy fellow you just lied to us about. By the way, that king won't walk," he said, laying down an ace of diamonds. "This woman was a nurse at the VA hospital in Louisville and fell in love with one of her patients, a good-looking, mild-mannered fellow with a cyst in his brain that popped and gave him amnesia."

"Now, there's something you don't hear every day," the engineer said, trumping the ace with a bang.

"He didn't know what planet he came from," the pilot said stiffly. "A few months later they got married and he went to work in a local iron plant. After a year he began wandering away from work at lunchtime. So they fired him. He spent a couple of weeks walking up and down his street and all over Louisville, looking into people's yards and checking passing buses for the faces in the windows. It was like he was looking for someone but he couldn't remember who. One day he didn't come home at all. For eighteen months this pretty little nurse was beside herself with worry. Then her nephew was at a rock concert downtown and spotted a shaggy guy in the mosh pit who looked familiar. He was just standing there like he was watching a string quartet. Between songs, he asked him if he had amnesia, which is a rather odd question, considering, and the man almost started crying because he figured he'd been recognized."

"That's a sweet story," the day fireman said, rubbing his eyes with his bear paw–sized hands. "Sydney, could you loan me your handkerchief? I'm all choked up."

"Choke this," the pilot said, trumping the fireman's jack. "Anyway, the little nurse gets attached to the guy again and is glad to have him back. She refreshes his memory about their marriage and all that and starts over with him. Things are better than ever, as far as she is concerned. Well, about a year of marital bliss goes by, and one evening there's a knock at the door. She gets up off the sofa where the amnesia guy is, opens it, and it's her husband, whose memory came back."

"Wait a minute," the deckhand said. "I thought that was her husband on the sofa."

"I never said it was her husband. She just thought it was her husband. It turns out that the guy on the sofa she's been living with for a year is the identical twin to the guy on the doorstep. Got an identical popped cyst, too."

"Aw, bullshit," the day fireman bellowed.

The engineer leaned back and put his hand on a valve handle. "I better pump this place out."

"Hey," the pilot yelled above the bickering. "I knew this girl. Her family lived across the street from my aunt. Anyway, after all the explanations were made, the guy who surfaced at the rock concert agreed it would be best if he moved on, and the wandering twin started back where he left off with his wife. Got his job back at the iron plant. But the wife wasn't happy anymore."

"Why the hell not?" the engineer asked, dealing the next hand. "She had two for the price of one."

"Yeah, well, even though those guys were identical in every way, something was different. We'll never know what it was, but she couldn't get over the second twin. Got so she would wander around herself, driving all over town looking for him."

"What the hell?" The deckhand threw down his cards. "She had her husband back, didn't she?"

"Oh, it was bad," the pilot continued. "She was driving down the street one day and saw the rock-concert twin, gets out of her car, runs into a park yelling and sobbing and throws her arms around him, crying, 'I found you at last. I found you at last.' Only it wasn't him."

"Jeez," the engineer said. "Triplets."

"No." The pilot shook his head. "It was worse than that. It was her husband, who was out on delivery for the iron plant, taking a break in the park after shucking his coveralls. Mild-mannered amnesiac or not, he was pretty put out at the way she was carrying on. But he didn't show it. He pretended to be his twin and asked her why she liked him better than her husband. And she told him. Now, don't ask me what it was. The difference was in her mind, way I heard it. But that guy disappeared again the next morning, and that was five years ago. They say you can go down in east Louisville and see her driving around today in a ratty green Torino, looking for one of those twins, this scared look in her eyes like she'll find one and'll never be sure which one she got hold of."

Raynelle pulled a pecan out of her overalls bib and cracked it between her thumb and forefinger. "That story's sadder'n a armless old man in a room full of skeeters. You sorry sons of bitches tell the depressingest lies I ever heard."

The deckhand lit up an unfiltered cigarette. "Well, sweet thing, why don't you cheer us up with one of your own."

Raynelle looked up at a brass steam gauge bolted to an I beam. "I did know a fellow worked in an iron foundry, come to think of it. His whole family worked the same place, which is a pain in the ass, if you've ever done that, what with your uncle giving you wet willies and your cousin bumming money. This fellow drove a gray Dodge Dart, the kind with the old slant-six engine that'll carry you to hell and back, slow. His relatives made fun of him for it, said he was cheap and wore plastic shoes, and ate Spam, that kind of thing." She turned the last card to show trumps, banging up a king. "Sydney, you better not bourrée again. You in this pot for thirty dollars."

The engineer swept up his hand, pressing it against his T-shirt. "I can count."

"Anyway, this boy thought he'd show his family a thing or two and went out and proposed to the pretty girl who keyed in the invoices in the office. He bought her a diamond ring on time that would choke an elephant. It was a *nice* ring." Raynelle looked at the six men around the table as if none of them would ever buy such a ring. "He was gonna give it to her on her birthday right before they got married in three weeks and meantime he showed it around at the iron foundry figuring it'd make 'em shut up, which basically it did."

"They was probably speechless at how dumb he was," the deckhand said out of the side of his mouth.

"But don't you know that before he got to give it to her, that girl hit her head on the edge of her daddy's swimming pool and drowned. The whole foundry went into mourning, as did those kids' families and the little town in general. She had a big funeral and she was laid out in her wedding dress in a white casket surrounded by every carnation in four counties. Everybody was crying and the funeral parlor had this lovely music playing. I guess the boy got caught up in the feeling, because he walked over to the coffin right before they was gonna screw down the lid and he put that engagement ring on that girl's finger."

"Naw," the engineer said breathlessly, laying a card without looking at it.

"Yes, he did. And he felt proud that he done it—at least for a month or two. Then he began to have eyes for a dental hygienist and that little romance took off hot as a bottle rocket. He courted her for six months and decided to pop the question. But he started thinking about the monthly payments he was making on that ring and how they would go on for four and a half more years, keeping him from affording a decent ring for this living girl."

"Oh no," the pilot said as the hand split again and the pot rolled over yet another time.

"That's right. He got some tools and after midnight went down to Heavenly Oaks Mausoleum and unscrewed the marble door on her drawer, slid out the coffin, and opened it up. I don't know how he could stand to rummage around in whatever was left in the box, but damned if he didn't get that ring and put the grave back together slick as a whistle. So the next day, he give it to the hygienist and everything's okay. A bit later they get married and're doin' the lovebird bit in a trailer down by the foundry." Raynelle cracked another pecan against the edge of the table, crushing it with the pressure of her palm in a way that made the welder and the oiler look at each other. "But there's a big blue blowfly in the ointment. She's showing off that ring by the minute and someone recognized the damned thing and told her. Well, she had a thirty-megaton double-PMS hissy fit and told him straight up that she won't wear no dead woman's ring, and throws it in his face. Said the thing gave her the willies. He told her it's that or a King Edward cigar band, because he won't get out from under the payments until the twenty-first century. It went back and forth like that for a month, with the neighbors up and down the road, including my aunt Tammy, calling the police to come get them to shut up. Finally, the hygienist told him she'd wear the ring."

"Well, that's a happy ending," the deckhand said.

Raynelle popped a half pecan into her red mouth. "Shut up, Jack. I ain't finished. This hygienist began to wear cowboy blouses and jean miniskirts just like the girl in the foundry office did. The old boy kinda liked it at first, but when she dyed her hair the same color as the first girl, it gave him the shakes. She said she was dreaming of that dead girl at least twice a week and saw her in her dresser mirror when she woke up. Then she began to talk like the foundry girl did, with a snappy Arkansas twang. And the dead girl was a country-music freak, liked the old stuff, too. Damned if in the middle of the night the guy wasn't waked up by his wife singing in her sleep all eleven verses of 'El Paso,' the Marty Robbins tune.

"He figured it was the ring causing all the trouble, so he got his wife drunk and while she was asleep slipped that sucker off and headed to the graveyard to put it back on that bone where he took it. Soon as he popped the lid, the cops was on him asking him what the living hell he was doing. He told them he was putting a diamond ring back in the coffin, and they said sure, buddy. Man, he got charged with six or eight nasty things perverts do to dead bodies, and then the dead girl's family filed six or eight civil suits, and believe me, there was mental anguish, pain, and suffering enough to feed the whole county. A local judge who was the dead girl's uncle sent him up for six years, and the hygienist divorced his ass good. Strange thing was that she kept her new hair color and way of dressing, began going to George Jones concerts, and last I heard she'd quit her job at the dentist and was running the computers down at the iron foundry."

"Raynelle, *chère,* I wish you wouldn'ta said that one." Simoneaux, the welder, never spoke much until late in the game. He was a thin Cajun, seldom without a Camel in the corner of his mouth and a high-crowned polka-dotted welder's cap turned backward on his head. He shrugged off a violent chill. "That story gives me *les frissons* up and down my back." A long stick of beef jerky jutted from the pocket of his flannel shirt. He pulled it out, plucked a lint ball from the bottom, and bit off a small knob of meat. "But that diamond shit reminds me of a old boy I knew down in Grand Crapaud who was working on Pancho Oil number six offshore from Point au Fer. The driller was puttin' down the pipe hard one day and my friend the mud engineer was takin' a dump on the engine room toilet. All at once, they hit them a gas pocket at five t'ousand feet and drill pipe come back up that hole like drinkin' straws, knockin' out the top of the rig, flyin' up in the sky, and breakin' apart at the joints. Well, my frien', he had a magazine spread out across his lap when a six-inch drill pipe hit the roof like a spear and went through and through the main diesel engine. About a half second later, another one passed between his knees, through the Playmate of the Month and the steel deck both, yeah. He could hear the iron comin' down all over the rig, but he couldn't run because his pants was around his ankles on the other side the drill column between his legs. He figured he was goin' to glory with a unwiped ass, but a worm run in the engine room and cut him loose with a jackknife, and then they both took off over the side and hit the water. My frien' rolled through them breakers, holdin' on to a drum of mineral spirits, floppin' around until a badass fish gave him a bite on his giblets, and that was the only injury he had."

"Ouch, man." The deckhand crossed his legs.

"What?" Raynelle looked up while posting her five-dollar bourrée.

The welder threw in yet another ante, riffling the dollar bills in the pot as though figuring how much it weighed. "Well, he was hurt enough to get the company to pay him a lump sum after he got a four-by-four lawyer to sue their two-by-four insurance company. That's for true. My frien', he always said he wanted a fancy car. The first thing he did was to drive to Lafayette and buy a sixty-five-thousand-dollar Mercedes, yeah. He put new mud-grip tires on that and drove it down to the Church Key Lounge in Morgan City, where all his mud-pumpin' buddies hung out, an' it didn't take long to set off about half a dozen of them hard hats, no." Simoneaux shook his narrow head. "He was braggin' bad, yeah."

The engineer opened his cards on his belly and rolled his eyes. "A new Mercedes in Morgan City? Sheee-it."

"*Mais,* you can say that again. About two, tree o'clock in the mornin' my frien', he come out, and what he saw woulda made a muskrat cry. Somebody took a number-two ball-peen hammer and dented every place on that car that would take a dent. That t'ing looked like it got caught in a cue-ball tornado storm. Next day he brought it by the insurance people and they told him the policy didn't cover vandalism. Told him he would have to pay to get it fixed or drive it like that.

"But my frien', he had blew all his money on the car to begin with. When he drove it, everybody looked at him like he was some kind of freak. You know, he wanted people to look at him—that's why he bought the car—but they was lookin' at him the wrong way, like 'You mus' be some prime jerk to have someone mess with you car like that.' So after a week of havin' people run off the road turnin' their necks to look at that new Mercedes, he got drunk, went to the store, and bought about twenty cans of Bondo, tape, and cans of spray paint."

"Don't say it," the deckhand cried.

"No, no," the engineer said to his cards.

"What?" Raynelle asked.

"Yeah, the poor bastard couldn't make a snake out of Play-Doh but he's gonna try and restore a fine European se-dan. He filed and sanded on that poor car for a week, then hit it with that dollar-a-can paint. When he finished up, that Mercedes looked like it was battered for fryin'. He drove it around Grand Crapaud and people just pointed and doubled over. He kept it outside his trailer at night, and people would drive up and park, just to look at it. Phone calls started comin', the hang-up kind that said things like 'You look like your car,' *click,* or 'What kind of icing did you use?' *click.* My frien' finally took out his insurance policy and saw what it did cover. It was theft.

"So he started leaving the keys in it parked down by the abandoned lumberyard, but nobody in Grand Crapaud would steal it. He drove to Lafayette, rented a motel room, yeah, and parked it outside that bad housing project, with keys in it." The welder threw in another hand and watched the cards fly. "Next night he left the windows down with the keys in it." He pulled off his polka-dotted cap and ran his fingers through his dark hair. "Third night he left the motor runnin' and the lights on with the car blockin' the driveway of a crack house. Next mornin' he found it twenty feet away, idled out of diesel, with a dead battery. It was that ugly."

"What happened next?" The pilot trumped an ace like he was killing a bug.

"My frien', he called me up, you know. Said he wished he had a used standard-shift Ford pickup and the money in the bank. His wife left him, his momma made him take a cab to come see her, and all he could stand to do was drink and stay in his trailer. I didn't know what to tell him. He said he was gonna read his policy some more."

"Split pot again," the deckhand shouted. "I can't get out this game. I feel like my nuts is hung up in a fan belt."

"Shut your trap and deal," Raynelle said, sailing a loose wad of cards in the deckhand's direction. "What happened to the Mercedes guy?"

The welder put his cap back on and pulled up the crown. "Well, his policy said it covered all kinds of accidents, you know, so he parked it in back next to a big longleaf pine and cut that sucker down, only it was a windy day and soon as he got through that tree with the saw, a gust come up and pushed it the other way from where he wanted it to fall."

"What'd it hit?"

"It mashed his trailer like a cockroach, yeah. The propane stove blew up and by the time the Grand Crapaud fire truck come around, all they could do was break out coat hangers and mushmellas. His wife what lef' ain't paid the insurance on the double-wide, no, so now he got to get him a camp stove and a picnic table so he can shack up in the Mercedes."

"No shit? He lived in the car?"

The welder nodded glumly. "Po' bastard wouldn't do nothin' but drink up the few bucks he had lef' and lie in the backseat. One night last fall we had that cold snap, you remember? It got so cold around Grand Crapaud you could hear the sugarcane stalks popping out in the fields like firecrackers. They found my frien' froze to death sittin' up behind the steering wheel. T-nook, the paramedic, said his eyes was open, starin' over the hood like he was goin' for a drive." The welder pushed his down-turned hand out slowly like a big sedan driving toward the horizon. Everybody's eyes followed it for a long moment.

"New deck," the engineer cried, throwing in his last trump and watching it get swallowed by a jack. "Nick, you little dago, give me that blue deck." The oiler, a quiet olive-skinned boy from New Orleans's west bank, pushed the new box over. "New deck, new luck," the engineer told him. "You know, I used to date this ol' fat gal lived in a double-wide north of Biloxi. God, that woman liked to eat. When I called it off, she asked me why, and I told her I was afraid she was going to get thirteen inches around the ankles. That must have got her attention, because she went on some kind of fat-killer diet and exercise program that about wore out the floor beams in that trailer. But she got real slim, I heard. She had a pretty face, I'll admit that. She started hitting the bars and soon had her a cow farmer ask her to marry him, which she did."

"Is a cow farmer like a rancher?" Raynelle asked, her tongue in her cheek like a jawbreaker.

"It's what I said it was. Who the hell ever heard of a ranch in Biloxi? Anyway, this old gal developed a fancy for steaks, since her man got meat reasonable, being a cow farmer and all. She started putting away the T-bones and swelling like a sow on steroids. After a year, she blowed up to her fighting weight and then some. I heard she'd about eat up half the cows on the farm before he told her he wanted a divorce. She told him she'd sue to get half the farm, and he said go for it. It'd be worth it if someone would just roll her off his half. She hooked up with this greasy little lawyer from Waveland and sure enough he got half the husband's place. After the court dealings, he took this old gal out to supper to celebrate and one thing led to another and they wound up at her apartment for a little slap-and-tickle. I'll be damned if they didn't fall out of bed together with her on top, and he broke three ribs and ruined a knee on a night table. After a year of treatments, he sued her good and got her half of the farm."

The deckhand threw his head back and laughed—*ha-ha.* "That's a double screwin' if ever there was one."

"Hey, it don't stop there. The little lawyer called up the farmer and said, 'Since we gonna be neighbors, why don't you tell me a good spot to build a house?' They got together and hit it off real good, like old drinkin' buddies. After a couple months, the lawyer went into business with the farmer and together they doubled the cattle production, specially since they got rid of the critters' worst predator."

Raynelle's eyebrows came together like a small thunderhead. "Well?"

"Well what?" The engineer scratched an armpit.

"What happened to that poor girl?"

All the men looked around uneasily. Raynelle had permanently disabled a boilermaker on the *St. Genevieve* with a corn-bread skillet.

"She got back on her diet, I heard. Down to one hundred twenty pounds again."

"That's the scary thing about women," the day fireman volunteered, putting up three fingers to ask for his draw. "Marryin' 'em is just like cuttin' the steel bands on a bale of cotton. First thing you know, you've got a roomful of woman."

Raynelle glowered. "Careful I don't pour salt on you and watch you melt."

The engineer released a sigh. "Okay, Nick, you the only one ain't told a lie yet. Let's have some good bullshit."

The young oiler ducked his head. "Don't know none."

"Haw," Raynelle said. "A man without bullshit. Check his drawers, Simoneaux, see he ain't Nancy instead of Nicky."

Reddening, the oiler frowned at his hand. "Well, the cows remind me of something I heard while I was playing the poker machines over in Port Allen the other day," he said, a long strand of black hair falling in his eyes. "There was this Mexican guy named Gonzales who worked with cows in Matamoros."

"Another cow farmer," the deckhand groaned.

"Shut up," Raynelle said. "Was that his first name or second name?"

"Well, both."

"What?" She pitched a card at him.

"Aw, Miss Raynelle, you know how those Mexicans are with their names. This guy's name was Gonzales Gonzales, with a bunch of names in between." Raynelle cocked her ear whenever she heard the oiler speak. She had a hard time with his New Orleans accent, which she found to be Bronx-like. "He was a pretty smart fella and got into Texas legal, worked a few years and became a naturalized citizen, him and his wife both."

"What was his wife's name?" the pilot asked. "Maria Maria?"

"Come on, now, do you want to hear this or don'tcha?" The oiler pushed the hair out of his eyes. "The cattle industry shrunk up where he was at, and he looked around for another place to try and settle. He started to go to Gonzales, Texas, but there ain't no work there, so he gets out a map and spots Gonzales, Louisiana."

"That that rough place with all the jitterbug joints?"

"Yep. Lots of coon-asses and roughnecks, but they ain't no Mexicans. Must have been settled a million years ago by a family of Gonzaleses, who probably speak French and eat gumbo nowadays. So Gonzales Gonzales gets him a job working for two brothers who are lawyers and who run a horse farm on the side. He gets an apartment on Gonzales Street, down by the train station." The oiler looked at a new hand, fanning the cards out slowly. "You know how badass the Airline Highway cops are through there? Well, this Gonzales was dark and his car was a beat-up smoker, so they pulled him one day on his way to Baton Rouge. The cop stands outside his window and says, 'Lemme see your license,' to which Gonzales says he forgot it at home on the dresser. The cop pulls out a ticket book and says, 'What's your last name?' to which he says, 'Gonzales.' The cop says, 'What's your first name?' And he tells him. That officer leans in the window and sniffs his breath. 'Okay, Gonzales Gonzales,' he says real nasty, 'where you live?' 'Gonzales,' he says. 'Okay, boy. Get out the car,' the cop says. He throws him against the door hard. 'And who do you work for?' Gonzales looks him in the eye and says, 'Gonzales and Gonzales.' The cop turns him around and slams his head against the roof and says, 'Yeah, and you probably live on Gonzales Street, huh, you slimy son of a bitch.' 'At Twelve twenty-six, apartment E,' Gonzales says."

The deckhand put his cards over his eyes. "The poor bastard."

"Yeah." The oiler sighed. "He got beat up and jailed that time until the Gonzales brothers went up and sprung him. About once a month some cop would pull him over and give him hell. When he applied for a little loan at the bank, they threw his ass in the street. When he tried to get a credit card, the company called the feds, who investigated him for fraud. Nobody would cash his checks, and the first year he filed state and federal taxes, three government cars stayed in his driveway for a week. Nobody believed who he was."

"That musta drove him nuts," the welder said, drawing four cards.

"I don't think so, man. He knew who he was. Gonzales Gonzales knew he was in America and you could control what you was, unlike in Mexico. So when the traffic cops beat him up, he sold his car and got a bike. When the banks wouldn't give him no checks, he used cash. When the tax people refused to admit he existed, he stopped paying taxes. Man, he worked hard and saved every penny. One day it was real hot and he was walking into Gonzales because his bike had a flat. He stopped in the Rat's Nest Lounge to get a root beer, and they was this drunk fool from West Texas in there making life hard for the barmaid. He come over to Gonzales and asked him would he have a drink. He said sure, and the bartender set up a whiskey and a root beer. The cowboy was full of Early Times and pills, and you coulda lit a blowtorch off his eyeballs. He put his arm around Gonzales and asked him what his name was, you know. When he heard it, he got all serious, like he was bein' made fun of or something. He asked a couple more questions and started struttin' and cussin'. He pulled out from under a cheesy denim jacket an engraved Colt and stuck it in Gonzales's mouth. 'You jerkin' me around, man,' that cowboy told him. 'You tellin' me you're Gonzales Gonzales from Gonzales who lives on Gonzales Street and works for Gonzales and Gonzales?' That Mexican looked at the gun and I don't know what was going through his head, but he nodded, and the cowboy pulled back the hammer."

"Damn," the welder said.

"I don't want to hear this." Raynelle clapped the cards to her ears.

"Hey," the oiler said. "Like I told you, he knew who he was. He pointed to the phone book by the register, and after a minute, the bartender had it open and held it out to the cowboy. Sure enough, old Ma Bell had come through for the American way and Gonzales was listed, with the street and all. The cowboy took the gun out his mouth and started crying like the crazy snail he was. He told Gonzales that he was sorry and gave him the Colt. Said that his girlfriend left him and his dog died, or maybe it was the other way around. Gonzales went down the street and called the cops. In two months he got a six-thousand-dollar reward for turning in the guy, who, it turns out, had killed his girlfriend and his dog, too, over in Laredo.

He got five hundred for the Colt and moved to Baton Rouge, where he started a postage stamp of a used-car lot. Did well, too. Got a dealership now."

The day fireman snapped his fingers. "G. Gonzales Buick-Olds?"

"That's it, man," the oiler said.

"The smilin' rich dude in the commercials?"

"Like I said," the oiler told the table, "he knew who he was."

"Mary and Joseph, everybody is in this hand," the pilot yelled. "Spades is trumps."

"*Laissez les bons temps rouler,*" the welder sang, laying an eight of spades on a pile of diamonds and raking in the trick.

"That's your skinny ass," Raynelle said, playing a ten of spades last, taking the second trick.

"Do I smell the ten-millionth rollover pot?" the engineer cried. "There must be six hundred fifty dollars in that pile." He threw down a nine and covered the third trick.

"Coming gitcha." Raynelle raised her hand high, plucked a card, and slammed a jack to win the fourth trick. That was two. She led the king of spades and watched the cards follow.

The pilot put his hands together and prayed. "Please, somebody, have the ace." He played his card and sat up to watch as each man threw his last card in, no one able to beat the king, and then Raynelle leapt like a hooked marlin, nearly upsetting the table, screaming and waving her meaty arms through the steamy engine room air. "I never won so much money in my life," she cried, falling from the waist onto the pile of bills and coins and raking it beneath her.

"Whatcha gonna do with all that money?" the oiler asked, turning his hat around in disbelief.

She began stuffing the bib pockets on her overalls with half-dollars. "I'm gonna buy me a silver lamé dress and one of those cheap tickets to Las Vegas, where I can do some high-class gamblin'. No more of this penny-ante stuff with old men and worms."

Five of the men got up to relieve their bladders or get cigarettes or grab something to drink. The pilot stood up and leaned against a column of insulated pipe. "Hell, we all want to go to Las Vegas. Don't you want to take one of us along to the holy land?"

"Man, I'm gonna gamble with gentlemen. Ranchers, not cow farmers, either." She folded a wad of bills into a hip pocket.

Nick, the young oiler, laced his fingers behind his head, leaned back, and closed his eyes. He wondered what Raynelle would do in such a glitzy place as Las Vegas. He imagined her wearing a Sears gown in a casino full of tourists dressed in shorts and sneakers. She would be drinking too much and eating too much, and the gown would look like it was crammed with rising dough. She would get in a fight with a blackjack dealer after she'd lost all her money, and then she would be thrown out on the street. After selling her plane ticket, she would be back at the slot machines until she was completely broke, and then she would be out on a neon-infested boulevard, her tiny silver purse hanging from her shoulder on a long spaghetti strap, one heel broken off a silver shoe. He saw her at last walking across the desert through the waves of heat, mountains in front and the angry snarl of cross-country traffic in the rear, until she sobered up and began to hitch, picked up by a carload of Jehovah's Witnesses driving to a convention in Baton Rouge in an unair-conditioned compact stuck in second gear. Every thirty miles the car would overheat and they would all get out, stand among the cactus, and pray. Raynelle would curse them and they would pray harder for the big sunburned woman sweating in the metallic dress. The desert would spread before her as far as the end of the world, a hot and rocky place empty of mirages and dreams. She might not live to get out of it.

The Courtship of
Merlin LeBlanc

The baby woke up after lunch, and her grandfather changed her on the sofa, spooning baby food into her until she spat it back at him. It was then he realized that his daughter had left no toys for the child. He spread out a blanket on the floor, turned on the television, and went out of the room for a minute. When he came back, the baby had the TV cord in her mouth, and he realized with a pang that he couldn't keep his eyes off her for a minute. The baby stared at him and he stared at the baby. He went into his bedroom and fumbled through a box in his closet where he kept his shotgun shells, then returned with twenty or so, giving them to the child as playthings. There were shiny red Remingtons, green Federals, yellow Winchesters, and a cheap all-plastic orange variety he had bought at Wal-Mart. They were waterproof and too big to choke on, so he figured they'd be safe.

After the ten o'clock news, he drank a shot glass of strawberry wine. He fancied that the hot medicinal charge he felt in his stomach relaxed him enough to go to sleep at once. Two hours before, he had sung to his granddaughter so she would sleep. As far as he could remember, it was the first time he had sung anything. Maybe he had sung the National Anthem once, when he was in the service, but he wasn't sure. Not knowing any lullabies, he had sung "Your Cheating Heart." He lay down, and after he had drifted off, the telephone on his bed table rang out. He jumped for it, thinking at once of the sleeping baby.

The voice on the phone had the sad, official sound of a state policeman. He told Merlin LeBlanc that at about four o'clock a small airplane his daughter was riding in had come down out of a cloud bank over the Gulf of Mexico and crashed next to a Monrovian freighter. The accident happened over a hundred miles from shore in a thousand feet of water.

Merlin sat up in the dark and shook his head, thinking he was having a bad dream. "Where is my daughter?" he asked, his words husky with sleep.

"The ship's crew looked for survivors for two hours," the voice said. "The plane fell straight down in a dive. The crewmen got the plane number, and we found a manifest for it from Lakefront Airport here in New Orleans." The voice dragged on for several minutes, told Merlin he would be called again in the morning and hung up. He got out of bed, turned on his lamp, and walked over to where the baby was sleeping on a pallet. He could talk until he was blue, and the baby wouldn't know that her mama was at the bottom of the Gulf at the side of some slicked-back lounge-lizard pilot who ran a plane so ratty it couldn't even stay in the sky. He was not angry or sorry, just amazed. All of his children, all three of them, were now dead. Merlin junior had run off a bridge drunk, John T. was shot dead in a poker game, and now Lucy had fallen out of the sky like a bomb in a white trash's airplane.

The loss of his first two children had saddened him, but he had denied or concealed the sorrow in his life. Now he sensed an unavoidable change coming, as though he were being drafted by the army at his advanced age. He looked at the blond head on the blanket, and a powerful fear overcame him. What would he do with her? he wondered.

He thought of the day before, when he had pulled his old tractor under the lean-to and had noticed his daughter waiting for him on the porch. He had shaken his head. Whenever she stood leaning on that post by the steps, he knew she was upset and wanted to unload on him before he got into the house. He looked away, over his fields. The strawberry harvest was finally over, the land stripped of black plastic, the played-out plants disked under, and he looked forward to a short glass of wine, an hour of TV, and the coolness of his little white wooden house. Probably not, he thought, looking over at his daughter.

Even at this distance he could tell she'd been crying. He was fifty-two years old and had never once understood crying, or at least he failed to understand how people got themselves into predicaments that made them cry. He least understood his daughter, who was his oldest child, thirty-four, and who had been married twice, abandoned by both husbands, had been an alcoholic, a drug abuser, had been detoxified twice, and now had a seven-month-old daughter by a Belgian tourist she had met in a bar in New Orleans. Merlin was a man who assumed that the world was a logical place and that people were born into it with logical minds, the way they came with the ability to breathe and eat.

He walked across the close-clipped St. Augustine that grew up to the porch and looked at her. His daughter's dirty-blond hair was pulled back into a limp ponytail, and her eyes were baggy and pained. They were looking at him, but they had a faraway quality he had seen before and never tried to understand. "You comin' by for lunch?" he asked.

"No, Daddy. I had a cup of coffee and some toast late." She put her hands in the pockets of her jeans, not work jeans, Merlin noticed, but what she called "preworn," for people too lazy to wear out their own clothes. "The baby's asleep inside on the sofa."

"Okay," was all he said as he pushed past her and put his hand on the screen.

"Daddy, the reason I came by was I have to get away for a couple days. I mean, I'm just going nuts hanging around Ponchatoula doing nothing."

He stopped, his hand on the screen door handle and looked at her. "And?" he asked. He couldn't figure his children out, but he knew there was always an "and" in a conversation like this. He saw his daughter maybe five times a year even though she lived but three miles away in a little duplex built by the government for folks down on their luck. When she showed up, there was always an "and."

"And I want you to keep Susie for me while I'm gone," she said, smiling fearfully.

He looked inside at the infant on the sofa and back at her. "Get Mona to keep her."

"Mona's husband couldn't find work, so they've moved to Georgia."

"Get Doreen."

"Dorees wants money. I don't have any money, Daddy. Look, I got all the baby food and Pampers you'll need. It'll only be two days, and I know you finished with the field today, so you'll have lots of time."

"I can't care for a little thing that size," he protested. But his daughter began to cry and tell him how he never really helped her out and how she met this airplane pilot in La Place who wanted to fly her to Mexico for a couple of nights and half a dozen other things, until he ran his left hand through his silver hair and told her to take off and not tell him any more. He didn't want to hear about yet another deadbeat she was going out with, and though he was tempted to tell her she was making a mistake, he held his tongue, as he always had with his children. He was a man who never offered his children advice yet always marveled at how stupidly they behaved.

In the past he had watched over Susie for three hours at a time, so he figured he could fill her mouth and mop her bottom for a couple of days. Not much more trouble than a puppy, he thought. He went inside and his daughter put her face against the screen door and peered at him. "It'll be all right, Daddy. When I get back I'll fix you a big pot of shrimp okra gumbo like Momma used to make."

"Awright," he told her. He thought briefly of his wife, dead now six years, standing at the stove stirring a pot.

"Now don't get mad if she cries," she said. "Remember, it'll only be a couple days."

"Awright," he barked, walking into the dark kitchen to fix himself a lunch-meat sandwich.

The morning after the crash he got up with the baby, then fed and burped her. She smelled sour, so he put her in the big claw-footed bathtub and washed her down with Lifebuoy soap. She kept slipping out of his fingers, and he was glad finally to fish her out of the suds and rub her dry like a kitten. He dressed her in only a disposable diaper, since it was a warm day. The phone rang and it was the policeman's voice again, telling him that they were searching, but after all it was over one thousand feet of water and they weren't exactly sure where the plane had hit and other bits of unpromising news. Merlin sat in the rocker on the front porch, the baby in his lap playing with a Remington dove load, and tried to think about his daughter as a baby, but he couldn't remember a thing. His wife had tended the children just as he had tended the pigs they used to have in back of the tractor shed. He wondered if what went wrong was that he had treated his children like animals. You don't, after all, explain to an animal how to do what it's supposed to do. It goes through the gates, eats where the food is put, lies where it's proper to lie, and, when it's time, lines up to be hit or shot. He put his hand over his eyes when he thought this. Why do you have to tell children things? Why don't they do what's logical?

He was still rocking when his father pulled into the yard at ten o'clock. Etienne LeBlanc was seventy-five, feeble, and forgetful, but he had been that way for twenty years. He sat in the other porch rocker and Merlin told him about Lucy. The old man cried and mumbled into a bandanna he fished out of his overalls, and all the time Merlin looked off at his tractor, trying to remember if the oil needed changing. After a while the baby reached for her great-grandfather, and he took her into his lap, where she pulled at the copper rivets on his bib, trying to pluck them like berries. The old man began to talk to her in French.

"Daddy," Merlin asked, "what am I going to do with that little thing?"

His father, a balding, straight-backed man, sun-freckled and big-boned, made a face as the baby put her thumb up his great nose. "Only one thing to do."

"What's that?"

"You got to get married. We got no one to give Susie to."

Merlin blinked.

"And she's got to be a little younger than you."

"I could use someone to cook and clean up."

The old man tucked the baby into the crook of his left arm and looked at his son hard. "I'm not talking about a cleanin' lady." He said this very loudly. His upper plate fell down with a click. "You got to find someone you can care about."

"What?" Merlin gave his father a questioning look.

Etienne looked into his son's eyes for a while, then lay back against the rocker. "Aw hell," he said, shaking his head. "I forgot who I was talking to."

"Du," Susie said, pulling at a tobacco tag dangling from the old man's overalls.

For two weeks, everywhere Merlin went, the baby went also, until he felt that he had somehow grown an extra uncooperative limb that he had to drag around at all times. He spoon-fed her, washed her few clothes by hand in the big bathtub, hung them out to dry, washed her, convinced her to sleep at naptime, dealt with her crying at five in the afternoon, set her on his stomach to watch the news and *Wheel of Fortune,* bought her a playpen and plastic things to chew on, and, in the evening, sang to her and bounced her on the edge of the bed to cajole her to sleep at bedtime. Only then, between eight and his own bedtime, could he read the paper, or change the air filter in the truck, or bathe himself. At six it started all over again. He thought of his dead wife and was ashamed of himself. On the fourteenth night, after he had thought long and hard on what his father had told him, he decided he would at least try to talk to a single woman. The next night was Saturday, and in the morning he called his father to come over and keep Susie. About five o'clock the old man was sprawled on the sofa, the child beating him on the head with a plastic hammer. Merlin steamed himself clean in the big tub, then dug around in the medicine cabinet for something to make himself smell good. He found a green bottle with no label and slapped on some of its contents. His face caught fire and then he remembered that the liquid was a foot liniment his wife had bought. He pictured her rubbing her white feet in the evenings after a day of working the packing shed and running the kitchen. He washed his face quickly and found an oval blue bottle, sniffed it carefully, and splashed the liquid on. There was a bottle of lard-colored hair oil plugged with a twisted piece of newspaper, and this he massaged into his hair until the silver in it shone. In his bedroom he stood in his boxer shorts before his closet and wondered what he owned that would attract the eye of a female. Other than khaki pants and shirts, he had only two pairs of green double-knit slacks, one white shirt, an orange knit shirt, and a yellow knit shirt with a little animal embroidered over the heart. Merlin pulled it off the hanger and examined it closely— the animal was a possum.

He cleared the seed catalogs and fence staples off the seat of his truck and drove into Ponchatoula, where the dim neon sign of the Red Berry Lounge caught his eye. When he walked in, Aloysius Perrin, who owned the farm next to his, spotted him from across the dance floor and yelled over the pounding jukebox, "Hey, looka this. Clark Gable done come to the Red Berry." Merlin grinned in spite of himself and looked down at his tight yellow shirt and green slacks. Several of his old friends were in the bar, and he settled in with them for an hour or so, keeping a weather eye out for any unattached ladies. Sure enough, around eight, two women, Gladys Boudreaux and her older sister, came in and took a table across from the jukebox. Gladys had lost her husband two years ago to heart trouble, and she was ten years younger than Merlin, so he thought that maybe she was out on the prowl. He played a slow song on the jukebox and walked over to ask her to dance. She said no, she didn't believe she would. She told him she'd just come in to drink a beer, that she and her sister were taking a break from fixing a five-gallon pot of sausage gumbo for tomorrow night's Knights of Columbus dance.

"But you can come over to my place in the next block and help me and sis ladle out the stuff into the Tupperware if you want," she said, giving him a cute little gumbo-ladling smile. He followed the two women to their house and discovered that what they really needed was a man to wrestle the five-gallon pot off the back burners of a huge Chambers range and over to a low table. After he helped them, they gave him a bowl of gumbo and he sat there in the kitchen eating, feeling like a stray dog enjoying a handout. The gumbo was made with cheap sausage, and his bowl had a quarter inch of grease floating on top.

" 'Scuse me, Gladys," he said. "Did you fry this sausage before you put it in the gumbo?"

"No. Why? There's nothing wrong with it, is there?"

He spooned up a tablespoon of clear oil and dumped it out on the plate. "Well, no. It's just fine. I'm just wondering if it wouldn't be quite so slick if you heated some of the fat out of the meat before you put it in the gumbo."

"Oh, that ain't fat, Merlin. That's just juice."

"Juice," Merlin repeated.

"Yeah. Kind of like clear sauce. Now, don't stare at it like that. Just stick your spoon in and eat it up." She smiled at him again in a way that made him wonder if she wanted him to scrub the big pot and put it on the top shelf in her kitchen, too.

He stared at his gumbo and understood why her husband had died from a bad heart. He ate slowly, worrying about all his friends in the Knights of Columbus.

He returned to the Red Berry Lounge, where Aloysius introduced him to a bleached blonde named Alice. They danced once or twice and sat at a table by the bar while she told him her life story, her dead husband's life story, and the problems her four sons had with the law. It occurred to Merlin that marrying someone his own age would probably make him father of several young men and women who would soon be after him for hand tools and car-insurance payments. Despite this, he told Alice about his granddaughter. She made a face and said, "Well, let me tell you, I don't want anything to do with a kid in that yellin' and stinkin' stage. I already done my time." When he finished his beer, Merlin excused himself and walked to the bar, standing under the rotating Schlitz sign and surveying the twenty or so folks in the room, all more or less his age. The Red Berry was known as an old folks' bar, what they called a tavern in other parts of the country. The crowd that was in here now was the same one that had started coming right after the Korean War. He spotted Gwen Ongeron, whose husband had been killed in a ferryboat collision, and she waved with one hand and adjusted the bottom of her permanent with the other. So he went over through the smoke and cowboy music to ask her to dance. They danced to two records, and in that time she asked him how much land he owned, how much he had saved up in the bank, and what year his tractor was made. He didn't follow her back to her table.

Out in the parking lot he sat in the grass-seed smell of his truck and wondered what the hell he was doing looking for a wife in a honky-tonk. It was like trying to find a good watch in a pawnshop. He tried to think back to when he had been nineteen and had asked his wife to marry him. What had he felt when he held her hand? What had he wanted thirty-three years before that he could still want now? He couldn't remember how he'd felt the day he married, couldn't remember one thing he had said to his wife. After all those years of marriage he hadn't known much about her but that she was honest and a good cook. Now, for the first time in his life, he wondered what he should look for in a wife. Whatever it was, he had had it once, didn't realize it, and was now ashamed.

He drove home and found his father asleep in an oak rocker next to the reading lamp, a photo album open in his lap. He walked up to him quietly and bent over to see what he had been studying. The old man's pointing finger was resting on a picture of Merlin's children and wife. They were all grinning like fools, Merlin thought, seated on the front bumper of a 1958 Chevrolet. He didn't think he had taken the photograph. Where had he been? Why wasn't he in it? He nudged his father and the gray eyes opened over a slow, wrinkled smile. "Hey, boy," he said, straightening up a bit. "Have any luck with the ladies?"

"Nah. What you looking at, Daddy?" He bent to study the album more closely.

"It's Merlin junior, John T., and Lucy," he said.

"And Bee."

The old head nodded. "And Bee. God, that woman could cook. Two minutes in the house with a fresh cut-up rabbit, and the onions and bell peppers would be a smokin' in the skillet."

Merlin focused on the smiles in the picture. "Makes you wonder what went wrong." He stood up, looked down on his father's bald and spotted head. The statement hung in the air like an unanswered question. "I was never mean to them."

Etienne LeBlanc turned his head slowly and looked up toward the screen door as though someone was standing there. "Maybe you should have been," he said. "At least that would've been something."

On the first Monday of each month, Our Lady of Perpetual Help Nursing Home would bring Merlin's grandfather over for a daylong visit. About eight-thirty a white van pulled into the farm lot and two attendants rolled out Octave LeBlanc in his wheelchair and installed him on the porch. There wasn't much left to him. Sixty-five years before, he had been a millwright with the F. B. Williams Lumber Company in the bayous of St. Mary Parish, but now he was a pale eighty-pound rack of bones. He was blind, but he could still think and talk. Etienne drew up a rush-bottomed chair on one side of him and Merlin and the baby sat on the other side in the swing. The old man blinked his dead eyes, flung a gray arm against the weatherboard of the house, and dragged his palm along the wood. "You gonna have to paint next year, Merlin." The voice was thin and whispery, like a broom sweeping a wood floor.

Merlin looked at the peeling paint under the eaves. "It might last longer."

"It might not."

The baby moved in Merlin's arms, subsiding and yawning, dangling a naked foot over his arms, testing the air. Merlin was so full of worry about the child, he could hardly pay attention to his grandfather. He couldn't raise her. What if he died? Worse, what if he didn't do any better with her than he had with his own?

"You got a beer for me?"

"No," Etienne said. "You don't need no beer at eight something in the morning."

"What," the old man said, "you scared it's going to kill me?"

Etienne leaned back in his chair and laughed. "Poppa, if we give you a beer, you'll sleep through your visit."

The old man turned his head quick as a bird. "It's a hell of a thing you won't give me one son-of-a-bitchin' beer." He flung a hand toward his son, who crossed his arms against his overalls and leaned back against a peeling white roof support.

The baby stuck her tongue out and blew a bubble over it. It was very warm outside, and she was in a diaper only. She made a fist with her left hand, put it into her right palm, pulled them apart, and made a noise like a laugh. Octave's head turned. "What the hell's that?"

"A possum," Merlin said.

"Let me see." The old man held out two trembly arms bound with black veins. The baby went at once to him. "Ow," the old man said as she settled in his lap. He ran his hand over her head and over her stomach. "Merlin," he said fondly, a smile showing his cracked dentures, "you tricky bastard."

"Granpop."

"This ain't no possum." He put his hand between the baby's legs and gave the diaper a quick squeeze. "This ain't no lil' boy, either."

Etienne leaned over to help the baby find its foot. Merlin bent down, picked up a shotgun shell, and handed it to the child.

"Whose baby is this?" Octave asked, finding the girl's nose with his fingers and gently pushing it like a button. The baby opened her mouth and sang a note.

"Lucy's," Merlin said. "Remember, we told you about the airplane."

"That's right. Didn't that girl know no better than to go up in one of them damn things?" And then he turned his eyes on Merlin as though he could see, and said, "Didn't you teach her nothin'?" and Merlin shuddered like a beef cow hit with the flat side of an ax. The old man had always told people what he thought and what they should think. Merlin feared his directness, didn't understand it. But he was ninety-three years old and all his children were still alive.

"Don't be hard on me, Granpop."

The old man turned his head toward where he thought his son was sitting. "Somebody shoulda," he accused.

"Come on, now." Etienne lost his smile.

Octave bent over and planted a shaky, slow kiss on the top of the baby's head. She looked up and burped. "Ha-haaaa," Octave rasped. "You feel some better now for sure, eh, *bébé*?" His hand found the shell she was playing with and seized it. "What's this?" He picked up his face and aimed it at Merlin.

"A play toy," Etienne said.

"She likes it to play with." Merlin and his father exchanged worried looks.

Octave ran his forefinger around the rim. "Feels like a number-six play toy with a ounce-and-a-quarter shot." He tossed it over the back of the wheelchair, where it bounced on the porch and rolled off into the grass. "You don't give no baby a damn shot shell to play with." His voice was little, but it spoke from a time and experience Merlin could not imagine. One of his stiff legs fell off its step on the wheelchair. "I ought to be put in jail for causing two muskrats like you. You lying to me just because I can't move out this chair and get you."

Etienne put a meaty hand on his father's shoulder. "Easy, Poppa."

" 'Tien, what I told you. Talk to the boy. He got no more heart than a alligator. All he cares about is his berries and his tractor." The old man's eyes began to brim with a filmy moisture.

"Hush," Etienne said, looking at the porch floor.

"Perrin came in the home last night. He told me about Valentino in a yellow shirt. I heard it and I believed it."

"Hush, now. This won't do no good."

The old man grimaced as he moved the baby over in his lap. She put four fingers in his limp green shirt pocket and pulled. "I know what I know. Merlin in a damn barroom lookin' for a woman like a pork chop."

Merlin put his hands together and stared at the baby. Old men made him feel weak and ignorant, because he trusted them and believed what they said about things. They had been where he was going. Here was his grandfather, ninety-three years old, his blood and his bone telling him what he was afraid to hear.

Octave coughed deeply and his whole chest caved in, his eyes closing and even his ears moving forward with the slope of his shoulders. It was a while before he got his breath back, and then his voice was weaker than ever. "Looking for a woman like a damn toaster he can bring home and take in the kitchen and plug in. Plug in and forget it. Hot damn." He began coughing again, but he had so little wind in him, his cough was more like a slow aspirate rattle. He seemed to be drowning in a thimbleful of liquid deep in his chest. Merlin took the baby and brought her inside while his father bent over Octave. When he came back out, Etienne's face was red, and tears were streaming down.

"What is it?" Merlin asked, holding on to the screen door handle.

"I don't know. I guess he's asleep. His heart's just like a little bird, you can't hardly hear it at all." He sat down and began to feel for a pulse in the soft skin of his neck. "You know," Etienne began, "what he said about you is true. You never felt much about your children. You never had no kind of emotions." He placed a huge spotted hand on Octave's forehead.

Merlin sat back in his chair, pulled a handkerchief, and mopped the sweat from his face. "Daddy, I don't know what's going on, but I'm not no rock like you and Granpop make out."

Etienne looked over at the lean-to and the dull red tractor it sheltered. "When you was thirteen I took you to a movie in town. Before it started up, the Movietone news come on and showed four fellows killed by a tornado, laid out next to they barn. When you saw that picture you said, 'Look, Daddy, them fools nailed the seams wrong on that tin roof.' " He looked down at the floor and blinked. "I shoulda pulled you outside and talked to you right then."

Merlin sat in the swing and put his head in his hands. A breeze slowly stirred high in the pecan tree by the porch, the way a spirit might rattle the leaves passing through. He thought about the women in town. He might try again. Maybe at church. Maybe at the KC bingo game. And he wouldn't look for a toaster.

"Merlin." His father called his name. He was staring at the old man's face, which was the color of wood ash. "I think he's gone at last."

Merlin swung close. "You want me to call the ambulance?"

"What can they do? Look." Etienne nudged Octave's open mouth shut and pulled down his eyelids.

"Damn," Merlin said. "And I didn't let him have a beer."

"They's a lot of things we didn't let him have." Etienne turned his wet face away and looked over the disked-up fields to a group of starlings wheeling along the edge of the far tree line. "When you first got married, you was young. We all married young. We didn't know no more about raising children than a goat knows about flying. He knew," Etienne said, straightening up and touching his father's shoulder. "I told you what he told me, but you looked like you . . . aw, what the hell. When I saw how you was ignoring your kids, I should have come over and whipped your ass good three or four times and thrown you in the slop with the pigs." He put his head down and placed a hand on his father's cool leg.

It was not easy for Merlin to touch his father, but he reached over and swatted him on the shoulder.

"Damn it," Etienne cried, "he told me to do it, too." He jerked his thumb at the still form in the wheelchair.

"I bet," Merlin said. He heard the baby stirring in her new playpen and beginning to whimper. He got up and went to her, bending to pick her up the way he would lift a puppy, then changing his mind and slipping his palms under her arms. Returning to the porch, he stood next to Octave and stared down. The baby made a noise. Octave turned his head in reflex. "Hot damn, where that baby?" he said.

Etienne sat back in his chair so hard he lost his balance and tumbled off the porch onto the grass. Merlin froze, his mouth open. Only the baby spoke, singing *laaaaaaaaa* and holding out a fist to the old man, who sensed where she was and touched her foot.

"We thought you was dead," Merlin said at last.

Octave did not change the faraway smile on his face. "Oh, I come and I go. The nurses said I passed away three times last week." His hands, blue and trembly, pulled the baby toward him.

Etienne sat up on the lawn, his hand on his shoulder. "I'm all right," he said to Merlin. "Just give me a minute." He seemed to be caught between pain and laughter.

"What's this baby's name?" the old man asked in his whispery voice.

"Susie."

He grunted. "No, sir. Her name is Susan. Susie sounds like someone you gonna meet in the Red Berry after ten o'clock."

"Yes, sir," Merlin said.

"Her name is Susan. Su-san. You hear that? You gonna keep her here and raise her even if you don't find no wife."

"Yes, sir." Merlin sat in the swing and held on to the chain.

"You gonna talk to her every day about everything. Tell her about dogs and salesmen."

"Yes, sir."

"Tell her about worms and bees." Here he wiggled his finger into Susan's belly and silver giggles rang from her round red mouth.

"Yes, sir."

"About cooking and cars and poker and airplanes."

"Oh sweet Jesus." Merlin got up and went down the two steps to help his father. Making a face, Etienne reached under his bottom and pulled out the shotgun shell. He banged it upright on the edge of the porch. Octave's head wavered above the baby's bright face as he swung a foot off the wheelchair stirrup and kicked the shell back down to the ground. Merlin hugged his father under the arms and hoisted him up, keeping his hold after they were standing, trying for balance. The two of them stood there in the sunshine, chastened but determined, amazed by the smiles on the porch, where Octave and Susan whispered and sang.

Navigators of Thought

At ten-thirty Friday morning, Bert was in the wheelhouse of the company's oldest tugboat, trying to figure out its controls. The jagged squawks of the shortwave set were interrupted by Dixon's trombone voice. "*Phoenix,* come back."

Bert turned and stared at the peeling machine, wondering why his boss was on the air instead of the dispatcher. He grabbed the microphone. "*Phoenix* by." Please, not a towing call, he thought. Not already.

"Doc, are you cranked and hot?"

Bert made a face at the expression. "Max had some trouble with the engines, but he's got them started now."

"Hang by the set," Dixon told him. "A tanker hit the fleet above Avondale Bend and some barges are coming down. If the other tugs can't catch them, you might have to go out and lasso one."

Bert placed a palm on the top of his bald head. "You want us to chase a barge downriver?"

"What's the matter, Doc? Don't your speaker work?"

"You can't send the Mexican fellows after it?" Dixon's crews were hired by their captains, and the *Sonny Boy* was run by Henry Gonzales, who had employed all his relatives. The *Aspen* gleamed under the attentions of its Vietnamese operators, and the *Buddy L* twanged around the New Orleans harbor with a crew from Biloxi.

"Gonzales hung up a hawser in his prop. You might see a big grain hopper coming down in a half hour. Look out." In a tearing snort of static, Dixon was gone, replaced by a low, whistling fabric of dismembered voices. Bert hung the mike on the set and looked upriver through the wheelhouse door. The Mississippi was a gray deserted street. He sat on the stool behind the spokes of the varnished wheel and thought of how his crew had trouble tying on to drifting equipment. Like the other captains, he had been allowed to hire his own people, so he gathered men like himself, college teachers who had been fired. He wondered whether they could change form in midlife like amphibians.

He thought back to the week before, when he had been at the controls of the new *Toby,* shoving a small barge to a dock downriver from the city. He had jerked the throttle levers into reverse, and the boat had hauled back on the barge, her engines shuddering. His mouth fell open when he saw the starboard and port lines seeming to untie themselves, paying overboard as the barge charged the dock at an angle, hammering two pilings into kindling.

Several stevedores wandered over to see what had caused all the thunder. Two of them pointed at the *Toby* and laughed. Bert shoved the throttle levers up, easing the bow against the barge to keep it pinned in place. Thomas Mann Hartford and Claude McDonald, the deckhands, appeared on the push knees, and on the third try attached a rope to their tow, turning when they had finished to look warily up to the wheelhouse. Bert pushed open a window.

"Clove hitches on a barge? You've got to be kidding." His deckhands sometimes reminded him of the cloudy-eyed freshmen in the backwoods college where he had taught for four years.

Thomas Mann lowered his small blond head to look at one of the ropes that had come undone. Bert studied his unraveling dress slacks and greasy Izod shirt, waiting for him to look up. "I'm really sorry, Bert, but a couple of hours ago when we were picking up the barge, Claude told me about the new book on John Donne's poetry, and I went to his bunk to see it." The deckhands had been denied tenure at a small state college and were unable to find full-time work anywhere. Thomas Mann looked up at the shattered pilings. "We forgot to ratchet up the cables after we made the preliminary tie-off."

Bert leaned out farther to get a better look at the damage. "I can't believe you expected two rowboat knots to hold that thing. What the hell do you think Dixon is going to say when he finds out you two were twittering over seventeenth-century metaphors when you should have been lashing a barge?"

Claude McDonald shook the mane of dark curls clustered over his thick glasses. "It's a formidable consideration," he said.

At seven the next morning, the five-man crew of the *Toby* had filed onto the deep carpet of their employer's office. Dixon was the owner of two tugboat fleets, a person who could appreciate the true value of intellectuals. At sixty-six, the former deckhand still looked out of place in his fine office, his gray suit. He sat back in a tall leather chair and popped his knuckles. A series of wrinkles ran vertically across his forehead like hatchet scars. "Please don't try to explain nothin'," he said. "I wouldn't understand what you was talking about if you did. Last month, you ruined three hundred dollars' worth of cable, and you had me believing it was my fault, like I wrapped it around that ferryboat myself." He looked at them hard, and Bert watched the old eyes, which were like two olives forgotten in the bottom of a jar. The crewmen kept back from the big desk, afraid for their jobs. The middle-aged cook, Laurence Grieg, was trembling, facing the loss of the first employment he had found in two years.

The engineer, a bony man with Nordic features, was Maximilian Renault, a Romantics scholar given to slow, spooky movements and inappropriate smiles. Dixon threw a hard look his way and Max backed up a step, running long fingers through his dark hair.

"You guys have tore up more machinery in six months than the other five crews put together." Dixon looked at them carefully, his intellectuals, sorry at the expense they had caused him, but at the same time enjoying their failures. The college boys, all Ph.D.'s, would never make the money he had made. "I realize," he continued, turning a heavy white-gold ring on his left hand, "that times is bad. All the good professor jobs been sucked up years ago." He paused, letting the obvious sink in. If these had been ordinary crewmen, they might have traded glances, told Dixon to go to hell, and walked out.

But discarded teachers would take anything. "So I'm gonna keep you on, but remember this," he said, falling forward in his chair and aiming his chopped face at them. "I pay you damn good money—union scale. I deserve better for my boats than you been doing. If you can't do better, I got to let all of you go."

The five men were silent. The tension had been broken, and they waited to be told to leave. Dixon sent a bored glance out over the grassy median of Carrollton Avenue, where a green-roofed streetcar clattered past. "I can't let you stay on the *Toby*. She cost too much. Today, I'm gonna put all the Cajuns on her. I'll sell their tug and you can go on the spare."

"The spare?" Bert looked over his shoulder at Max, who shrugged.

Mr. Dixon pulled a form from his desk and began writing. "The *Phoenix Three*," he said.

"The old red tug tied up against the willows?"

"That's it," Dixon said, sucking his teeth and looking up to study Max's frayed Arrow shirt. "It was built in the twenties out of carbon steel and rivets. Even you people can't tear it up." He looked Bert in the eye. "Go on down to the dock and get familiar with the boat. It's got old controls. Steering it will be like dancing with a cow."

And now Bert stood in the wheelhouse of the *Phoenix III,* pulling mud daubers' nests off the control levers and gauges. A gummy spar varnish darkened the oak cabin, and the windows were cloudy with dust and soot. He looked around at the tarnished brass, the old-fashioned curved-front cabin, worrying about the ragged machinery. Bert always suspected that Dixon had hired him as a mean joke, and now he'd played another on him.

After he'd lost his teaching appointment, his wife had to find work as a secretary, and his children were taken out of private school. During the year of fruitless applications and interviews, his family buckled down as though waiting out a stubborn malady. There were no offers of jobs, only mild interest expressed by junior colleges in Alaska, Saudi Arabia, and a fundamentalist high school in West Virginia.

Once a week he'd ridden the Jackson Avenue ferry to collect his unemployment check. He liked the gritty smell of the Mississippi that met him at the landing, and the red-and-white tugs and broad, rusty freighters sometimes floated along the channels of his dreams. The throbbing vessels moved with the power and grace of great poems.

He got the idea to apply to a towing company for work. Dixon had laughed out loud when he saw Bert's resumé. He disliked the idea of a man like Bertram Davenport so much that he hired him on the spot. He wanted to let the college man roast his brains on the steam tug *Boaz* with the backwoods savages from Arkansas he'd hired to run her. He was sure they'd throw him overboard first trip out.

However, Bert got along with the Arkansas men, who were not really savages but only easily angered farm boys from around Camden. He became an excellent harbor wheelman, learning the currents and signals as though they were in his blood. Dixon was grudgingly impressed. A smart wheelman avoided thousands of dollars in dry-dock work on smashed bows and bent propeller shafts.

Bert should have been satisfied with his success, but it only told him that he was a better river man than he had been a teacher. When he recalled how he had often bored his students and become disoriented while dealing with complex ideas in his lectures, he suspected that the English department was right in getting rid of him.

After two years, Bert was given his own small boat and was allowed to recruit men for his crew as replacements became necessary. The first scholar he'd hired was Max, his old graduate school roommate, an amiable but directionless man who worked on car engines for extra money and who had earned his final degree at forty-one after taking dozens of diverse and ill-chosen courses and then writing a seven-hundred-page dissertation on Byron and Nietzsche.

Dixon thought it a fine joke to have two scholars on one of his tugs, and he encouraged the hiring of more, so when Bert needed to employ a cook, he enlisted his old confidant, Dr. Laurence Grieg, who had been fired two years before for failing too many students, and whose hobby was preparing French cuisine. The two deckhands, Thomas Mann Hartford and Claude McDonald, were hired last.

From the wheelhouse, Bert heard an old generator engine rattle alive below, and the cabin's lights came on slowly, like newly lit candles. A compressor began to chatter, and after a few minutes Max turned over one of the huge engines down in the hold, and it thundered alive, sending convulsions of black smoke from the tug's stack. Bert pulled the wheel around and saw a swirling comma of water sail out from under the stern. At least the steering worked. On the boat's long stern, he saw a deckhand making notations in a spiral-bound book. Every professor Bert knew wrote essays with the dream of earning some share of fame and a position at a well-known university. When he and his crew were languishing on the decks waiting for a towing call, most of them brought manuscripts to revise, add to, and argue over.

A month earlier, tied up in blinding fog below the Belle Chasse locks, they had met in the galley and had passed around one another's works. For hours the men sat hip-to-hip, hunched over cramped handwriting or poor typing. The conversation was stiff and polite. The pedantic, graceless ordinariness of the writing showed in the faces of the scholars gathered under the pulsing lights of the small compartment. Bert read an article in progress by Claude McDonald, a man who was a true academic, very intelligent, but so educated that he was unable to compose two coherent paragraphs in a row. After a few pages he put the paper down and wondered whether his own work was half as taxing. He smiled faintly and nodded at Claude, who was sitting two stools to the left of him, struggling with Max's enormous work on Byron. Bert turned to his right, putting his hand on Max's shoulder. "Sometimes I think we think too much," he told him.

Max frowned above a handwritten page. "Thought is life."

Bert took back his hand. "Someone could just as well say, 'Navigation is life.' That's what we are now—navigators." He liked the sound of the word.

Max turned his dark eyes on him. "We're navigators of thought."

Bert set the wheelhouse clock and then climbed down to the galley, where Laurence Grieg had just made coffee in a half-gallon enamel pot. Bert held a hot ironware mug in both hands and studied Laurence, how his shoulders were rounding into middle age, worn that way like a boulder in a creek by his wife, who was constantly on his back about returning to an academic job. Laurence would never work again, for his dossier contained a damning letter from his department head.

"How's Laura?" Bert asked, sitting at the counter that ran down one wall of the galley, a narrow compartment spanning the width of the boat. Laurence Grieg, who had lately begun dressing in khaki work clothes, all his polycottons and tweeds finally wearing out, adjusted the tiny gas range so the coffee would not boil.

"Laura is Laura." He showed Bert a beleaguered smile. "She's complaining about the smell of oil in my clothes," he said, shaking his shiny head.

Maximilian lumbered in, got a cup of coffee, and left immediately. He seemed unaware that anyone else was in the galley. Thomas Mann poked his blond head in the door. "Bert, someone is on the radio for you."

Bert put his cup down and went out into the wind, zipping up his corduroy jacket and climbing the flaking stairs to the wheelhouse. He picked up the receiver and spoke to the dock dispatcher, who told him that his boat might be sent to the mouth of the river to pull a ship from a sandbar. He signed off and saw that Max had followed him up. His face was weighted with embarrassment. "Bert, Loyola has rejected my application," he said, looking away quickly, his face growing darker. He was not a man who liked to admit that he was in trouble. None of them were.

"What about the other applications?"

"The same. Tulane's letter was very snide. The search committee said they did not employ industrial workers as professors." He thrust his hands into his pockets. "It's finally happened," he said, looking down to the corrugated deck. "I didn't tell you at first because I was ashamed." He snuffled once, bringing a crisp new work-shirt sleeve up to his nose.

Bert imagined him in the classroom fumbling with notes. "Why are you ashamed?"

The engineer looked past him at a small gaily painted excursion boat grinding up the river, its decks speckled with tourists pointing their cameras at the old tug. Four of them waved with enthusiasm. "I'll never be in the classroom again."

Bert waved back absently. "Is that the worst that can happen?"

Max looked surprised. He replied only after he had thought fully half a minute. "The worst is what we think it is." He smiled quickly, catching himself. He sat down in the wheelman's chair. "I don't think I can face it. The change, I mean. Giving up on teaching. Maybe, when my manuscript finds a publisher . . ."

"Max, you're making a good living on this job." Bert turned away, jamming his hands into his coat pockets, feeling his ring of keys, one of which fit an office door a thousand miles away.

Max pressed a palm on the glass of the wheelhouse window. His voice was low and steady. "Will any of us get back to where we belong?"

Bert broke another mud dauber's nest off an overhead gauge and threw it sidearm over the rail.

And then at eleven that Friday morning, there it was, Dixon's voice on the radio like a tearing tarp. "*Phoenix,* come back."

Bert grabbed the microphone quickly. "*Phoenix* by."

"Doc, can you move out in a flash?"

"What? Are we going down to the jetties?"

"Lord, no. It's a rodeo upriver. They're lassoing runaway barges like crazy. Somebody's chasing all but the lead barge. Go catch it."

Bert squeezed the mike like a lemon and looked upriver. "Couldn't you call out another boat? We're—"

"Make it smoke, Doc. I don't want to tell you twice."

"I don't know if we can catch it. I'll have to think about—"

"Don't think. Do." Dixon was flashing into anger. The two deck-hands, hearing the broadcast, crowded into the wheelhouse, little Thomas Mann shivering and Claude McDonald squeezing one joint of a finger in his book. Bert looked upriver and saw a long grain barge nose around the bend, riding high in the water, doing about seven miles an hour.

"Doc?" Dixon's portentous voice tore through the old gray short-wave set. "You think you got tenure here or something?"

Bert looked at Claude's arms, wondering how much was muscle. "Okay," he sang, "we're heading out. *Phoenix Three* over." Without thinking, he began to give orders. Soon, Thomas Mann was hopping about on the landing barge like a blond monkey, untying the lines. Claude rattled down the steps to the pointed foredeck, where he began making up a bowline. Bert gave four short blasts of the whistle, and Max stuck his head out of the engine room door.

"Bertram. Where're we going?" He gestured with a manuscript in his gloved hand.

"Just study your engines for a change," he called. "We'll need all the power they've got."

Bert swung the steering wheel, leaned on the throttle levers hard, and felt the tug surge away from the landing barge. A cloud of black smoke billowed from the exhaust ports in the stack, the engines trembled like old horses, and Bert imagined he could hear Maximilian shouting encouragement to the machinery. He reached up for the whistle cord and blew another danger signal. The river was clear of traffic except for one ascending ore freighter, which he called to advise. The *Phoenix III* headed straight out toward the barge while Bert judged its speed and weight. Several options occurred to him instantly, not the result of deliberation. If he were to run the boat ahead and gradually slow down, letting the barge catch up to the stern and stop against it, the slanted bow might climb the rear deck and sink the tug. If he tried to tie on and control it from the side and couldn't, it might drag the *Phoenix* downriver sideways and capsize it. He decided to catch it from the rear with a bowline and yelled for Claude to tie a hundred feet of two-and-a-half-inch nylon rope to the front towing bitts and to form the free end into a loop. He could hear Maximilian below, beating on something with a hammer or wrench, and suddenly the engines, their teeth-rattling vibration gone, surged smoothly with added power.

He piloted the tug to within thirty feet of the barge, cutting the engines to half speed and following the vessel downstream, letting its rusty sides slip past. Its mooring cleats were twelve feet above Claude's head, and Bert hoped his deckhand could throw a rope that far.

As the stern of the barge slid past his bow, Bert revved the engines to keep up. Claude climbed on the hemp fender and swung the yellow hawser back and forth underhand as Thomas Mann waited behind him. He tossed the loop toward a cleat on the barge's deck, but the line tangled in itself and fell short, splashing into the churning river. Bert cut back the engines to keep from nudging the barge into a spin, then blew another series of short warning blasts to alert any boats that might be ascending Carrollton Bend.

Thomas Mann retrieved the rope and coiled it on the deck so that it would pay out smoothly. He seemed not to be thinking about anything; perhaps there was not an abstraction in Thomas Mann's head for the first time in years as he spread his legs wide, bent his back, and threw the rope into an orderly coil. When the boat rounded Carrollton Bend, Bert could see the willowy foot of Walnut Street on the east bank, and abreast of it, three-quarters of a mile below him, two excursion vessels, a tanker in midriver, and a towboat shoving a raft of barges past the tanker on the west, all ascending.

Claude climbed high on the bow, and Thomas Mann coached him on his swing. The big man's black curls fluttered in the wind as he practiced swinging one, two, three times, and on the fourth swing, he flung his arms open like springs, tossing the noose spinning, spinning, up to the mooring cleat, where it hung on the metal like a cowboy's lariat.

"Eeeeeh-haaaah," Dr. Claude McDonald yelled as Thomas Mann pulled in the slack behind him, whipping it around the double towing bitts in four quick figure eights. Bert set the engine-control levers into full reverse, and the nylon line began to tighten like an archer's bowstring. The barge slowed to a crawl as the propellers bit into the river. The hawser turned to rock, complaining on the bitts, creaking and popping on the painted iron.

"Get off!" Claude screamed at Thomas Mann, who was standing on the bitts, inspecting his knot. He jumped free and both men ran amidships as the line parted with a sound like cannon fire, whipping back to where the deckhand had stood, hitting the metal like a thunderbolt. The tug surged backward, and the barge was taken again by the current. Bert killed the engines and looked over the runaway hopper barge to the ascending tow. He saw the low profile and red vents of loaded petroleum barges. Sliding open a stubborn wheelhouse window, he yelled down, "Get Max out of the engine room, latch the doors on the first deck, and climb to the bunk deck with Laurence."

Looking over at the ascending towboat, Bert could see its crew coming to the rails, donning life jackets. The big boat was trapped between the freighter and the bank, and both vessels had cut their engines. The *Phoenix III* and the barge drifted down on them. Horns and whistles filled the river, and the shortwave gave off a jam of panicked voices. Bert's own crew of four watched at the rail below him as he made the old tug's engines rumble. Soon they were sloshing alongside the barge, drawing close. When the tug's bow was amidships and five feet off from the runaway's side, Bert turned the wheel, jolting into the barge and holding the bow against its flank. The *Phoenix III*'s stern swept around and the tug began to capsize. It was taking the river sideways, leaning over into the current like an old drunkard falling down slowly. The barge began to respond and move sideways into the lower bank of Nine Mile Point, but water was roaring over the tug's port rail. The crew scrambled to starboard and looked up to the wheelhouse for a signal to jump. Bert noticed that they had buckled their life vests correctly for once. They had no time to think about what they were doing.

The ascending tow was blowing shorts and the tanker contributed sonorous blasts of its steam horn. When the hopper was thirty feet from the bow of the leading petroleum barge, it swung clear into the dead water under Nine Mile Point, the *Phoenix III* heaving it toward the bank on a hard rudder. Bert looked behind, past the storm of his wheelwash, and saw the petroleum barge slide toward his stern, and he braced for the impact. The tug surged against the rusty, buckling steel, and the far side of the runaway began to rise in the air as it rode up onto a mud flat. Behind, the petroleum barge slid clear, brushing the hemp fender on the *Phoenix*'s stern. Then an empty lunch box slid off a shelf above the radio and banged to the floor and the port door swung out. A shout went up from the men at the rail as the boat went into a dying roll. Bert pulled back on the engine controls, but it was too late. The boat was heeling over, and with his crew Bert scrambled out onto the near-horizontal bunk deck wall.

Max swung down to the engine room door, pulled it open, and ducked under as it slammed like a gong. At once the crew slid toward the water and pulled at the latches on the oval steel door. They saw Max inside, struggling in a surf of brown water roiling in through the vents and up through the bilge.

"Max," the cook shouted, leaning in. "What are you doing?"

The engineer didn't look up. "My manuscript," he yelled.

The generator sucked up a charge of water and banged to a halt, the compartment falling dark. Bert jumped in, feet first, landing on the side of a stair ramp. "Forget it. Come on." He grabbed Max by the shirt collar and hoisted his head above the oily water, but he shook out of his grasp.

"It's the only copy," he wailed, plunging in again, disappearing against the port wall. The river began to pour in the open door.

"It's not worth it," Claude MacDonald yelled at Max's emerging head. "It'll never be published."

Thomas Mann Hartford hung upside down into the engine room. "Max," he pleaded. "Give it up. It's a piece of crap."

"No." He rose into a shaft of water-jeweled light falling through the door. "It will get me out of here," he told them, going under again. Before Bert could reach him, the boat shifted to a pure horizontal, and the water reached the hot manifolds of the towering port engine, filling the engine room with steam. Bert yelped and jumped for the outstretched hands of his crew, who hauled him up through a muddy waterfall, for the boat was going down, the river storming into the open door. An explosion of steam and trapped air propelled them into deep water, the men clinging together like a raft of ants in a flood. They were swept by the current while the *Phoenix III* turned over, flashed its corroded propellers, and went down headfirst.

Bert looked over to the geysers of air breaking the river's surface and tried to think of something to say, but his mind would make no words.

Five minutes later the cook watched the Dixon fleet's crew boat approach at a chopping roar. "I hope the old man gives us a strong cup of hot coffee before he fires us." The hull came up to them, and Dixon himself, dressed in a wool suit and overcoat, helped pull them out of the water and hustle them into the small cabin. "Where's that Renault guy?" he asked, his face flushed and worried.

No one could say anything for a long moment. "He's in the engine room," Bert finally said. Dixon turned his head and gave the river a long, openmouthed look. Bert peered out at the dull water while the crew boat's pilot radioed an approaching Coast Guard cutter about the lost man. "We tried."

Dixon sat down and pushed the wrinkles out of one side of his face. "I saw what happened on radar. I heard it on the radio." He looked over at the rescued hopper barge. "It's fifty feet deep where it went down. Maybe I can have it raised." He shook his head once. "Jeez, why couldn't he get out of the engine room?"

The men looked at one another, and Dr. Grieg, the cook, cleared his throat. "I guess he got trapped."

For a moment, Dixon hid his face in his soft, spotted hands. "What? Did the door slam on him?"

Bert looked out at the river, which renewed itself every flowing moment without a thought. "Something like that," he said, watching a little white cutter begin to circle above the wreck, two divers looking in the water for something to make them jump.

People on the
Empty Road

Wesley and his girlfriend were parked in his father's driveway on Pecan Street, arguing in his old Pontiac Tempest. Bonita was a sulky brunette with a voice as hard as a file. She wanted him to get the forty-dollar tickets to the Travis Tritt concert, and he tried to explain that the twenty-dollar tickets were a better deal. He looked down the humpback asphalt lane to where it turned off at Le Phong's Country Boy Cash Grocery and ground his teeth. He sensed he was going to lose his temper again, the way a drunk feels in his darkened vision that he is about to fall off a stool. Bonita crossed her arms and called him the cheapest date in Pine Oil, Louisiana, and Wesley crushed the accelerator, leaving the car in neutral, letting the racket do his talking. The engine whined up into a mechanical fury until a detonation under the hood caused everything to stop dead, as if all the moving parts had welded together. Wesley cursed and got out, followed by Bonita, who spat her gum against a pin oak and put her hands on her hips. "Now you done it," she told him. "When are you gonna calm down?"

Wesley examined a volcano-shaped hole in the hood of his car where a push rod had blown through like a bullet. "You can walk home and wait for Travis Tritt to climb in your window with a bouquet of roses," he yelled. "But don't wait for me."

She started down the street, then turned and shouted back to him, "When you gonna grow up?"

"When I'm old enough to."

Bonita continued toward her rental house in the next neighborhood. Wesley turned and went into the kitchen. The old man was at the table, home from his supermarket, sipping a glass of iced tea.

"That's the second engine this year, Wes. How many can you afford?"

"I know. She got me so damned mad." He fell into a chair. "I think we just broke up."

His father ran a hand over his gray hair and then loosened his tie. "It's just as well. She was common. Her sister who used to check for me on register six was kind of rough. What was her name, Trampoline?"

"Trammie-Aileen," Wesley corrected. "She works for Le Phong now." He put his head down and his red hair fell forward like a rooster's comb.

"Know what I think?" his father asked.

"What?"

"I think you ought go come back cutting meat in the store. You were the fastest trimmer I ever had. With a rolled rump, you were an artist."

Wesley held up the nub of his left forefinger, and his father looked out the window. "I want to do something else for a while, Daddy."

"I think you'll be safer cutting meat for me here in Pine Oil than off driving for that gravel company. You don't have the disposition for that."

Wesley's face became as tight as a rubber glove. "You mean I'm reckless, don't you?"

"You just got to find a girl who'll calm you down. Only thing'll do that is a good girl and time."

Wesley put his head back down in his hands. "I don't want to hear this."

"Well, when's it gonna happen? You're twenty-four and been through eight cars." His father took a swallow of tea and softly grabbed a fistful of his son's hair. "That old Tempest wasn't any good, but it was transportation."

"I can afford Lenny's rusty T-Bird. It's for sale."

His father clamped the coppery strands in his fingers, an old game, his way of saying, "Calm down. Come back to earth." Then he said, "I'll get you a better car if you come back to work for me."

Wesley pulled free and moved toward the window. "I've got to go roll some gravel. I'm good at it."

"I don't like you running those tight schedules."

Wesley leaned on the wooden window frame and watched a wisp of oil smoke rise from the puncture in his hood. "The construction folks want the rock quick. If we can't get it to them when they need it, someone else gets the contract."

His father rubbed his eyes. "Your boss is making money on your lack of patience. You need to slow down and find a girl who thinks there's more to life than fast cars and cowboy music."

Over the next month he made more runs than any other driver at the gravel pit. His boss, old man Morris, pear-shaped, with skin like barbecued chicken, told him, "Boy, you're a natural."

"A natural what?" Wesley asked, stepping up into a blue Mack.

The old man spat on a wheel rim. "A natural way to get my rock moved faster than Ex-Lax."

Each day, his truck clipped a minute off the time to the big casino site in New Orleans, but each fast trip shaved a little off his nerves, the way the road wore down tires to the explosive air at the center of things. He couldn't help the urge to sail across the twenty-four-mile-long causeway over Lake Pontchartrain like a road-bound cargo plane weighted down with many tons of pea gravel. A big sedan might be in the right lane doing sixty-five and he would be coming up from behind at ninety, water showering up from his wheels, a loose tarpaulin flying over the forty-foot trailer wild as a witch's cape. Near his left rear mud flap there'd be another car, and the time to change lanes was exactly then or the people in the big sedan would be red pulp, so after one click of his blinker he would roll out like a fighter plane, road reflectors exploding under his tires like machine-gun bursts.

He used his recklessness like a tool to get the job done. After every twelve-hour day, he would tear out of the gravel pit in his rusty Thunderbird, spinning his wheels in a diminishing shriek for half a mile. The road turned through worthless sand bottoms and stunted growths of pine, and the car would surge into the curves like electricity, Wesley pushing over the blacktop as if he were teaching the road a lesson, straightening it out with his wheels. When he would charge off the asphalt at eighty onto a gravel road, he would force the low sedan over a rolling cloud of dust and exploding rock as though he were not in danger at every wheel skid and shimmy of slamming into a big pine like a cannonball. For Wesley, driving possessed the reality of a video game. After thirty miles, he would skid to a stop, a half ton of dust boiling in the air behind him.

His destination was a dented sea-green mobile home parked in an abandoned gravel pit. He would pull at its balky door until the whole trailer rocked like it was caught in a hurricane, and finally inside, he would sit at his little kitchen table and watch his hands shake with something beyond fatigue.

One morning at six o'clock he was awakened by an armadillo rummaging in his kitchen. The animals were all over the place and had come in before. Wesley soft-kicked it through the open door frame like a football and watched it land in a pit of green water on the other side of his car. He sat down to listen to a radio talk show coming from the AM station in Pine Oil.

"Wouldn't you say that giving a man the death penalty for stealing two cows is a bit excessive?" The host's voice was pleasant and instructive.

"If they was *your* cows, sweetie, you'd want him to fry like bacon," a tubby voice said.

Wesley forced himself to eat breakfast, and sometime between the cereal and the orange juice, he began to relax. The woman announcer's voice was smooth as a moonlit lake, and he remembered meeting her at the store when she did a remote from the meat aisle during Pine Oil Barbecue Days. After breakfast, he sat on the galvanized step below his warped door frame, folded his hands, and rested his chin on his knuckles. He wondered how fast he would be driving in another month.

Wesley watched a lizard race from under the step. When the pit around the trailer had been operating, years before, a watchman had lived here. Spread over it for two hundred acres were green ponds shaped like almonds or moons or squares. To the south was an abandoned locomotive, its wheels sunk into the sand. Shards of machinery and cable lay about as though rained down from the clouds. He had lived in the center of the wreckage for six months and not one person had been to see him. He needed a new girlfriend—his father had said it—one who would make him go to the movies, barbecue hamburgers over a lazy fire, read magazines with no girlie pictures in them. He remembered the woman on the radio.

Turning up the ivory-colored Zenith left behind by the watchman, he listened to Janie, dealing with the farmers' wives. She ran from six to twelve, starting each program with a simple question, such as: "Do you think people should send money to TV evangelists?" or "Should the federal government spend more on welfare?" Many of her callers were abusive or made inflammatory statements far beyond the boundaries of simple ignorance. Most, Wesley decided after weeks of listening to the program, were people too stupid to be trusted with jobs, so they just sat around the house all day thinking up things to call the radio station about. He turned up the volume.

"Hello, you're on the air." The voice laid hands on him.

"Miz Janie," a high-pitched old-lady voice whined.

"Good morning."

"Miz Janie?"

"Yes, go on. Today's topic is the library tax." The voice was seasoned with a bright trace of kindness.

"Miz Janie, ain't it a shame what the law did those poor boys down in Manchac?"

"Ma'am, the topic is the library tax."

"Yes, I know. But ain't it a shame that those poor boys got put in jail for killing birds?"

"You're referring to the Clemson brothers?"

"That's right."

"They killed over two thousand Canada geese," she said, not the least hint of outrage in her voice.

"Birds is all," the old lady said. "Them boys is people. You can't put people in jail for what they do to birds."

Wesley balled up his fists and glared at the radio, remembering Elmo, his pet mallard from childhood.

"Ma'am," the smooth voice said, "if everybody killed all the geese they wanted to kill, soon there'd be no more geese." Wesley searched for some bitter undercurrent in the voice but found not one molecule. The announcer gradually guided the old woman through a long channel of logic that led to the day's topic, the library tax.

"Miz Janie, everybody wants to raise our taxes. It's hard to made ends meet, you know."

"This tax is twenty-five cents a month." That was slick, Wesley thought.

"Well, it's the principle of the thing," the old voice complained. "Seems like we're paying people just to sit around and read when they ought to be out doing something else. If everybody would quit hanging around the library and get out on the highway picking up trash paper instead, we'd have a clean community, now wouldn't we?"

Wesley glared at the dusty radio. But the lady announcer continued to speak with honesty and openness until the woman on the line lost interest and hung up.

The next caller was an old man. "What the hail we need to spend money on a damned library for? Let them what wants to read go down to Walgreen's and buy they own magazines. The old library we got's plenty enough for such as needs it."

The next caller agreed with the millage proposal, but then a straight-gospel preacher came on the air and told that only one book ought to be in the library, and then another voice said he wouldn't mind voting for the millage if they got rid of the ugly librarian. "I mean, if they want to renovate, let's *really* renovate and get rid of the old warthog at the front desk." The announcer, her words like April sunshine, explained that Mrs. Fulmer was a lovely person as well as a certified librarian. Wesley turned up the radio, got out the brushes and Comet, and scrubbed his trailer like a sandstorm, wondering whether the announcer was single and trying to remember what she looked like. Her voice made her seem young, in her mid-twenties maybe, like he was. Then the phone rang, and he was called for two runs to New Orleans.

Down at the pit, he drew King Rock, a vast expanse of red enamel and chrome, the soul of the gravel yard. The foreman swung his gut out of the scale shack and climbed onto the truck's step, shoving his bearded face through the window. "If you can't push the son of a bitch to New Orleans by nine," he said, "you better keep going, hock the truck, and leave the country."

Wesley pulled a steel bar from under the driver's seat, got down, and walked around the rig, beating the tires as if he was angry with them, testing for flats. It was an extra-long trailer heaped with wet gravel. Wesley drove the rig onto the twisting two-lane blacktop, stomping the accelerator at every shift of the gears. He couldn't make himself think about the danger, so he again chose to see the windshield as a big video-game screen he could roar through with the inconsequence of a raft of electrons sliding up the face of a vacuum tube. The challenge was time, and he would lose if he drove a real road. He checked his watch—five after eight. The New Orleans site had to mix cement by nine or send a shift of workers home. King Rock loped under his feet like a wolf after deer.

Wesley streaked past a speeding Greyhound bus at the bottom of a grade, cut into the right lane, hit a curve, and felt the heart-fluttering skitter of nine tires trying to leave the ground. "Good God," he said aloud, surprised and frightened. But when he came to a straight section, as empty and flinty as a dull lifetime, he raced down it. He turned on the radar detector and thought of the two trips he had to make. The order had come in at seven: triple money for a load before nine in downtown. He was the only man who could make the ride.

Soon the truck was singing up to eighty. Wesley tapped his trailer brakes and drew ghosts of smoke from his rear tires. The video game had to be perfect now, for any mistake would cause a fierce yellow flash on the screen, the loss of a man.

He saw pines swarm past his window until he rose over the crest of Red Top Hill, the descending road tumbling away from him, deserted and inviting speed. He tried not to think about how fast he could go; he just rode the machinery as though it were only noise instead of iron and rock, and when he slid into the curve at the bottom of the hill, he was not really alarmed at the rear of the stopped school bus ahead with its silly tin signs flopped out and a dozen children strung across the highway.

Wesley stood on the brakes and hung on the air horn while his tires howled and a cumulus of blue smoke rolled up behind. Gravel hammered the roof of King Rock's cab, and he could hear the retreads tear off the tires. He fell out of his video game when he saw the faces of the children, real kids whose only mistake in life was to cross a road ten miles down from a greedy man's gravel pit.

The truck slid, and the trailer wagged from side to side. The hair on Wesley's arms bristled, the muscles in his legs cramped. Finally, like a child recoiling from a father's slap, he closed his eyes tight and yelled, not seeing what happened as his truck dove past the bus.

When he opened his eyes, the rig had begun to slide off the blacktop and into a roadside slough. The bumper bit a ton of mud that surfed over the windshield and roof, and the truck stopped at last. Wesley's arms and legs felt rubbery and bloodless. His head turned to the all-seeing expanse of his side mirror, which would at least miniaturize the disaster behind. No one lay in the road, though several children were cowering under the bus. Three or four heads popped up out of a roadside ditch, and he found comfort in the fact that they were looking in his direction, that perhaps there were no bodies to see. Wesley jumped to the ground, where he heard his tires hissing in the mud, and began running limp-legged to the bus. A river of powdered rubber lay on the roadway, and the air stank. The grammar school kids picked themselves up and stood silently on the grassy roadside, and he could see that no one was hurt. Standing next to the bus, trembling and accused by the young eyes, he felt a presence behind him and looked into the face of the driver, a veteran gray-haired housewife who watched him through the vent window as though he were a snake creeping on the highway. "They'll ticket you, and you'll be back on the road again soon as you clean your pants," she said, her face quivering with anger.

When the parish deputies showed up, they handcuffed him, and Wesley panicked, twisting against the steel loops as he sat in the backseat of the cruiser. His movement was taken, and all he could do was squirm and try not to consider what he had done. No one talked to him except to utter quick, bitten-off questions, and he longed for a helpful voice. When the deputies unlocked the gnawing cuffs at the jailhouse, Wesley shook out his arms like wings warming up for flight.

His boss claimed a favor from the sheriff and made his bail. That night about eight, Wesley drove down to Pine Oil as slowly as he could bear, found out where Janie Wiggins, the radio announcer, lived, and went to her apartment building. He was as shaky and light-headed as a convert come from a tent meeting. When he knocked on the door, a blond woman about thirty years old answered.

"Miz Janie?" he asked.

The woman examined him politely, trying to place him. She had a pleasant face that was a bit round, and bright, alert eyes. "Do I know you?" she asked, her voice just like the one on the radio.

"I'm Wesley McBride. I met you in the meat department at McBride Mart." He picked up his left foot and shined the top of a loafer on the back of his slacks. "I'm one of your . . . well, fans." He briefly wondered if announcers on five-hundred-watt radio stations had fans. "I've always wanted to meet you again."

Her mouth hung open a bit, and he could see she felt complimented. "You're the guy who does the fancy-cut rib racks. Well, I'm glad to meet you, Wesley, but I guess you ought to come by the radio station if you want to discuss advertising."

"I don't work for the store anymore. I've got a new job, and I'd like to talk to you a little about it now, if that's all right with you. Maybe we could meet at the coffee shop down the street and sit a while."

She looked at him harder now, studying his features. "Talk about what?" He liked the way she ticked off her words like a northerner.

"I want to know about how you're so patient with people." He had never once in his life thought that he would say such a thing, and he turned red.

She looked at him carefully for a moment, shrugged, and told him she would meet him for a cup of coffee in a half hour. Before she closed the door, he saw that her apartment was nearly bare, had blond paneling, cottage-cheese ceiling, rent-to-own furniture, a nubby couch.

At Slim's Coffee Hut Wesley began to tell her about himself, how he was always impatient, even as a kid, but how over the past year he'd been losing control. He showed her his shortened finger, told her about his driving and about the school bus. His hands began to sweat when he mentioned the children, and he put his palms on his knees. She reminded him of a nurse the way she listened, like someone trying to comprehend symptoms. It occurred to him that she might not be able to tell him anything.

"Let me see if I understand," she said. "You want to know how I can be patient with the folks that call me on the air?" He nodded. "Well, I've got bad news for you. I was born patient. I just don't see the point in getting angry with anyone." Wesley frowned. Was she suggesting he had some sort of birth defect? He looked down and saw grains of masonry sand in the penny slots of his loafers. His boss, old man Morris, had given the sheriff two loads of driveway gravel to tear up Wesley's tickets, and he wanted him back on the road in a few days. Wesley wondered how long it would be before he killed someone.

"I'm sorry to bother you so late," he said, looking into her eyes and giving her the easiest smile he could manage. "It's just that I've been sort of waiting for things to turn around in my life. Right now, I got the feeling I can't wait any longer."

"Oh God," she said, her face crinkling like crepe paper, burgundy flushes coming under her eyes. "Don't say that."

"Say what?"

"That you're tired of waiting for things to turn around." She put a hand palm up on the table. "My favorite uncle used to say something close to that, over and over. Nobody knew what he really meant until we found him on his patio with a bullet in his temple."

Wesley straightened up. "Hey, I ain't the kind for that."

She stood awkwardly, almost upsetting her water glass. "I found him. You don't know how that made me feel. The missed connection." She stared out at the street, and he saw a flash of panic in her eyes. Her expression made him think of something his father used to say: that good times never taught him one crumb of what bad times had. "Come on," she said, "I want to show you something." He followed her out, and in the middle of the block she made Wesley get into the driver's seat of her car, a boxy blue Checker, a civilian version of a taxi.

"Where'd you get this big old thing?"

"My uncle," she explained, settling in on the passenger side. "He said it was slow, relaxing to drive, and one of the only things that brought comfort to his life." She rolled down the window. "He left it to me in his will."

"Where we going?" Wesley asked.

"Just drive around Pine Oil. I want to watch you." So he drove down the main street a mile to the end of town as she directed. Then he drove back on a parallel street, then west again, until he had done every east-west street in the checkerboard village. She told him to pull over at the edge of town at the Yum-Yum drive-in, a cube of glass blocks left over from the fifties.

"How'd I do?"

"Awful," she said.

Wesley thought he had never had a milder drive. The heavy Checker had floated over the city streets as though running on Valium. "What'd I do?"

"You rode the bumper on two elderly drivers," she told him. "Then you signaled for dimmers from two cars who had their low beams on. And Wesley," she said in her flutelike voice, "six jackrabbit starts, and at the traffic light you blew your horn."

"The old lady with the bun didn't move when the light changed."

Her face rounded off into a tolerant smile. "Wesley, this is Pine Oil. Nobody blows his horn at anyone else unless he spots a driver asleep on the railroad track. That woman was looking in her purse and would have noticed the light in a second. And where were *you* going? To a summit meeting?" She put her hand on his shoulder like a sister. "You've got to pay attention to how you're doing things." Her voice held more touch than her hand.

The fat woman wedged in the little service window of the Yum-Yum stared at them. "Okay," he said. "I'll try most anything." Janie then bought him a deluxe banana split, and even though he told her he hated bananas, she made him eat it with a flimsy plastic spoon.

Later, she made him drive the whole town, north to south, from poor brick-paper neighborhoods next to the tracks to the old, rich avenues of big drowsy houses. Janie lay back against the door, twisting a strand of hair around a finger. Finally, she asked him to take her home. When he pulled up to her apartment and turned off the motor, the quiet flowed through him like medicine.

"How do you feel, Wesley?" she asked with that voice.

"Okay, I guess. Just tired." He felt he had dragged her huge car around town on a rope slung over his shoulder.

"You did better." She straightened up and looked out over the long hood. "I have no idea what's wrong with you. I just want you to know that, and I really don't think you need to see me again." She smiled at him politely. "Just be patient like you were when you were driving tonight. You have to wait for things to turn around."

That's that, Wesley thought, as he helped her into the late-night air and walked her to the apartment.

The next morning he was sitting in the door of his trailer, drinking a cup of instant coffee and eating a Mars bar, wondering if he could get a job on the railroad, or even go back to work for his father. He heard the rattle and snap of gravel and saw Janie's navy-blue Checker lumber toward him through the mounds of gravel and sand. Swinging the door open quickly, she dropped from the front seat, fluffing out a full leaf-green skirt. "Wesley, you have got to be kidding."

"Ma'am?"

"Why're you living in a place like this? You can do better."

He nodded slowly, taking the last bite of his candy bar and staring at her. "My boss rented it to me the day I was hired. I guess I thought it came with the job." In daylight, she was prettier, though he could see better the cautious cast of her eyes.

"It wasn't easy locating you, let me tell you." She looked around at the junk as if to get her bearings, then settled her worried gaze on him. She was direct and moved precisely, unlike any woman he'd been around. "Can you take a ride right now?" He saw the white arm move out from her side.

He put down his coffee cup. "I reckon so. Where we going?"

She smiled. "I like the way you say 'reckon.' "

Where they went was out on 51, the sluggish two-lane that bisected the parish. She had him pull up to a stop sign and wait. A pickup truck rattled by, and he started to pull out. "Not yet," she said.

They waited five minutes, watching lumber trucks and motorcycles pass. Janie craned her neck and studied the southbound lane carefully. Finally she saw something that seemed to draw her interest. "That cattle truck," she said. "It's perfect. Get in behind it."

Wesley stared at the tinged sides of the slowly approaching trailer. "Aw, no," he pleaded.

"Follow it to Pine Oil," she commanded as the truck packed with heaving cows rocked by. He pulled into the wall of stench and began to follow at forty miles an hour. After five miles, he begged her to let him pass.

"No," she said. "You'll remember this trip for the rest of your life and realize that if you can wait out this, you can wait out anything." She turned her face to the side of the road, and the sunlight bounding off the hood brightened her high cheeks and made her beautiful. "A road is not by itself, Wesley, even if it's empty. It's part of the people who live on it, just like a vein is part of a body. Your trouble is you think only about the road and not what might come onto it."

He made a face but followed in silence, down through Amite, Independence, and a half a dozen redbrick and clapboard communities with countless red lights and school zones. Arriving among the low tin-and-asbestos buildings of Pine Oil, he was white-faced and nauseated.

"You look awful," she said, leaning over, her green eyes wide. "Does being patient upset you this much?"

"No, ma'am," he lied.

"Well, let's see." She had him drive to Wal-Mart and stand in the longest line to buy a can of paste wax. They went over to her apartment, where she told him to get busy waxing the car. For three hours she sat in a folding chair under a volunteer swamp maple growing by the street, watching and occasionally calling for him to go over spots he'd missed. "Polish slower," she called. "Rub harder." Wesley thought he'd like to sail the green can of wax a block down the street and tell her to go to hell, but he didn't. His face began to develop slowly in the deep blue paint of her car.

Later, she set him in a straight-back chair in her plain living room and made him read a short story in *The Atlantic* and then talk to her about it. To Wesley, this was worse than following the cattle truck. He stared down at the glossy page. What did he care about a Chinese girl who couldn't make herself look like Shirley Temple to please her mother? Then Janie drove him home and they sat in the Checker outside his trailer. He leaned over and kissed her, long and slow, once.

"Wesley," she began, "what did the story in the magazine mean to you?"

"Mean?" he repeated, suspicious of the word. "I don't know." He knew what she was doing. She was trying to make him patient enough to think.

She asked him again, this time in her nicest radio voice. He told her about the Chinese girl's guilt and about her will be independent. They talked for an hour about the story. Wesley thought he was going crazy.

The next day he did not see her, but he did listen to the radio. The topic was how to get rid of weeds in the yard. One caller, a wheezy old man, recommended pouring used motor oil along fences and sidewalks.

"But Mr. McFadgin," Janie began, using her most patient voice, "used motor oil is full of toxic metals such as lead."

"That's right, missy," the old man said. "Kills them weeds dead."

Wesley listened to her program for three hours and did not become enraged once.

The following night she called him to meet her at the Satin Lounge, a sleepy nightclub for middle-aged locals next to the motel. In a blue dress with a full skirt, she looked like a schoolteacher, which was all right with Wesley. They talked, Wesley about his father trying to control his life and Janie about her uncle, how he had raised her, how he had left her alone. They ordered a second round of drinks, and Janie did not test him for patience for an hour. Then, someone played a slow number on the jukebox, and she stood up and asked him to dance. "Now slow down," she said, after they had been on the floor about ten seconds. "This is not a Cajun two-step. Barely move your feet. Dance with your hips and shoulders." He felt the controlling movement of her arms, of her soft voice, and realized that she was leading. After a while—he didn't know how it happened—he was leading again, but slowly. He felt like a fly struggling in sap, but he willed himself to dance like this all the way through the lengthy song.

Later on, two men sat at a table next to them. One was round and bearded, wearing a baseball cap with *Kiss My Ass* embroidered across the crown. The other, a short man with varnished blond hair, stared at Janie and once or twice leaned over to his companion, saying something behind a hand. Wesley watched him walk over to their table. The little man smiled, showing a missing tooth. He asked Janie to dance, and when she replied in a voice that made being turned down an honor, he scowled. "Aw, come on, sweetie. I need to hug me some woman tonight."

"I'm sorry, but I don't want to dance right now. Maybe someone at one of the other tables would enjoy your company." She smiled, but it was a thin smile, a fence.

He grinned stupidly and leaned over the table, placing his hands down on the damp Formica. "That sounds like a line a crap to me, sweetie."

Wesley caught her glance but couldn't read her face. He figured that she would want him to stay calm, to avoid an argument, to sit expressionless and benign, like a divinity student. Maybe this would be another test, like polishing her mountain of a car.

"We really would like to be alone," she said, her confident voice weakening. The man smelled of stale cigarette smoke and beer. He looked at Wesley, who did not move, who was thinking that her voice was betraying her.

"Looks like you are alone," he said, grabbing her wrist and giving it a playful tug.

Wesley was sitting on his emotions the way he used to sit on his little brother in a backyard fight. When he saw Janie's wrist circled by a set of nubby fingers, he said in a nonthreatening voice, "Why don't you let her go? She doesn't want to dance."

The blond man cocked his head back like a rooster. "Why don't you just sit there and cross your legs, little girl."

Wesley looked down at the table as Janie was towed over to the tile dance floor. He relaxed in his fury and watched them. The little man couldn't jitterbug, his steps had nothing to do with the music, and he cramped Janie's arms on the turns. At the end of the song, he pulled her close and said something into her ear. She pushed him away, and the little man laughed.

When she stormed over to Wesley, her face was flushed, her voice a strained monotone. "I am so embarrassed," she said, staring straight ahead. "Why didn't you do something instead of just sitting there like a worm?"

Wesley felt a rush of blood fill his neck. He imagined that the back of his head was ready to blow out. "Do you know how hard it was for me to sit here and not pop him one in the face?"

She rubbed her right arm as though it hurt. "I felt so awkward and helpless while he was limping around out there."

"I was being patient. The only thing that would've made the little bastard happy is if I'd whipped his ass and gotten us all pitched out on the street or arrested."

She seemed not to hear. "I needed help and you just sat there." She stirred her drink with a swizzle stick but did not lift it. "I felt abandoned." She looked down into her lap.

Wesley's face was red, even in the dim light of the Satin Lounge, and the muscles in his neck rolled and twitched. He told himself to hold back. She wanted him patient and slow. "Hey, no harm done. It's over."

Janie stood up, sending her chair tumbling, and slammed her purse on the table. "Right," she yelled. "It's over."

By the time he paid the tab and ran into the parking lot, all he saw were the crimson ovals of the big Checker's taillights swerving around a distant curve. In the hot night air hung the sound of her uncle's car grinding through its gears, gaining momentum as though it might never stop.

The next morning he called Janie four times at the station, and each time she hung up on him. He sat on the sun-warmed iron steps to the trailer and tried to figure out why she was so upset. He had done what he thought she'd wanted him to do. He looked over at the abandoned locomotive buried axle-deep in the sand and shook his head.

Around eight o'clock the telephone rattled. Big Morris, his boss, was on the line. "Hey, boy. Mount that T-Bird and fly over here. We got called on a full load of masonry sand for the south shore by nine-thirty."

Wesley stared through a cracked window at his ten-year-old car. "It'll be a pinch."

"C'mon. You can do it."

"Call Ridley."

"He went through the windshield yesterday over in Satsuma. Be out for three weeks. Listen," Big Morris said with the cracked and weathered voice of an old politician, "you're my man, ain't you? You're the fastest I got."

Wesley looked at the warped and mildewed trailer, then out at the junk stacked around it. "I think I'm going to lay off driving for a while."

"What? You're good at speeding gravel, son."

"I know. That's why I'd better quit."

Two weeks later he was cutting meat in his father's grocery store, doing a fine job trimming the T-bones and round steaks, though now and then he jammed the slicer when he hurried the boiled ham. It was a new store, and the cutting room was pleasant, with lots of fluorescent lights, red sawdust on the floor to soak up the fat, and an auto-parts calendar on the wall showing Miss Rod Bearing. He always worked the one to nine P.M. shift, but today he had to cover the morning stretch. While he was in the back pulling meat out of the cooler, he noticed a familiar voice on the janitor's boom box, and he stopped, a rib cage cocked under his arm, to listen to Janie. She was dealing with Raynelle Bullfinch, a motorcycle club president from up near the Mississippi line.

"Who cares if we don't put no mufflers on our hogs, man," Raynelle growled. "Last time I looked, it was a free country."

Janie's voice slid out of the radio. "The ordinance in Gumwood is limited to neighborhood streets, Raynelle. It wouldn't affect your driving through town."

"Yeah, well what if one of us wants to take a leak or something, and we have to buzz in off the highway? Those fat cops in Gumwood will jump on us like bottle flies."

"You don't think anyone should mind being inconvenienced by your racket?" The voice was a little thinner, and Wesley arched an eyebrow.

"Hey, everybody has to put up with some BS."

"Yes, but ugly noise is—"

"Aw, what the hell do you know, girlie. You never rode a Harley. You never get out of that radio station."

"Yes, but—"

"You got a leather jacket?"

There was a second of dead air. "Why would I want one?" The voice was flat and poisonous. Wesley leaned closer to the radio.

Raynelle shouted out, "What?"

Another second of dead air, and then Janie's voice splintered, trantrumlike and shrill. "Why would I want to dress like a bull dyke who thinks the highest achievement of Western civilization is a stinking motorbike that makes a sound like gas being passed?" Wesley dropped the rib cage, then caught it up quickly at his ankles and hoisted it onto the cutting table.

"You bitch," Raynelle screamed.

Janie said something that made Wesley sit back against the meat, hold his nub, and stare at the radio. Just then, his father came through the back door, shaking rain off his hat.

"What you frownin' at, Wes? You look like somebody just had a accident." He began pulling off a raincoat.

"Aw hell, I don't know," he said. Janie played a commercial and then broke for the national news. Turning on the band saw, he positioned the ribs, watching the steel flash through the meat.

The next morning Wesley tuned in the local station on a new stereo in his apartment. A male voice filled his living room, an old guy with a scratchy throat who hung up on people when they disagreed with him. Wesley was surprised, the way he'd felt when something unexpected had come into the road in front of his gravel truck. He called the station and talked with the secretary, but she wouldn't tell him anything. For two mornings he listened for Janie but heard only the disgruntled voice, a sound rough and hard-nosed, a better match for the backwoods folks of the parish than Janie could make herself be. He called her at home, but the phone had been disconnected. He went to her apartment, but it was being cleaned by a Vietnamese woman who said she was getting it ready for the next occupants. Finally, he stopped at the station, which was upstairs over Buster's Dry Cleaning, and found the manager in his littered office.

"Hey, I'm Wesley, a friend of Janie. I wonder if you could tell me how to get up with her."

The manager, a tall, square-shouldered man in his sixties, invited him to sit down. "I'm kind of curious about her whereabouts myself. After she lost control with a caller the other day, she just jerked the headset out of her hair and threw it. She ran down the stairs with this damned angry look on her face and I haven't seen her since."

"Does she have any relatives around here?"

The manager looked at his desk a long time before answering. "She moved here with an uncle when she was a kid. He had to raise her, don't ask me why. She never mentioned any parents."

Wesley bit his cheek and thought a moment. "She told me about the uncle."

The manager shook his head and looked across the hall to the broadcast booth. "She was the best voice I ever had. I don't know what happened. I don't care about what she did the other day."

"She sounded great all right." The two men were silent a moment, savoring Janie's words as though they were polite touches remembered on the back of the neck.

"I wish I could tell you something, Wesley, but to me, at least, she was mainly a voice. It did everything for her—it was her hands and feet." The manager leaned closer to him and narrowed his eyes. "After she lost her uncle, I listened to her, and she didn't sound any different." He motioned to a dusty speaker box over his door. "But if you looked in her eyes, you could see how everything but that voice had been taken out of her. Do you know what I mean?"

"I think so," Wesley said, standing up to go. He tried to picture her walking in and out of the studio's dowdy tiled rooms, but he couldn't see her.

The manager followed him to the door and put a hand on his back. "She sounded like she knew it all, didn't she?"

"She could give advice," Wesley told him, "but she couldn't follow it." Together they stared through the soundproof glass at a fat man scratching his bald liver-spotted skull with the eraser of a pencil, an unfiltered cigarette bobbing on his lips as he berated a caller.

He looked for her off and on for six months, writing letters and calling radio stations throughout the South. Sometimes he'd be cutting meat, hear a voice by the display cases, and go out and search the aisles. His father tried to match him with one of the cashiers, but it didn't work out. One evening he was helping the old man clean the attic of his house on Pecan Street when they found a wooden radio behind a box of canceled checks.

Wesley studied the Atwater Kent's dials and knobs. "You stopped using this before I was born. You reckon it still works?"

His father walked over to where Wesley knelt under a rafter. "Don't waste your time."

"Let's plug it into the droplight there." He stretched to the peak of the low attic.

"You won't get anything. You need a dipole antenna."

Wesley pulled a wire from the back and attached it to an aluminum screen door propped up sideways under the rafters. "Didn't you tell me these old sets could bring in Europe?"

His father sighed and sat Indian-style in the attic dust next to Wesley. "You're crazy if you think you'll find her on that," he said. They watched the Ivorine dial build its glow, heard a low whine rise as the screen door gathered sound from the air. Outside, it was sundown, and all over the country the little stations were signing off to make room for the clear-channel fifty-thousand-watt broadcasters coming from Del Rio and New Orleans, Seattle and Little Rock. Wesley turned the knob slowly, the movement of his fingers like a clock's minute hand. He passed a station in Baton Rouge, then brought in Mexico City on a rising whistle.

"This thing's got some power," Wesley said.

His father shook his head. "All you'll get is junk from all over the world, especially at night. What's that?"

"*Bonjour* is French. Are we getting France?"

"Maybe Canada. It's hard to tell." For ten minutes, as the roof timbers ticked and cooled above them, they scanned the dial for used cars in Kansas City, propaganda in Cuba, Coca-Cola in someplace where children sang a clipped language they had never heard before, the voices coming clear for a moment and then fading to other tongues even as Wesley kept his hand off the dial, the radio tuning itself, drifting through a planetful of wandering signals. And then, a little five-hundred-watter from another time zone where it was not yet sundown skipped its signal for a moment over Pine Oil, Louisiana, and Wesley heard a woman's liquid voice as she ran the tail of a talk show off toward nightfall.

"Oh, it's usually not as bad as you think it is," she was saying.

A sour voice answered, an angry sound from the inner city. "You're not in my shoes. How do you know what I feel?" Somewhere lightning struck, and the words began to stutter and wane. Wesley grabbed the walnut box and put his head down to the speaker.

His father let out a little groan. "It's not her. Don't be such a fool."

"I can't know how you feel," the announcer said. "But are you saying there's nothing I can tell you?"

The response was lost in a rip of static, and the woman's voice trembled away from Wesley's ears, shaking like his father's dusty hand pulling back on his hair.

The Bug Man

I t was five o'clock and Felix Robichaux, the Bug Man, rolled up the long, paved drive that ran under the spreading live oaks of the Beauty Queen's house. He pulled a one-gallon tank from the bed of his little white truck and gave the pump handle five patient strokes. When a regular customer was not at home and the door was unlocked, the Bug Man was trusted to spray the house and leave the bill on the counter. Her gleaming sedan was in the drive, so he paused at the kitchen door and peered through the glass. A carafe of steaming coffee was near the sink, so he knew Mrs. Malone was home from the office. When he tapped on the glass with the shiny brass tip of his spray wand, she appeared, blond and handsome in her navy suit.

"Mr. Robichaux, I guess it's been a month? Good to see you." He always thought it funny that she called him Mr., since he was five years younger, at thirty-one the most successful independent exterminator in Lafayette, Louisiana.

"You been doing all right?" He gave her a wide smile.

"You know me. Up's the same as down." She turned to place a few dishes in the sink. He remembered that a touch of sadness lingered around the edges of nearly everything she said, around the bits and pieces she had told him about herself over the years, about her dead husband. Why she told him things, the Bug Man was not sure. He noticed that most of his customers told him their life stories eventually. He began to walk through the house, spraying a fine, accurate stream along the baseboards. He treated the windowsills, the dark crack behind the piano, her scented bathroom, the closets hung with cashmere and silk. Soon he was back in the kitchen, bending behind the refrigerator and under the sink.

"Would you like a cup of coffee?" she asked. Then, as he had done off and on for five years, he sat down with her at the walnut breakfast table and surveyed her fine backyard, which was planned more carefully than some people's lives, a yard of periwinkle beds skirting dark oaks, brick walks threading through bright, even St. Augustine, and in the center an empty cabana-covered pool. The Beauty Queen had been a widow for four years and had no children. He called her the Beauty Queen because she once had told him she had won a contest; he forgot which—Miss New Orleans, maybe. Each of his customers had a nickname he shared only with his wife, Clarisse, a short, pretty brunette who worked as a teacher's aide. She liked to be near children, since she couldn't have any of her own.

"Hey," he began, "have you seen any bugs since the last time?"

She turned three spoons of sugar into his cup and poured his cream. He stirred. "Just a couple around the counter."

"Little ones, big ones, or red ones?"

"Red ones, I think. Those are wood roaches, aren't they?" She looked at him with her clear cornflower blue eyes.

"They come from outside. I'll spray around the bottom of the house." He put a hairy arm on the table and raised the cup to his mouth, sipping slowly, inhaling the vapor. "You don't have newspaper piled up anywhere, do you?"

She took a sip, leaving a touch of lipstick on the ivory cup. "I quit reading the newspaper. All the bad news bothers me more than it should."

Felix looked down into his coffee. He thought it a waste for such a fine woman to live an empty life. Clarisse, his wife, kept too busy to be sad, and she read every word in the newspaper, even police reports and the legals.

"I'd rather read sad stuff than nothing," he said.

She looked out through the large bay window into one of her many oaks. When she turned her head, the natural highlights of her fine hair spilled into his face. "I watch TV, everybody's anesthesia. On my day off, I shop. More anesthesia." She glanced at him. "You've seen my closets."

He nodded. He had never seen so many shoes and dresses. He started to ask what she did with them all, since he guessed that she seldom went out, but he held back. He was not a friend. He was the Bug Man and had his place.

In a few minutes he finished his coffee, thanked her, and moved outside, spraying under the deck, against the house, even around the pool, where he watched his reflection in a puddle at the deep end, his dark hair and eyes, his considerable shoulders rounding under his white knit shirt. He saw his paunch and laughed, thinking of his wife's supper. Turning for the house, he saw the Beauty Queen on her second cup, watching him in an uninterested way, as though he might be a marble statue at the edge of one of her walks. He was never offended by the way she looked at him. The Bug Man lived in the modern world, where, he knew, most people were isolated and uncomfortable around those not exactly like themselves. He also believed that there was a reason people like Mrs. Malone opened the doors in their lives just a crack by telling him things. He was a religious man, so everything had a purpose, even though he had no idea what. The Beauty Queen's movements and words were signals to him, road signs pointing to his future.

After Mrs. Malone's coffee stop came Felix's last job of the day, the Scalsons'; he had nicknamed them "the Slugs." As the Bug Man, he had seen it all. Most customers let him wander unaccompanied in and out of every room in the house, through every attic and basement, as though he had no eyes. He had seen filthy sinks and cheesy bathrooms, teenagers shooting drugs, had sprayed around drunken grandfathers passed out on the floor, had once bumbled in on an old woman and a young boy having sex. They had looked at him as though he were a dog that had wandered into the room. He was the Bug Man. He was not after them.

Even so, he faced the monthly spraying of the Scalsons' peeling rental house with a queasy spirit. Father Slug met him at the door, red-faced, a quart bottle of beer in his hand. "Come on in, Frenchie. I hope you got some DDT in that tank. The sons of bitches come back a week after you sprayed last time."

"I'll give it an extra squeeze," Felix told him. But he realized that the entire house would have to be immersed in a tank of Spectracide to get rid of the many insects crawling over the oily paper bags of garbage stacked around the stove. When he opened the door under the sink, the darkness writhed with German roaches.

He finished in the kitchen, then walked into the cheaply paneled living room, where Mr. Scalson was arguing with a teenaged son, Bruce.

"It won't my fault," the son screamed.

Mr. Scalson grabbed the boy's neck with one of his big rubbery hands and slapped him so hard with the other that his son's nose began to bleed. "You shoulda never been born, you little shit," he told him.

Felix Robichaux sprayed around the two men as though they were a couple of chairs and went on. He glanced out the window, to see Mrs. Scalson burning a pile of dirty disposable diapers in the backyard, stirring them with a stick. In an upstairs bedroom, he found the round-shouldered daughter playing a murderous video game on an old television that was surrounded by half-eaten sandwiches and bowls of wilted cereal. In another room, the sour-smelling grandfather was watching a pornographic movie while drinking hot shots of supermarket bourbon.

The tragedy of the Scalsons was that they didn't have to be what they were. The grandfather and father held decent jobs in the oil fields. Their high school diplomas hung in the den. Yet the only thing the Bug Man ever saw them do was argue and then sulk in their rooms, waiting like garden slugs dreaming of flowers to kill.

Felix Robichaux lived on what was left of the family homestead outside of Lafayette. The house was a white frame situated a hundred yards off the highway, one big pecan tree in front and a live oak out back between the house and barn. Rafts of trimmed azaleas floated on a flat lake of grass. He thought the shrubs looked like circles of children gossiping at recess. He ate his wife's supper, a smoky chicken stew, and helped her clear the dishes from the Formica table. While she washed them under a noisy cloud of steam, he swept the tile floor and put away the spices. Then they went out on the front porch and sat on the yellow spring-iron chairs that had belonged to his father.

Clarisse and Felix lived like a couple whose children had grown and moved out. They felt accused by the absence of children, by their idleness in the afternoons, when they felt they should be tending to homework or helping at play. They had tried for all their married life, ten years, had gone to doctors as far away as Houston, and still their extra bedrooms stayed empty, their nights free of the fretful, harmless sobs of infants. They owned a big Ford sedan, which felt vacant when they drove through the countryside on idle weekends. They were short, small-boned people, so even their new motorboat seemed empty the day they first anchored in a bayou to catch bream and to talk about where their childless lives were going. Overhead, silvery baby egrets perched in the branches of a bald cypress, and minnows flashed in the dark waters, sliding like time around the boat's hull.

Clarisse stared from their porch to the pecans forming in the branches of the tree in their front yard. She slowly ran her white fingers through the dark curls at the back of her neck. Felix watched her pretty eyes, which were almost violet in the late-afternoon light, and guessed at what she would say next. She asked him whose house he had sprayed first, and he laughed.

"I started out with Boatman."

"That's Melvin Laurent. A new one?"

He nodded. "Then Fish, Little Neg, Mr. Railroad, the Termite Twins." He stared high into the pecan tree and flicked a finger up for each name. "Beauty Queen and the Slugs."

She put her hand on his arm. "You should call them Beauty Queen and the Beasts," she said.

"I spray the Beasts tomorrow."

"That's right." Clarisse crossed her slim legs and held up a shoe to examine the toe. "It's too bad Mrs. Malone doesn't get married again. Just from the couple times I saw her working down at the bank, I could tell she's got a lot to offer."

Felix pursed his lips. "Yeah, but she needs a lot, too. You ought to hear all the droopy-drawers talk she lays out in the afternoon. Everything's sad with her, everything gets her down. She lost too much when her husband got killed." He thought of the Beauty Queen's eyes and what they might tell him.

"You think she's good-looking still?"

"Talk about."

She stared off at the highway, where a truck full of hay grumbled off toward the west. "Too bad we can't fix her up with somebody."

He rolled his eyes at her and put his hand on hers. "We don't know the kind of people she needs. What, you gonna get her a date with Cousin Ted?"

"Get off your high horse. Ted's all right since he's going to AA and got his shrimp boat back from the finance company." She pulled her hand away. "I could call names on your side, too."

As the lawn grew long in shadow, they brewed up a playful argument until the mosquitoes drove them inside, where their good cheer subsided in the emptiness of the house.

For the rest of the month he sprayed his way through the homes of the parish, getting the bugs out of the lives of people who paid him no more attention than they would a housefly, and on the thirty-first, in the subdivision where the Beauty Queen lived, he visited a new customer, a divorced lawyer named McCall. Even though it was the first time he had sprayed there, Felix was left alone by the tall, athletic attorney, who let him wander at will through the big house he had leased. Felix took his time in the living room so he could watch McCall and size him up. He sprayed in little spurts and stopped several times to pump up. The lawyer smiled at him and asked if he followed pro football.

"Oh yeah," the Bug Man said. "I been following the poor Saints since day one."

The other man laughed. "Me too. You know, I handled a case for a Saints player once. He sued a fan who came into the stadium tunnel after a game and bit him on the arm."

"No kidding?" Felix was fascinated at the story of a human insect, a biting football fan. He stayed a half hour and drank a beer with Dave McCall, discovering where he was from, what he did for fun, what he didn't do. After all, why wouldn't the lawyer tell him things? He was the Bug Man, who might not ever come again. The round little Cajun listened in his invisibility to things that might have significance.

"You should meet Mrs. Malone," he found himself saying. He had no idea why he said this, but it was as if a little blue spark popped behind his eyes and the sentence came out by itself, appearing like a letter with no return address. "She's a former beauty queen and a real nice lady." The lawyer smiled, seeming to think, What a friendly, meaningless offering. His smile was full and shining with tolerance, and Felix endured the smile, knowing he had done something important, had planted a seed, maybe.

On the fifteenth, he watered the seed when he had coffee with Mrs. Malone. She seemed empty, gray around the eyes, offering him only a demitasse, as though trying to hurry him off, though she was not brusque or distant. There was no need to spend brusqueness or distance on the Bug Man.

"You know," he began, delivering his rehearsed words carefully, "you ought to get out more."

She showed him a slim line of wonderful teeth. "I guess I do what I can."

He took a sip of coffee. "There's a single man your age just moved in down the street. I met him the other day and he hit me as being a nice guy. He's a lawyer."

"Are lawyers nice guys, Mr. Robichaux?"

The question derailed his train of thought. "Well, not all of them. But you know . . . uh, what was I talking about?"

"A new man in the neighborhood."

"Single man." He had run out of coffee; he tilted his cup to stare into it and then looked at the carafe. She poured him another sip. "I sprayed Buffa—I mean, Mrs. Boudreaux—this morning, and she said there was gonna be a neighborhood party at the Jeansonnes' tomorrow. This guy's supposed to be there."

"So you think I should check him out?" She wiggled her shoulders when she said "check him out," and Felix was worried that she was making fun of him.

"He's an awful nice man. Good-lookin', as far as I can tell."

"Would your wife, Clarisse, think he was good-looking?"

He bit his lip at that. "Clarisse thinks I'm good-looking," he said at last, and the Beauty Queen laughed.

That night Clarisse and Felix sat on their porch and listened to the metallic keening of tree frogs. The neighbors had just gone home with their two young children and Felix put his hand on a damp spot near his collar where the baby had drooled. He caught the cloth between his fingers and held it as though it contained meaning. Clarisse sat with her left arm across her chest and her right fist on her lips. "If we had had a little girl, I wonder who she would have looked like."

"Dark curly hair and eyes deep like a well," he said. The frogs in the yard subsided as he spoke. They sometimes did that, as though wanting to listen.

After a long while, she said, "Too bad," a comment that could have been about a thousand different things. One by one the frogs commenced their signals, and the moon came out from behind a cloud like a bright thought. Across the road a door opened and a mother's voice sang through the silvery light, spilling onto the lawn a two-note call—"Ke-vin"—playful but strong, and then, "Come out of the dark. You've got to come out of that dark."

The next week he showed up off schedule at Mrs. Malone's house, later than usual, and found her in the backyard looking at the empty pool.

"Since the weather's been so damp, I thought I'd give a few sprays around while I was in the neighborhood."

She nodded at him as he walked by her and began spraying the cracks in the pool apron. "I appreciate the service," she told him, a hint of something glad lingering around her mouth.

"Uh, you been goin' out any? You know, chase the blues away?" He drew a circle in the air as if to circumscribe the blues.

"Thinking about it," she said, hiding her mouth behind a ringless white hand.

"Yeah, but don't think too long," he said. "Might be time to check it out." He wiggled his shoulders and blushed. The Beauty Queen bit a nail and turned her back on him slowly.

When he sprayed the lawyer's house, he spent an hour with him, marveling at both Mr. McCall's charm and two bottles of imported beer.

Three weeks later the Bug Man went down to LaBat's Lounge for a beer after supper. As he was driving down Perrilloux Street, he passed the Coachman Restaurant, an expensive steak house. He saw a BMW parked at the curb, and stepping out of it smoothly were the long legs of Mrs. Malone. The lawyer was holding her door and looking like he had been cut with scissors out of a men's fashion magazine. In the short time he had to look, Felix strained to see her face. It was full of light and the Beauty Queen was smiling, all unpleasant thought hidden for the night at least. Her blond hair spilled over her dark dress, and at the throat was a rill of pearls. The Bug Man drove on, watching them in his rearview mirror as they entered the brass door of the restaurant. When he reached LaBat's old plywood barroom, he drank a Tom Collins instead of a beer, lost three dollars in the poker machine and won four in a game of pool with two cousins from Grand Crapaud, and for the rest of the night celebrated his luck.

The next day was the fifteenth, and Mrs. Malone served him coffee and no sad talk, but not one morsel of what was going on between her and the lawyer. And the Bug Man could not ask. He made himself satisfied with the big cup of strong coffee she fixed for him and the sight of the new makeup containers on the vanity in her bedroom. He finished up carefully and went to spray the Slugs'. Even the visible stench of the Slugs' bathrooms could not dampen a deep, subtle excitement Felix felt, almost the anticipation and hope a farmer feels after he has put in a crop, a patient desire for a green future.

Mr. and Mrs. Scalson were having an argument as Felix was trying to spray the kitchen. She got her husband down on the floor and beat at him with a flat-heeled shoe. Her lip was split and her brows and cheeks were curdled and swollen. Mr. Scalson broke away from her, grabbed a pot of collard greens from the stove, and slung it, hitting her in the legs. The screaming was a worse pollutant than all the rotten food stacked against the stove. Felix watched the greens fly across the floor, the water splashing under the cabinets, a hunk of salt meat coming to rest under the table, where he knew it would stay for a week. The young daughter ran into the kitchen, a headset tangled in her hair, and began pulling ice from the refrigerator for her mother's burns. The Bug Man left without waiting to be paid, jogging down the drive toward his white truck, which waited, scoured and shiny, a reminder that some things can be kept orderly and clean.

The summer months rolled into August, and Felix Robichaux mixed his mild, subtle concoctions, spraying them around the parish in the homes of good and bad people, talking to anybody, drinking anyone's coffee, and seeing into private lives like the eye of God, invisible and judging. He began using a new mixture, which was odorless and, unlike the old formula, left no cloudy spots or drips, and now there was even less evidence that he had been in the world, had passed along the ways of people's lives, and that was all right with him.

He became even more curious about Mrs. Malone, and he stepped over the understood boundary between them to ask about Mr. McCall with a directness that made her eyes flick up at him. There was no doubt that for weeks she had been a happy woman, asking about Clarisse, telling him about plans for putting her pool back in service, since she'd found out that the lawyer liked to swim.

But then there was a change. In mid-August she let him in without speaking, going to the sink and doing dishes left over from the day before. While he was spraying the living room, he heard her gasp and drop one of her expensive plates to the tile floor. He put his face in the kitchen doorway.

"Let me clean that up for you," he said. "I know where the dustpan's at."

"Thank you. I'm a bit shaky today." Her color was good, he noticed, but there was a worried cast to her usually direct, clear eyes. He knelt and carefully swept the fragments into a dustpan, then he wet a paper towel and patted the floor for splinters of china.

"You want me to make you some coffee?" he asked.

She put her head down a bit and shaded her eyes. "Yes," she said.

The Bug Man set up the coffeemaker, then sprayed the rest of the house while the machine dripped a full pot. When he came back, she had not moved. He knew where the cups and the spoons were in hundreds of houses, and the first cabinets he opened showed him what he wanted.

"What's gone wrong?" he asked, pouring her a cup.

"Oh, it's nothing. I'm just not myself today." She crossed her legs slowly and pulled at her navy skirt.

"Mr. McCall been around?"

"Mr. McCall has not been around," she said flatly. "He tells me he will never be around."

The Bug Man shook his head slowly. Mrs. Malone and the lawyer looked like the elegant, glittering people on the soap operas his mother watched, people he could never figure out. He was not an educated man and had never set foot in a country club unless it was having a roach problem, but he guessed that many wealthy people were complicated and refined, that those qualities made it harder for them to be happy. But he had no notion of why this was so. He thought of Clarisse, and felt lucky. "I'm sorry to hear that," was all he could think of to say. "I thought you two were hitting it off real good."

She grabbed a napkin from the table and began crying then. Embarrassed, he looked around the kitchen, raised his hands, then dropped them. "Yes," she said, and then she looked at him with such an intensity that he glanced away. He could have sworn that she really *saw* him. "We've been hitting it off very well. I thought David was a little like my late husband." She looked toward the backyard, but her gaze seemed to waver. "I thought he was a man who carried things through."

"Aw, Mrs. Malone, these things have a way of working out, you know?"

"I'm pregnant," she told him. "And David wants nothing to do with me."

Felix Robichaux took a swallow of hot coffee, opened his mouth to say something, but his mind was blasted clean by what she had said. A light seemed to come on in the back of his head. "What are you going to do?" he said at last.

"I'm not sure, exactly." She narrowed her gaze and watched him carefully. "Why?" He scooted back his chair and ran his left hand down his white uniform shirt, his fingers pausing just a second on the green embroidery of his last name.

"I mean, do you think you'll keep it or give it up for adoption or what?" His eyes grew wide and he slid his round bottom to the edge of the chair.

Her voice chilled a bit with suspicion. "I shouldn't be discussing this with you." She looked down at the glossy tile.

"Mrs. Malone, Clarisse and me, we've been trying for years to have a baby, and if you're going to give up the one you got, we'd be happy to get it, let me tell you." The Bug Man was blushing as he said this, as though he was trying to become intimate and was unsure how to proceed.

The Beauty Queen straightened up in her chair. "We're not talking about a cast-off sofa here, Mr. Robichaux."

"Mrs. Malone, don't get mad. You know I'm just a bug man and can't talk like a lawyer or a businessman." He opened his thick palms toward her. "Just think about it, that's all."

She stood and held the door open for him, and he picked up his tank and walked outside. "I'll see you in a month," she said. When she closed the door, the smell of her exquisite perfume fanned onto the stoop. For a moment, it overcame the smell of bug spray in Felix's clothes.

For the next month he made his rounds with a secretive lightness of spirit, not telling Clarisse anything, though it was hard in the evenings not to explain why he held her hand with a more ardent claim, why he would suddenly spring up and walk to the edge of the porch to look in the yard for something, maybe a good place to put a swing set. The closer the days wound down to the fifteenth of the month, the more hopeful and fearful he became. When he sprayed the lawyer's house, McCall let him in without looking at him, disappearing into a small office upstairs, leaving him alone in the expensive, empty house. The Bug Man decided to name him Judas.

Finally, at a little before five on the fifteenth, the Beauty Queen let him in, and he went about his business quickly, finishing, as usual, by spraying under the sink in the kitchen. He noticed that she had prepared no coffee. He looked for her in the hall and in the living room, retracing his route, giving embarrassed little shots in corners as though he was going over a poor job. He found her in the bedroom, with her back against the headboard, reading a book.

"I left a check for you on the counter," she said.

"I saw it. How you doin', Mrs. Malone?"

"I'm fine." But the stiffness of her mouth and the deep-set hurt in her eyes said otherwise. She rested the book on top of her dress, a dark print with lilies against a black background. "Is there something you forgot to spray?"

"Yes, ma'am. Usually I mist under your bed. Every now and then you leave a snack plate and a glass under the edge." He got down on his knees, adjusted the nozzle on the tip of his wand, and sprayed. "You decided what to do about the baby yet?" He wondered if she sensed the wide gulf of anticipation behind the question.

"I'm having an abortion tomorrow," she said at once, as though she was reading a sentence from the book in her lap.

His thumb slipped off the lever of his sprayer. He was frozen on his knees at the foot of her bed. "It would be such a fine baby," he said, straightening his back and staring at her across a quilted cover. "You, a beauty-contest winner, and him, a good-looking lawyer. What a baby that would make." He began to say things that made his face burn, and he felt like a child who had set his heart on something, only to be told that he could never have what he wanted. "Clarisse would be so happy," he said, trying to smile.

Mrs. Malone drew up her legs and glared at him. "Mr. Robichaux, what would you do with such a baby? It wouldn't be like you and Clarisse. It would look nothing like you."

He stayed on his knees and watched her, wondering if she had planned a long time to say what she had said. He reflected on the meanness of the world and how for the first time he was unable to deal with it. "It'd mean a lot to us" was all he could tell her.

"It would be cruel to give this child to you. Why can't you see that?" For a moment her face possessed the blank disdain of a marble statue in her backyard. "Would you please just get out," she said, looking down at her book and balling a white fist against her forehead.

The Bug Man left the house, forgetting to close the door, feeling his good nature bleed away until he was as hollow as a termite-eaten beam. In twenty minutes, as he pulled into the littered drive of the Scalsons', his feelings had not changed. He was late, and the Slugs were seated at their hacked table, arguing bitterly over parts of a fried chicken. Felix stood in the door, pumping up his tank, looking into the yellowed room at the water-stained ceiling, the spattered walls, the torn and muddy linoleum, the unwashed and squalling Scalsons. The grandfather dug through the pile of chicken, cursing the children for eating the livers. The mother was pulling the skins from every piece and piling them on her plate while the children gave each other greasy slaps. They tore at their food like yard animals, spilling flakes of crust and splashes of slaw under the table. "Gimme a wing, you little son of a bitch," Mr. Scalson growled to his son.

"It doesn't have to be like this," Felix said, and everyone turned, noticing him for the first time.

"Well, I'll be damned. It's the Frenchman. You must have water in that tank of yours, because the bugs have been all over us the past month. What'd I pay you good money for anyway, Shorty?"

Ever since he had opened the door the Bug Man had been pumping his tank, five, ten, twenty strokes. He adjusted the nozzle to deliver a sharp stream, pressed the lever, and peeled back Mr. Scalson's left eyelid. The heavy man let out a yell and Felix began spraying them all in their faces, across their chests, the grandfather in the mouth with drilling streams of roach killer. The family sat stupidly for several moments, sputtering and calling out when they were sprayed again in the eyes as though being washed clean of some foul blindness. One by one the Scalsons scampered to their feet. The father swung at the Bug Man, who ducked and then cracked him across the nose with his spray wand. The grandfather came at him with an upraised chair, and the Bug Man snapped the brass wand across the top of his head, leaving a red split in the dull meat of his skull.

The next evening the weather was mild, and at dusk Felix and Clarisse were sitting in the yellow spring-iron chairs, whose backs were flattened metal flowers. He had told her everything, and together they were staring at a few late fireflies winking on the lawn like the intermittent hopes of defeated people. Across the road a mother called her child for the second time, and they watched for him as he bobbed out of a field.

In the house the telephone rang, and Felix got up slowly. It was Mrs. Malone, and she sounded upset.

"What can I do for you?" he asked. He twisted the phone cord around his fist and closed his eyes.

"I was in the clinic waiting room this afternoon," she began, her voice stiff and anesthetized, "and I read the local newspaper's account of the attack."

He winced when she said "attack" and looked down at the dustless hardwood of his living room. "I'm real sorry about that." He thought of the expression on his wife's face when she had brought the money for his bail.

"And you did it right after you left my house," she said, her voice rising. "I didn't know what to think."

"Yes, ma'am." He listened to her breaths coming raggedly over the phone for at least a half minute, but he didn't know what else to say. He wasn't sure why he had hurt the Scalsons. At the time, he had wanted to keep them from damaging the world further.

"I don't want you to work for me anymore. I just can't have you in the house."

"I wouldn't bother you again, Mrs. Malone."

"No." The word came quick as a shot. "You'll stay away."

And that was it.

The Bug Man went back to his work at dawn, and for that day and every workday for the next ten years he walked through houses and lives. His business expanded until he had to hire three easygoing local men to spray bugs with him. He erected a small building with a storage area and office, hiring a young woman to manage appointments and payments. Clarisse attended the local college, became a first-grade teacher, and labored in her garden of children. With his spare time he began attending a local exercise club and soon lost his bulky middle, though much of his hair left with it.

Felix had been thirty-seven when the other independent exterminator in town decided to sell the business to him. These new routes were profitable, and Joe Brasseaux, Felix's best sprayer, tended them religiously, never missing an appointment for two years, except for one day when he called in sick. Felix looked over Joe's route for the afternoon, and when he saw the addresses, he decided to treat the houses himself.

About four o'clock, he pulled into the long drive that led to the Beauty Queen's house. Getting out of the truck, he looked up at the oaks, which had changed little, and at the pool in back, which swirled with bright water. The plantings were mature and lush, rolling green shoulders of liriope bordering everything.

The driveway was empty, but in the door was a key with a pair of small plastic dice hanging from it. He rang the bell and bent down to pump up his tank. When he raised his face, the door opened, and standing there was a young boy with sandy hair and blue eyes, a boy with a dimpled chin, an open, intelligent face, and, Felix noticed, big feet. "Yes, sir?" the child said, adjusting the waistband on what appeared to be a soccer uniform.

For a moment, Felix couldn't speak. He wanted to reach out and feel the top of the boy's head, but he pointed to his tank instead. "I've come to spray for bugs."

"Where's Joe? Joe's the one takes care of that for us."

The Bug Man looked inside hopefully. "Is your mother Mrs. Malone?"

"She's not here, and I'm sorry, but she told me not to let in anyone I don't know." The boy must have noticed how Felix was staring, and stepped back.

"You don't have to be afraid of me." Felix gave him his widest smile, all the while studying the child. "I'm the Bug Man."

The boy narrowed his bright eyes. "No sir. Not to me you aren't. You'd better go away."

At once he felt shriveled and sick, like a sprayed insect, and he wondered whether he should tell the boy that he knew his mother, that he knew who he was, but the Bug Man was by now a veteran of missed connections and could tell when a train had left a station without him. He scanned the child once more and turned away.

Pulling out of the drive, he saw in the rearview a small fair-skinned figure standing on the steps, looking after him, but not really seeing him, he guessed. He allowed himself this one glance. One glance, he decided, was what he could have.

Little Frogs in a Ditch

Old man Fontenot watched his grandson draw hard on a slim cigarette and then flick ashes on the fresh gray enamel of the front porch. The boy had been fired, this time from the laundry down the street. The old man, who had held only one job in his life, and that one lasting forty-three years at the power plant, did not understand this.

"The guy who let me go didn't have half the brains I got," Lenny Fontenot said.

The old man nodded, then took a swallow from a warm can of Schlitz. "The owner, he didn't like you double-creasing the slacks" was all he said, holding back. He watched a luminous cloud drifting up from the Gulf.

"Let me tell you," Lenny said with a snarl, his head following a dusk-drawn pigeon floating past the screen, "there's some dumb people in this world. Dog-dumb."

The grandfather rolled his head to the side. Lenny was angry about his next paycheck, the one he'd never get.

"They was dumber back in my time," the grandfather told him.

Lenny cocked his head. "What you talking about? People today can't even spell *dumb.*" He pointed two fingers holding the cigarette toward the laundry. "If it wouldn't be for dumb people, modern American business couldn't keep doing its thing selling fake fingernails and fold-up fishing rods."

"Give it a rest," the old man said, looking down the street to the drizzle-washed iron roof of the laundry, where a lazy spume of steam rose from the roof vent. His grandson was living with him again, complaining of the evils of capitalism, eating his food, using all the hot water in the mornings. The grandfather pulled a khaki cap over his eyes and leaned back in his rocker, crossing his arms over a tight green knit shirt. Lenny would never hold a job because he suffered from inborn disrespect for anybody engaged in business. Everybody was stupid. All businessmen were crooks. At twenty-five his grandson had the economic sense of a sixty-year-old Russian peasant.

"No. Really. Other than food and stuff you need to live, what do you really have to buy?" He took a searing drag on the last of six cigarettes he had borrowed from his girlfriend, Annie. "A car? Okay. Buy a white four-door car, no chrome, no gold package, no nothing. But wait. Detroit wants you to feel bad if you buy a plain car. You got to have special paint. You got to have a stereo makes you feel Mr. Mozart is pluckin' his fiddle in the backseat. You got to have a big-nuts engine for the road. You got to have this, you got to have that, until that car costs as much as a cheap house. If you buy a plain car, you feel like a donkey at the racetrack."

His grandfather took a swig of Schlitz. "If you work on your attitude a little bit, you could keep a job."

Lenny stood up and put his nose to the screen, sniffing, as if the grandfather's statement had a bad odor. "I can keep a job if I wanted. I'm a salesman."

"You couldn't sell cow cakes to a rosebush." The old man was getting tired. His grandson had been out on the porch with him for two hours now, pulling cigarettes from his baggy jeans, finding fault with everybody but his skinny, shaggy-haired self.

Lenny threw down his cigarette and mashed it with the toe of a scuffed loafer. "As dumb as people are today I could sell bricks to a drowning man."

Grandfather Fontenot looked at the smudge on his porch. "No, you couldn't."

"I could sell falsies to a nun."

"No, you couldn't."

"I could sell"—Lenny's mouth hung open a moment as he looked down into the cemented side yard and toward the old wooden carport at the rear of the lot—"a pigeon."

His grandfather picked up his hat and looked at him. "Who the hell would buy a pigeon?"

"I could find him."

"Lenny, if someone wanted a pigeon, all he'd have to do is catch him one."

"A dumb man will buy a pigeon from *me*." He pushed open the screen door and clopped down the steps to the side yard. At the rear of the lot was a broad, unused carport, swaybacked over useless household junk: window fans, a broken lawn mower, and a wheelbarrow with a flat tire. He looked up into the eaves where the ragged nests of pigeons dripped dung down the side of a beam. With a quick grab, he had a slate blue pigeon in his hands, the bird blinking its onyx eyes stupidly. He turned to his grandfather, who was walking up stiffly behind him. "Look. You can pluck them like berries under here."

Old man Fontenot gave him a disgusted look. "Nobody'll eat a pigeon."

Lenny ducked his head. "Eat. I ain't said nothing about eat." He smiled down at the bird. "This is a homing pigeon."

The grandfather put a hand on Lenny's shoulder. "Look, let's go fix a pot of coffee and open up the *Picayune* to the employment ads. We can find something good for you to do. Come on. That thing's got fleas like a politician. Put it down." The old man pulled at his elbow.

Lenny's eyes came up red and glossy. "Your Ford's got a crack in the head and you can't even drive across the bayou for groceries. I'm gonna sell birds and get the damn old thing fixed."

His grandfather sniffed but said nothing. He knew Lenny wanted the car for himself. He looked at the bird in his grandson's hands, which was pedaling the air, blinking its drop of dark eye. The old man had never owned a dependable automobile, had always driven junk to save money for his kids and grandkids. He remembered a Sunday outing to Cypress Park when his superannuated Rambler gave up in the big intersection at Highway 90 and Federal Avenue, remembered the angry horn of a cab, the yells of his son and wife as they argued about a tow truck fee while Lenny sat on the floor by a misshapen watermelon he had stolen with care from a neighbor's garden for the picnic that never happened.

"This bird," Lenny said, turning it back into its nest," is gonna get your car running."

"I told your parents I wouldn't let you get in any more trouble." He watched Lenny make a face. Maybe his parents couldn't care less. The grandfather remembered the boy's big room in their air-conditioned brick rancher, the house they sold from under him to buy a Winnebago and tour the country. They had been gone four months and had not called once.

For two days he watched Lenny sink deeper and deeper into a red overstuffed sofa, a forty-year-old thing his wife had won at a church bingo game. It was covered with a shiny, almost adhesive plastic, broadly incised with X's and running with dark, fiery swirls. The big cushions under Lenny hissed as he moved down into the sofa's sticky grasp. For Lenny, sitting in it must have been like living with his parents again. They were hardworking types who tried to make him middle-class and respectable, who frowned on his efforts to manage the country's only Cajun punk salsa band, which was better, at least, than his first business of selling cracked birdseed to grammar school kids as something he called "predope," or "pot lite." One day Lenny had come home from a long weekend and everything he owned was stacked under the carport, a SOLD sign in front of the house. For a long while, he had lived with his friends in Los Head-Suckers, but even the stoned longhairs tired of his unproductive carping and one by one had turned him out.

Lenny folded back the classified section to the pet column and found his ad, which read "Homing pigeons, ten dollars each. Training instructions included," and gave the address. His grandfather read it over his shoulder, then went into the kitchen and heated two links of boudin for breakfast and put on a pot of quick grits. Lenny came in and looked over at the stove.

"You gonna cook some eggs? Annie likes eggs."

"She coming over again?" He tried to sound miffed, but in truth, he liked Annie. She was a big-boned lathe operator who worked in a machine shop down by the river, but he thought she might be a civilizing influence on his grandson.

Lenny rumbled down the steps, and his grandfather watched him through the kitchen window. From behind the carport he pulled a long-legged rabbit cage made of a coarse screen called hardware cloth, and two-by-two's. He shook out the ancient pellets and set it next to the steps. With his cigarette-stained fingers, he snatched from the eaves a granite-colored pigeon and clapped him in the cage. Most of the other birds lit out in a *rat-tat-tat* of wings, but he managed to snag a pink-and-gray, which flapped out of its nest into his waiting hands. The old man clucked his tongue and turned up the fire under the peppery boudin.

Annie came up the rear steps, lugging a rattling toolbox. By the time Lenny came in and joined her, the old man had finished breakfast and was seated in the den beyond the kitchen. He didn't like being with both of them at the same time, because he felt sorry for the girl. He didn't understand how she could put up with Lenny's whining. Maybe he was the only man who would pay attention to her. She got a second helping and sat at the breakfast table, spooning grits and eggs into herself.

"Annie, baby." Lenny plopped down across from her.

"I saw that ad. The one you told me about." She broke open a loaf of French bread. "Why would anybody buy a pigeon? They're all over the place. Our backyard shed's full of 'em." She flipped her fluffy blond hair over her shoulders. "What are you trying to do?" she asked. "Prove something?" She looked up from her plate, her square jaw rising and falling under her creamy skin.

"I want to scare up some money to fix the old guy's car."

"And what else?" She chased a lump of grits out of a cheek with her tongue and brought her large cobalt eyes to bear on his.

He bunched his shoulders. "I don't know. It might be fun to see people throw away their money. You know. Like people do."

"You maybe want to find out why they do it? Or maybe you're just mad you don't have any to throw away. Am I reading your mind?"

He looked down at the table, shaking his head. "We been going out too long."

A voice came from the den. "I'll buy fifty shares a that."

Lenny spoke loudly. "I mean, she knows how I think." He put a hand palm up on the little table. "It's just that people throw money away on crazy stuff. It bothers the hell out of me. I could live for a year on what some people spend on a riding lawn mower or a red motorbike."

Annie took another bite and studied him. "You don't understand this?"

He looked away from her. "The more they get, the more they spend."

She put down her fork and glanced at her watch. She had to be down at Tiger Island Propeller by nine. "Lenny, in high school this teacher made the class read a play about an old guy was a king. I mean, it was hard reading, and she had to explain it or we wouldn't'ta got much out of it, but this old guy gave his kingdom away to his two bitchy daughters with the reserve that he could keep about a hundred old fishing buddies around to pass the time with. After a while one daughter gets pissed at all the racket around the castle and cuts his pile of buddies to fifty. Well, he hits the road to his other daughter's place, and guess what?"

Lenny looked at the ceiling. "She gives him his fifty guys back and sucks the eyeballs out of the other bitch's head, right?"

Annie blinked. "You got snakes in your skull, man." She raised a thick hand and pretended to slap him. "Pay attention. This second daughter cuts him back to twenty-five and the old man blows a gasket and calls her a dozen buzzards and like that. Then the first daughter shows up and says, 'Look, what you want with ten, five, or even one old buddy? You don't really *need* 'em.' "

Lenny snorted. "Damned straight. What'd he say to that?"

Annie ducked her head. "He told them even a bum had something he didn't need, even if it was a fingernail clipper. That if he only had the things he needed, he'd be like a possum or a cow."

Lenny made a face. "What's that mean?"

The voice from the den called out, "When's the last time you saw a possum on a red motorbike?"

"What?"

Annie put a calloused hand on one of his. "An animal can't own nothing. Wouldn't want to. Owning things is what makes people different from the armadillos, Lenny. And the stuff we buy, even if it's one of your pigeons, sometimes is like a little tag telling folks who we are."

He turned sideways in his chair. "I don't believe that for a minute. If I buy a Cadillac, does that tell people I'm high-class?"

Again the voice from the den: "You could buy a pack of weenies."

"I said a Cadillac," Lenny shouted.

Annie Meyer stood up and pulled on a denim cap. "Time for work," she announced. "Walk me to the bus stop." She put her arm through his. "Hear from the parents any?"

He shook his head. "Nothin'. Not a check, not a postcard."

The grandfather followed them with a plastic bag of trash in his hand. When they reached the street, they saw a white-haired gentleman standing there staring at a torn swatch of newsprint. He was wearing nubby brown slacks and a green checkered cowboy shirt. He stuck out his hand palm down and Lenny wagged it.

"I'm Perry Lejeune from over by Broussard Street. About ten blocks. I saw your ad."

Mr. Fontenot gave his grandson a scowl and pulled off his cap as if he would toss it.

Lenny straightened out of his slouch and smiled, showing his small teeth. "Mr. Lejeune, you know anything about homing pigeons?"

The other man shook his head once. "Nah. My little nephew Alvin's living at my house and I want to get him something to occupy his time. His momma left him with me and I got to keep him busy, you know?" Mr. Lejeune raised his shoulders. "I'm too old to play ball with a kid."

"Don't worry, I'll fill you in," he said, motioning for everyone to follow him to the back of the lot next to the junk-filled carport. He put his hand on the rabbit cage and made eye contact with Mr. Lejeune. "I've got just two left. This slate"—he nodded toward the plain bird—"is good in the rain. And I got that pink fella if you want something flashy."

Mr. Lejeune put up a hand like a stop signal. "I can't afford nothing too racy, no."

"The slate's a good bird. Of course, at this price, you got to train him."

"Yeah, I want to ask you about that." Mr. Lejeune made a pliers of his right forefinger and thumb and clamped them on his chin. Annie came around close, as though she wanted to listen to the training instructions herself. The grandfather looked at the bottom of his back steps and shook his head, wondering if this would be as bad as the fake pot debacle, when thirteen high school freshmen caught Lenny coming out of Thibaut's Store and beat him into the dusty parking lot with their knobby little fists.

Lenny put his hands in the cage and caught the pigeon. "You got to build a cage out of hardware cloth with a one-way door."

"Yeah, for when he comes back, you mean."

Lenny gave Mr. Lejeune a look. "That's right. Now to start trainin', you got to hold him like a football, with your thumbs on top of him and your fingers underneath. You see?"

Mr. Lejeune put on his glasses and bent to look under the pigeon. "Uh-huh."

"You go to your property line. Stand exactly where your property line is. Then you catch his little legs between your forefingers and your middle fingers. One leg in each set of fingers, you see?" Lenny got down on his knees, wincing at the rough pavement. "You put his little legs on the ground, like this. You see?"

"Yeah, I got you."

"Then you walk the bird along your property line, moving his legs and coming along behind him like this. You got to go around all four sides of your lot with him so he can memorize what your place looks like."

"Yeah, yeah, I got you. Give him the grand tour, kinda."

Annie frowned and hid her mouth under a bright hand. His grandfather sat on the steps and looked away.

Lenny waggled the bird along the ground as the animal pumped its head, blinked, and tried to peck him. "Now it takes commitment to train a bird. It takes a special person. Not everybody's got the character it takes to handle a homing pigeon."

Mr. Lejeune nodded. "Hey, you talking to someone's been married forty-three years. How long you got to train 'em?"

Lenny stood and replaced the bird in the cage. "Every day for two weeks, you got to do this."

"Rain or shine?" Mr. Lejeune's snowy eyebrows went up.

"That's right. And then after two weeks, you take him in a box out to Bayou Park and set his little butt loose. You can watch him fly around and then go home to wait. He might even beat you there, you know?"

The man bobbed his head. "Little Alvin's gonna love this." He reached for his wallet. "Any tax?"

"A dollar."

Mr. Lejeune handed him a ten and dug for a one. "Ain't the tax rate eight percent in the city?"

"Two percent wildlife tax," Lenny told him, reaching under the cage for a shoe box blasted with ice-pick holes.

When the man and bird had left the driveway, Lenny's grandfather cleared his throat. "I wouldn'a believed it if I didn't see it with my own eyes."

"That's capitalism—"

"Aw, stow it. You took that guy's money and he got nothin'." He started up the steps, pulling hard at the railing, but stopped at the landing to look down at them.

Lenny turned to the girl and said under his breath, "He'll feel better when I get that old Crown Vic running again." Turning to the carport, he fished out a young pigeon from the eaves, one the color of corroded lead.

"You think what you told him will work?" she asked, bending down for her glossy pink toolbox.

"Hell, I don't know what a bird thinks. Say, you got any cigarettes on you?"

"They don't let us smoke on shift." She looked at his back, which had begun to sag again. "I got to get to work," she said. "Try not to sell one to a cop, will you?"

That day Lenny sold pigeons to Mankatos Djan, a recent African immigrant who repaired hydraulics down at Cajun Hose, Lenny's simple cousin, Elmo Broussard, who lived across the river in Beewick, and two children who showed up on rusty BMX bikes. The next morning an educated-looking man showed up, made a face at Lenny's sales pitch, and got back into his sedan without a bird. Several customers had behaved like this, but by the third day he had sold a total of twenty-three pigeons and had enough to fix the leaf-covered sedan parked against the side fence. He had given everybody the same directions on how to train the birds. He told his grandfather that after two weeks, when the birds wouldn't come back at the first trial, they would chalk things up to bad luck, or maybe a skipped day of training. Not many things could take up your attention for two weeks and cost only eleven dollars, he argued.

Thirteen days after the ad first appeared, Lenny counted his money and walked up to the front porch, where his grandfather was finishing up a mug of coffee in the heat. He looked at the cash in Lenny's outstretched hand. "What's that?"

"It's enough money to fix the car."

His grandfather looked away toward the laundry. "I saw you take over twenty dollars from some children for a lousy pair of flea baits."

"Hey." Lenny drew back his hand as though it had been bitten. "It's for your car, damn it."

"That poor colored guy who couldn't hardly speak a word of English. Black as a briquette, and he believed every dammed thing you told him. My grandson sticks him for eleven bucks that'd feed one of his relatives living in a grass shack back in Bogoslavia or wherever the hell he was from for a year." He looked up at Lenny, his veiny brown eyes wavering from the heat. "What's wrong with you?"

"What's wrong with me?" he yelled, stepping back. "Everybody's getting money but me. I ain't even got a job, and I come up with a way, just like everybody else does, to turn a few bucks, not even for myself, mind you, and the old fart that I want to give it to tells me to shove it."

"You don't know shit about business. You're a crook."

"All right." He banged the money against his thigh. "So I'm a crook. What's the difference between me and the guy that sells a Mercedes?"

The grandfather grabbed the arms of his rocker. "The difference is a Mercedes won't fly off toward the clouds, crap in your eye, and not come back after you paid good money for it."

Lenny jerked his head toward the street. "It's all how you look at it," he growled.

"There's only one way to look at it, damn it. The right way." His grandfather stood up. "You get out of my house. Your parents got rid of you and now I know why. Maybe a few nights down at the mission will straighten you out."

Lenny backed up another step, the money still in his outstretched hand. "Gramps, they didn't get rid of me. They moved out west."

"And it was time they did. They shoved you out the house and got you lookin' for a job, you greasy weasel." He grabbed the money so hard he came close to falling back into his chair. "I'll take that for the poor folks that'll start comin' round soon for their money back."

"They'll get eleven dollars' worth of fun out the birds."

"Get out." The old man brought his thin brows down low and beads of sweat glimmered on his bald head. "Don't come back until you get a job."

"You can't put me on the street," Lenny said, his voice softening, his face trying an ironic smile.

"Crooks wind up on the street and later they burn in hell," the old man said.

Lenny walked to the screen door and stopped, looking down North Bertaud Street where its narrow asphalt back ran toward Highway 90, which connected with the interstate, which connected with the rest of the scary world.

He kicked the bottom of the screen and his grandfather yelled. A half hour later he was standing on the sidewalk in front, holding a caramel-colored Sears suitcase, listening to the feathery pop of wings as the old man pulled pigeons out of the rabbit cage and tossed them toward the rooftops.

He walked to Breaux's Café, down by the icehouse, drank a cup of coffee, and read the paper. Then he wandered his own neighborhood, embarrassed by the huge suitcase banging his calf, enduring the stares of the women sweeping porches. He swung by Annie's house even though she was still at work. Her father sat on the stoop in his dark gray plumber's coveralls, drinking a long-neck in the afternoon heat. He watched Lenny come to him the way a fisherman eyes a rain-laden cloud. "Whatcha got in the suitcase, boy?"

Lenny set it down on the curb and motioned down the street with a wag of his head. "The old man and me, we had a discussion."

Mr. Meyer laughed. "You mean he throwed your ass in the street."

Lenny tilted his head to the side. "He's mad at me right now, but he'll cool down. I just got to find a place to stay for a night or two." He glanced up at Mr. Meyer, who looked like a poor woman's Kirk Douglas gone to seed. "You couldn't put me up, you know, just for the night?"

Mr. Meyer didn't change his expression. "Naw, Lenny. What with Annie in the house and all, it just wouldn't look right." He took a long draw, perhaps trying to finish the bottle.

"That's okay. When it gets dark, I'll just go back and sleep in his car. The backseat on that thing's plenty big enough."

"You sell all your birds?"

"He put me out of the bird business. I was just doin' it for him. I thought it was a good idea. I didn't see no harm in it."

"That's what got him hot."

"What?"

"You didn't see no harm in screwing those people. I talked to Mr. Danzig over by the laundry. He said you didn't see no harm in putting one, two extra creases in a pair of slacks. He told me on Mondays some pants had more pleats than a convent-school girl's skirt. The trouble with you is, you ain't seeing the harm. You see what you want to see, but you ain't seeing the harm."

"I worked cheap for that old bastard. He could expect worse."

Mr. Meyer stood, took a last swig, then put the bottle in his hip pocket. "You hurt his business, boy."

"Business," Lenny said with a snarl. "It's bullshit. A business for people too lazy to iron their own clothes." He kicked his suitcase and it rolled over onto the grass, flattening an old dog dropping. Mr. Meyer threw back his head and laughed.

That night, the grandfather couldn't sleep, and he rolled up the shade at the tall window next to his bed, looking into the moonlit side yard at his old car parked against the fence. He thought about how Lenny was sweating and rolling like a log on the squeaky vinyl of the backseat, trying to sleep in the heat and mosquitoes. The old man knelt on the floor and folded his arms on the windowsill, thinking how Lenny should be back at the cleaners, smiling through the steam of his pressing machine. He remembered his own work down at the light plant, where he tended the thundering Fairbanks-Morse generators for forty years. Down in the yard, the Ford bobbled, and he imagined that Lenny was turning over, putting his nose in the crack at the bottom of the seat back, smelling the dust balls and old pennies and cigarette filters. The grandfather wondered if some dim sense of the real world would ever settle on Lenny, if he would ever appreciate Annie Meyer, her Pet-milk skin, her big curves. He had seen her once at her lathe, standing up to her white ankles in spirals of tempered steel as she machined pump rods and hydraulic pistons. Lenny talked with longing of her paychecks, nearly $2,400 a month, clear, all of which she saved. The grandfather climbed into bed but couldn't sleep because he began to see images of people Lenny had sold birds to—the dumb children, the African—and wondered why the boy had done them wrong. It was only eleven dollars he'd gotten. How could you sell your soul for eleven dollars?

At dawn he went down into the yard and opened the driver's door to the car. Lenny had used his key to turn on the power to the radio, the only thing in the car that still worked. He was listening to a twenty-four-hour heavy-metal station that was broadcasting a sound like the exhaust of a revving small-plane engine overlaid with an electrocuted voice screaming over and over something like "burgers and fries."

"That sounds like amplified puking," the old man said.

Lenny lay back against the seat and put his arm over his bloodshot eyes. "Aw, man."

His grandfather pushed on his shoulder. "You get a job yet?"

Lenny cocked up a red eye. "How'm I gonna get a job so soon? How'm I gonna get a job smelling bad, with no shave and mosquito bites all over me?"

The old man considered this a moment, looking into his grandson's sticky eyes. He remembered the inert feel of him as a baby. "Okay. I'll give you a temporary reprieve on one condition."

"What's that?" Lenny hung his head way back over the seat.

"St. Lucy has confessions before seven o'clock daily Mass. I want you to think about going to confession and telling the priest what you done."

Lenny straightened up and eyed the house. The old man knew he was considering its deep bathtub and its oversized water heater. "Where in the catechism does it say selling pigeons is a mortal sin?"

"You going, or you staying outside in your stink?"

"What am I supposed to tell the priest?" He put his hands in his lap.

His grandfather squatted down next to him. "Remember what Sister Florita told you one time in catechism class? If you close your eyes before you go to confession, your sins will make a noise."

Lenny closed his eyes. "A noise."

"They'll cry out like little frogs in a ditch at sundown."

"Sure," Lenny said with a laugh, his eyeballs shifting under the closed lids. "Well, I don't hear nothing." He opened his eyes and looked at the old man. "What's the point of me confessing if I don't hear nothing?"

His grandfather stood up with a groan. "Keep listening," he said.

After Lenny cleaned up, they ate breakfast at a café on Tulane Avenue, and later, walking back home, they spotted Annie coming up the street, carrying her toolbox, her blond hair splashed like gold on the shoulders of her denim shirt.

The old man tipped his cap. "Hi there, Miss Annie."

She smiled at the gesture. "Mr. F. Good morning."

Lenny gave her a bump with his hip. "Annie, you're out early, babe."

She lifted her chin. "I came to see you. Daddy told me you were wandering the street like a bum." She emphasized the last word.

"The old man didn't like my last business. . . ."

"It wasn't business," she snapped. Annie looked down at a work boot as though trying to control her emotions. "Lenny, yesterday morning I went walking over by Broussard Street. You know what I saw? Shut up. Let me tell you." She put down the toolbox and held out her hands as though she was showing him the length of a fish. "That old Mr. Lejeune, on his knees with that damned bird you sold him, wobbling down his property line."

Lenny laughed. "That musta been a sight."

Annie looked at the grandfather, then at Lenny's eyes, searching for something. "You just don't get it, do you?"

"Get what?" When he saw her expression, he lost his smile.

She sighed and looked at her watch. "Ya'll come on." She picked up her toolbox and started down the root-buckled sidewalk toward Broussard Street. After nine blocks they crossed a wide boulevard, went one more block, and stopped behind a holly bush growing next to the curb. Across the street was a peeling weatherboard house jammed between two similar houses separated by slim lanes of grass.

"This is about the time of day I saw him yesterday," Annie said.

"Who?" Lenny asked, ducking down as though afraid of being recognized.

"The old guy you sold the pigeon to."

"Jeez, you want him to see me?"

She looked at him with her big, careful blue eyes. The grandfather thought she was going to yell, but her voice was controlled. "Why are you afraid for him to see you?" She was backed into the holly bush, fresh-scrubbed for the morning shift and looking like a big Eve in the Garden.

Across the street, there was movement at the side of the house, and Mr. Lejeune came around his porch slowly, shuffling on his knees like a locomotive. The grandfather stood on his toes and saw that the old man was red in the face and that the pigeon looked tired and drunk. "Lord," he whispered, "he's got rags tied around his kneecaps."

"Yesterday I saw he wore the tips off his shoes," Annie told him. "Look at that." Behind Mr. Lejeune walked a thin boy, awkward and pale. "Didn't he say he had a nephew?" The boy was smiling and talking down to his uncle. "The kid looks excited about something."

"Two weeks," Lenny said.

"Huh?" the grandfather cupped a hand behind an ear.

"Today's two weeks. They'll probably go to Bayou Park this afternoon and turn it loose."

Mr. Lejeune looked up and across toward where they were standing. He bent to the side a bit and then lurched to his feet, waving like a windshield wiper. "Hey, what ya'll doing on this side the boulevard?"

The three of them crossed the street and stood on the short stretch of capsizing walk that led to a wooden porch. "We was just out for a morning walk," Lenny told him. "How's the bird doin'?" The pigeon seemed to look up at him angrily, blinking, struggling. Someone had painted its claws with red fingernail polish.

"This here's Amelia," Mr. Lejeune said. "That's what Alvin named her." He looked at his nephew. The grandfather saw that the boy was trembling in spite of his smile. His feet were pointed inward, and his left hand was shriveled and pink.

"How you doing, bud?" the grandfather asked, patting his head.

"All right," the boy said. "We goin' to the park at four o'clock and turn Amelia loose."

Lenny forced a smile. "You and your uncle been having a good time training old Amelia, huh?"

The boy looked over to where his uncle had gone to sit on the front steps. He was rubbing his knees. "Yeah. It's been great. The first day, we got caught out in a thunderstorm and I got a chest cold, but the medicine made me feel better."

"You had to go to the doctor?" Annie asked, touching his neck.

"Him, too," the boy volunteered in a reedy voice. "Shots in the legs." He looked up at Lenny. "It'll be worth it when Amelia comes back from across town."

"Why's it so important?" Lenny asked.

The boy shrugged. "It's just great that this bird way up in the sky knows which house I live in."

"Hey," Mr. Lejeune called. "You want me to put on some water?"

"No thanks," the grandfather said. "We had coffee already."

The old man struggled to his feet, untying the pads from his knees. "At least come in the backyard and look at the cage." He shook out his pants and tugged the boy toward the rear of the house to a close-clipped yard with an orange tree in the middle. Against the rear of the house was a long-legged cage shiny with new galvanized hardware cloth.

"That took a lot of work to build, I bet," the grandfather said to Lenny, who shrugged and said that he'd told him how to do it. The corners of the cage were finished like furniture, mortised and tenoned. In the center was a ramp leading up to a swinging door. The pigeon squirted out of the old man's hand and flew into the cage, crazy for the steel-mesh freedom.

"We'll let her rest up for the big flight," Mr. Lejeune said.

Lenny glanced over at Annie's face. She looked long at the pigeon, then over at where the boy slumped against the orange tree. "You know, if you decide you ain't happy with the bird, you can have your money back."

Mr. Lejeune looked at him quickly. "No way. She's trained now.

I bet she could find this house from the North Pole."

Lenny smiled. "I knew it. Another satisfied customer."

The grandfather told Mr. Lejeune how much he liked the cage.

"Aw, this ain't nothin'," he said. "Before my back give out, I was working for Delta Desk and Chair, thirty-six years in the bookcase division. Man, you could pass your hand over my seams and it felt like glass if you closed your eyes." He waved a flattened palm over the cage as if he was working a spell.

The grandfather touched Annie's shoulder and they said their good-byes. On the walk home, she was silent. When they got to his grandfather's, she stopped, rattled her little toolbox, and did not look at either of them. Finally, she looked back down the street and asked, "Lenny, what's gonna happen if that bird doesn't come back to the kid?"

He shook his head. "If she flies for the river and spots them grain elevators, she'll never see Broussard Street again, that's for sure."

"Two weeks ago you knew he was buying Amelia as a pet for a kid."

Lenny turned his palms out. "Am I responsible for everything those birds do until they die?"

The grandfather rolled his eyes at the girl. She wasn't stupid, but when she looked at Lenny, there was too much hope in her eyes.

Annie clenched and unclenched her big pale hands. "If I was a bad sort, I'd hit you with a crescent wrench."

Lenny blinked twice, perhaps trying to figure what she wanted to hear. The grandfather knew that she paid for their dates when the boy was out of work. She bought his cigarettes and concert tickets and let him hang around her house when something good was on cable. Often she looked at him the way she studied whatever gadget was whirling in her lathe, maybe wondering if he would come out all right.

Lenny lit up a cigarette and let the smoke come out as he talked. "I'm sorry. I'll try to think of something to tell the kid if the bird don't come back."

She considered this for a moment, then leaned over and kissed him quickly on the side of his mouth. As he watched her stride down the sidewalk, the grandfather listened to the Williams sockets rattling in her toolbox, and he watched Lenny wipe off the hot wetness of her lips.

That night, a half hour after dark, Annie, Lenny, and his grandfather were watching a John Wayne movie in the den when there was a knock at the rear screen door. It was Mr. Lejeune, and he was worried about Amelia.

"I turnt her loose about four-thirty and she ain't come back yet." The old man combed his hair with his fingers and peered around Lenny to where Annie sat in a lounger. "You got any hints?"

Lenny looked at a shoe. "Look, why don't you let me give your money back."

"Naw." He shook his head. "That ain't the point. The boy's gonna get a lift from seeing the bird come back." Alvin's pale face tilted out from behind his uncle's waist.

Annie, who was wearing shorts, peeled herself off the plastic couch, and the grandfather put a spotted hand over his eyes. Lenny turned a serious face toward Mr. Lejeune.

"Sometimes those birds get in fights with other birds. Sometimes they get hurt and don't make it back. What can I tell you? You want your money?" He put a hand in his pocket but left it there.

The old man sidestepped out onto the porch. "Me and Alvin will just go and wait. If that bird'd just come back once, it'd be worth all the crawling around, you see?" He held the boy's twisted hand and went down ahead of him one step at a time. Annie moved into the kitchen and broke a glass in the sink. The grandfather tried not to listen to what happened next.

Lenny went into the kitchen to see what had caused the noise, and met a rattle of accusations from Annie.

Then Lenny began to shout. "Why are you bitching at me like this?"

"Because you gyped that old man and the crippled kid. I've never seen you do nothing like that."

"Well, you better get used to it."

"Get used to what?" She used a big contrary voice better than most women, the grandfather thought.

"Get used to doing things the way I like."

"What, like stealing from old people and kids? Acting like a freakin' slug? Now I know why your parents left your ass in the street."

Lenny's voice came through the kitchen door thready and high-pitched. "Hey, nobody left me. They're on vacation, you cow."

"People on vacation don't sell their houses, leave the time zone, and never write or call. They left because they found out what it took me a long time to just now realize."

"What's that?"

And here a sob came into her voice and the grandfather put his head down.

"That there's a big piece of you missing that'll never turn up."

"You can't talk to me like that," Lenny snarled, "and I'll show you why." The popping noise of a slap came from the kitchen and the grandfather thought, *Oh no,* and struggled to rise from the sofa, but before he could stand and steady himself, a sound like a piano tipping over shook the entire house, and Lenny cried out in deep pain.

After the grandfather prepared an ice pack, he went to bed that night but couldn't sleep. He thought of the handprint on Annie's face and the formal numbness of the walk back to her house as he escorted her home. Now, he imagined Mr. Lejeune checking Amelia's cage into the night, his nephew asking him questions in a resigned voice. He even formed a picture of the pigeon hunkered down on a roof vent above the St. Mary Feed Company elevator, trying with its little bird brain to remember where Broussard Street was. About one o'clock he smacked himself on the forehead with an open palm, put on his clothes, and went down to the old carport with a flashlight. In the eaves he saw a number of round heads pop into his light's beam, and when he checked the section from which Lenny had plucked Amelia, he thought he saw her. Turning off the light for a moment, he reached into the straw and pulled out a bird that barely struggled. Its claws were painted red, and the grandfather eased down into a wheelbarrow to think, holding the bird in both hands, where it pecked him resignedly. He debated whether he should just let the animal go and forget the Lejeunes, but then he imagined how the boy would have to face the empty cage. It would be like an abandoned house, and every day the boy would look at it and wonder why Amelia had forgotten where he lived. He held the bird and thought of Lenny's parents probably parked in a Winnebago in some canyon in Utah, flown off that far to escape him, his mooching and his music. Why had they really left him? The old man shook his head.

At two-fifteen the grandfather walked down the side of Mr. Lejeune's house, staying close to the wall and out of the glow of the streetlight. When he turned the corner into the backyard, he was in total darkness and had to feel for the cage, and then for its little swinging gate. His heart jumped as he felt a feathery escape from his palms, and the bird squirted into the enclosure. At that instant, a backyard floodlight came on and the rear door rattled open, showing Mr. Lejeune standing in a pair of mustard-colored pajama bottoms and a sleeveless undershirt.

"Hey, whatcha doing?" He came down into the yard, moving stiffly.

The grandfather couldn't think of a lie to save his soul, just stood there looking between the cage and the back door. "I wanted to see about the bird," he said at last.

The other man walked up and looked into the cage. "What? How'd you get a hold of the dumb cluck? I thought she'd be in Texas by now." He reached back and scratched a hip.

The grandfather's mouth slowly fell open. "You knew."

"Yeah," Mr. Lejeune growled. "I may be dumb, but I ain't stupid. And no offense, Mr. Fontenot, but that grandson of yours got used-car salesman writ all over him."

"Why'd you come by the house asking about the bird if you knew it'd never come back?"

"That was for Alvin, you know? I wanted him to think I was worried." Mr. Lejeune grabbed the grandfather by the elbow and led him into his kitchen, where the two men sat down at a little porcelain-topped table. The old man opened the refrigerator and retrieved two frosty cans of Schlitz. "It's like this," Mr. Lejeune said, wincing against the spray from the pull tabs, "Little Alvin's never had a daddy and his momma's a crackhead that run off with some biker to Alaska." He pushed a can to the grandfather, who picked it up and drew hard, for he was sweating. Mr. Lejeune spoke low and leaned close. "Little Alvin's still in fairy-tale land, you know. Thinks his momma is coming back when school takes up in the fall. But he's got to toughen up and face facts. That's why I bought that roof rat from your grandson." He sat back and began rubbing his knees. "He'll be disappointed about the little thing, that bird, and maybe it'll teach him to deal with the big thing. That boy's got to live a long time, you know what I mean, Mr. Fontenot?"

The grandfather put his cap on the table. "Ain't that kind of mean, though?"

"Hey. We'll watch the sky for a couple days and I'll let him see how I take it. We'll be disappointed together." Mr. Lejeune looked down at his purple feet. "He's crippled, but he's strong and he's smart."

The grandfather lifted his beer and drank until his eyes stung. He remembered Lenny, asleep in the front bedroom with a big knot on the back of his head and a black eye. He listened to Mr. Lejeune until he was drowsy. "I got to get back home," he said, standing up and moving toward the door. "Thanks for the beer."

"Hey. Don't worry about nothing. Just do me a favor and put that bird back in its nest." They went out and Mr. Lejeune reached into the cage and retrieved Amelia, dropping her into a heavy grocery bag.

"You sure you doing the right thing, now?" the grandfather asked. "You got time to change your mind." He helped fold the top of the bag shut. "You could be kind." He imagined what the boy's face would look like if he could see that the bird had returned to the cage.

Mr. Lejeune slowly handed him the bag. For a moment they held it together and listened. Inside, the bird walked the crackling bottom back and forth on its painted toes, looking for home.

License to Steal

C urtis Lado rolled out of bed slowly, pulled on his wrinkled khakis, and walked into the kitchen, yawning and scratching the back of his head with both hands. He sat down at his chrome-legged dinette table and noticed that no pots murmured on the stove and no coffee smell hung in the air. He stared down at the note left on the worn Formica. "I had enough," the note said. It was his wife's handwriting. He got up and shoved open the rusted-out screen door, then walked into the backyard to look for her 1969 Torino, but it was gone. He stared at the empty gravel drive and said to himself, "What the hell?"

Curtis put on his brown vinyl bedroom slippers and walked down to the corner to use the pay phone outside the Mudbug Café to call his son, Nookey, who worked at a sausage plant in Ponchatoula.

"What you want?" Nookey yelled over the whir of a dozen grinders. "I got a pig to do here about the size of a Oldsmobile."

"Baby, Momma took off and I don't know where she's gone. Did she say anything to you?"

"Naw, nothing she ain't been saying since I was born. Said she was tired of living in Louisiana with somebody didn't bring home no money. Said she wanted to move to the United States."

"What the hell's that mean?"

"I don't know," Nookey whined. "And I don't know where she run off to. She did say something about not paying the light bill for two months because she needed the money for a trip. Hey, this pig had to be shot with a deer rifle to bring him down. I got to get busy."

"Just tell me where your brother is and I'll let you go."

"Buzzy's in jail."

"Which one?"

"Hammond."

"Okay. Maybe he'll know something." Curtis hung up and reached into his pocket for coins. He began dialing the jailhouse number, which he knew by heart. He got Buzzy on the phone, but his addict son didn't know what month it was, much less where his mother had driven off to that morning.

"Maybe she went to Biloxi," Buzzy suggested in his slow, faraway voice. "It's nice and sandy this time of year."

"Son, why would she leave me? Answer me that? I got to know where she is."

"Maybe she just went to the flea market."

"No, baby. She left me a letter and everything." His voice nearly cracked. The importance of what had happened was beginning to sink in. "I can't understand it, Buzz. She got a refrigerator that works, she got a nice brick-paper house, and she got us." But Buzzy, who hadn't seen his mother since he had been arrested for selling marijuana the week before, couldn't give a clue as to where she had gone. Curtis checked the coin-return slot and walked home.

He had a little folding money in his pocket from his wife's last check, but that was it. Though he had not held steady work since 1978, he knew he had to find a job fast. Without the money Inez had brought in from her job as a cashier, the power company would take his meter and Friendly Willy finance would show up to get the TV. His 1971 Dodge pickup was also not paid for. Though Curtis was convinced he had a weak heart and that work gave him a nervousness in his chest parts, he had to eat. So, in the tiny bathroom he scraped off his silver whiskers and added a shot of VO5 to his swept-back iron-gray mane. He pulled his best polyester cowboy shirt over his rounded shoulders and admired the pearly buttons in the mirror. On his way out the door, he lit up a Lucky Strike.

He drove up Highway 51 to Amite, where he saw a sign stating that a foundry was hiring. The receptionist in the main office said he would have to come back in an hour because the person who did the hiring was out, so Curtis drove back down 51 to get something to eat. At the Big Sicilian Lounge, a brown cinder-block structure huddled under a shot-up Dixie beer sign, he slid out from his truck. Inside, he hunched over the plywood bar and drank three beers quickly, as though he had come in from a two-day trip across a desert. "Give me a pickled egg," he said to Raynelle, the barmaid, a large redheaded woman with no eyebrows. "I need something good to eat."

"Why don't you try a pig lip," she said, hoisting onto the counter a gallon jar labeled with large black letters: FIFTY CENTS A LIP. He inspected shapeless parts floating coldly under a blond gluey film.

"Fish me out one," he told her. He finished off his meal on a paper towel, tossed down his last beer, and headed back to the foundry.

The personnel director at Deep South Metal Casting was a pretty thirty-year-old blonde who wore makeup and perfume like a cosmetics saleslady. Her name tag read TAMMY MICHELLE. She shook an application form at him, and he took it gravely, spending over an hour filling its tiny voids. Later, she read it in one minute flat. She put it down on her desk and looked at Curtis, who was seated across from her in a plastic chair. "Mr. Lado, I see you left school in the eighth grade."

"Yes, ma'am," he said. "I went further than anybody in my family. I always told my own boys how important it was to get a good education. My oldest is educated more'n anybody I know."

Tammy Michelle gave him a faint smile. "You mean he has something like a B.A. or M.A.?"

"Yes, ma'am. He got a GED."

The personnel director pursed her glossy lips and looked down at the smudged form on her desk. "I see that your longest employment was at a chicken plant for three years. Is that right?"

"Yes, ma'am, I was the neck and liver man." He gave her this information with great seriousness, as though she could not make a decision about him without it.

"Uh-huh. And you've been out of work for a number of years?"

Here, Curtis knew he had to be careful, because he didn't want to confess to the uncomfortable flutterings in his chest. Nobody hired an unhealthy man. "You see, my wife had this wonderful job that supported us to just the upmost, and I never was a greedy man. No, ma'am, I figured to work on the every now and then and enjoy one day at a time. My daddy used to say to me, 'Let the future take care of itself and never give a nail two licks when one'll make it hold.' My smartest, Nookey, he's just like me. Quit school in ninth grade when he caught on that all he had to do to get a diploma was lay out four years and then take a dinky little test."

Tammy Michelle made an unpleasant face, as if she smelled something out of the ordinary. "Mr. Lado, do you drink?"

"Not so that it affects my working, no, ma'am—just a few to wash down my meals, and at night with my podnuhs down in Hammond, but I seldom ever pop a top before breakfast." He gave her a big leery grin just to show he wasn't offended by the question.

"You know," Tammy Michelle began, flipping her shiny hair behind her shoulders with both hands, "I can't see much work experience that qualifies you for an opening here at the foundry. I notice you worked for a sawmill once. What exactly did you do?"

Curtis had to close his eyes to think, it had been that long ago. "I was a sawyer." He looked at the young woman and knew that she didn't understand. How could he explain what a sawyer was to someone who looked and smelled the way she did?

"Could you explain?"

"I guess so," he said. "I used to ride the carriage, that's a five-ton iron contraption, a frame on wheels pushed and pulled by a long steam piston. It goes back and forth holding a big log, running it against a saw blade and cutting it into boards. I had a bunch of levers to wrassle with, and I rode the machine feeling like a yo-yo. That was a real job, sure enough. Me and my podnuhs all worked the same mill those days, and we sure could make the lumber fly. I was real good at it. Real good. Thirty minutes into my shift, everybody handling the new boards was hollering for me to slow down." His voice trailed off as he thought about that first job. "But the mill closed down after two years."

Tammy Michelle seemed unimpressed. She gave her fluffed-out

hair a toss and told him that they didn't have a job he was qualified for.

He looked back at her, unblinking. "What about those boys that grind mistakes off the hot castings? A monkey could do that. I ain't asking for a job as a machinist." He felt Tammy Michelle's appraising eyes on his face. She might be sweet-flavored and colored like a gumdrop, but he realized with a pang that she had hired hundreds of men. He saw her take in the bags under his eyes, the red map of veins in his eyeballs. He saw her look at his hands, soft and nicotine-stained.

"Mr. Lado," she began, a hard edge creeping into her voice, "the casting shed is a place for young men. You're fifty-two years old." She folded his application and placed it in a folder with dozens of others. "You also need a high school diploma to work for us."

"I can work steady for as long as you need me," he said, getting up slowly. "I know there's been some gaps when I ain't worked much, but you can't work too steady if you're a Louisiana man. You got to lay off and smell the roses a bit, drink a little beer and put some wear on your truck."

Tammy Michelle looked down at the next application. "So long, Louisiana man," she said.

Curtis drove back to the Big Sicilian Lounge and drank one frosty can after another, washing down ten pickled eggs and four pig lips in three hours' time. All the while, he filled the husky barmaid's ear. Raynelle was sympathetic. "It's a shame they ain't got no place for a good soul like you, Curtis."

"All they're interested in is how educated a man is. They ain't interested in what all he knows that's practical." He took a long drag on a Lucky Strike, flicking the ash on the floor.

"Education, education, education. That's all I hear," Raynelle sang. "Why everybody's got to be so damned smart is beyond me. I never went past six grade and look at me." She spread her ample arms. "Hell, I ain't lacking nothing." Curtis looked at her sleeveless Ban-Lon shirt and agreed.

"Yeah," Curtis began, "used to be that all a man needed was guts and sweat to make money. All guts and sweat gets you now is laughed at." Raynelle snorted once and adjusted her bra straps, which sank into her shoulders like steel bands on a cotton bale.

By four o'clock Curtis felt that he was beginning to be drunk, so he figured it was time to take a drive. He climbed into his truck, started it with some difficulty, and stabbed at a tuning button to bring forth country music, but grazed it with his stubby forefinger. Off in the static-filled distance he heard his favorite song, "If You Don't Leave Me Alone, I'll Find Somebody Who Will." He lost his temper and hit the row of buttons with a fist. There was a crunch inside the radio and the little orange indicator lurched to the left side of the dial, lodging squarely on a Public Radio station. Strains of a string quartet filled the old Dodge's cab, and Curtis made a face as though a polecat had just crawled out from under the seat. He tried the buttons and the tuning knob, but the radio was forever jammed on violins and cellos. He cursed mightily and banged on the dash until he could stand no more of the delicate, weaving melody. He snapped the switch. No music at all was better than whatever that was.

He fishtailed out onto Highway 51 and headed south under a sky filled with puffy summer rain clouds. At a traffic light in Independence, his eyes managed to focus on a hand-painted sign that read HELP WANTED. He pulled over to the mud parking lot of a small metalworking shop, went inside the rusty tin building, and spoke to the young owner, breezily telling all he knew about welding log trucks together. Finally, the owner looked up and said, "I like you good enough, old man, but I just need someone who can read blueprints and work the math."

Curtis cocked his head like a feisty rooster observing a big yard dog. "Hey, I can cut iron real good. Ain't you got nobody can draw some lines on the iron what tell me where to cut?"

The owner shook his head. Curtis pleaded his case a few more minutes, but he finally gave up and left. He climbed back into his truck, but the engine only grunted twice. He got out and raised the hood. Sometimes when he let the sun shine on the battery to heat the acid, enough juice built up to start the engine. Two doors down from the metalworking shop was a bar promising a cool place to wait. Inside Anselmo's Oasis he began a lively argument with a group of strawberry farmers and pulpwood truck drivers about the value of education. One farmer told him that an education was important because you could maybe one day become a legislator and make millions of dollars. Most of the folks in Baton Rouge, he said, were real smart, lawyers even, and used what they knew to help their friends out in the construction industry by throwing an occasional bridge or firehouse job their way. "That's what democracy is all about," the old farmer said. "Spreading around the gravy."

But Curtis would not give up in the face of logic. Under the sway of six additional beers he grew cranky, grabbed the farmer by his shoulder and shook him.

"You're crazy. A Louisiana man ain't got to be a four-eyed egghead to throw away money. I could work that dog and pony show in the state capitol myself. If I had a three-hundred-dollar suit and a two-hundred-dollar secretary with a tight butt, I could steal tax money with the best of them."

The old men carped and hollered back and forth until Anselmo and a gravel truck driver grabbed Curtis and in a clop and skitter of boots threw him out the front door. He spun and weaved back to his truck, slammed down the hood, and succeeded in starting it up, getting it in the road, and aiming it toward home.

When he got to his house, he came in through the kitchen and hit the light switch. Nothing happened. Sure enough, checking the side of the house, he found that the electric meter had been removed. Back in the darkened living room, he sat in his torn vinyl recliner and let the house spin around his head. He felt nauseated, his eyes hurt, and his heart knocked away like a big woodpecker in a hollow tree. He wondered what had gone wrong with him. Going back in memory, he saw himself as an ironclad buck that no amount of liquor, cigarettes, or wildness could ruin. When he was young, he'd planned to live forever by the strength of his body and a dab of skill he could sell for enough to keep him in fun. There was always work. He thought of his sawmill job, his favorite, riding the carriage like a cowboy on a fast horse, charging back and forth, crashing logs into the humming blade. That had been twenty-five years before. Tonight he stared at the dark outline of his television, feeling sick enough to cry, and could not for the life of him figure out what was wrong.

The next day was Friday, Nookey's day off, and as usual he came over and got his daddy out of bed. His son was thin and big-boned, his shoulders rounding under a checkered long-sleeved shirt he wore winter and summer. His polka-dot welder's cap was pulled down over a pair of patient gray eyes. Nookey woke his father by pulling one leg out of bed and dropping it toward the floor as though it might be a limb on one of the carcasses down at the sausage plant.

Everything in the refrigerator smelled bad, so they closed it up and climbed into the truck to drive to the Mudbug for breakfast. As soon as Curtis turned the key, Nookey spun on the radio. The passionate voice of a soprano shrilled from the speaker, and Nookey jumped from the truck as though it had suddenly caught fire. "What the hail is that?" he yelled, stumbling about for a moment in the gravel.

"Aw, the damn radio is stuck on the longhair music station," Curtis complained, turning off the voice. "Quit fooling and come on."

"Man," Nookey hooted, climbing back into the Dodge. "Sounds like a tomcat hung up in a fan belt."

"That's just one more thing I got to pay to get fixed," Curtis said, looking over his shoulder as he backed out onto the street. "I got to get a job so's I can get the juice turned back on, too."

Nookey gave a sideways nod, like a hound blinking off a horsefly. "We'll get us some grits and eggs and I'll help you apply every place we can think of."

And that's what they did. But the veneer mill said they needed someone who could operate a computer. The lumberyard told Curtis he was too old. The cement plant needed someone good with weights and measures. Finally, the auxiliary power plant would consider his application. They needed someone as a watchman five days a week and three hours Saturday morning. Curtis was offended when he heard the schedule and told the man doing the hiring as much.

He was cranky by the time he got there, plus somewhat drunk, having found a handy bar after each turndown to build up his courage for the next application.

Afterward, in the Big Sicilian, Nookey tugged on the bill of his cap and tried not to sound like he was complaining. "Daddy, you shouldn'a called that man at the powerhouse a Communist just because he wanted someone to work on Saturday."

"And why the hell not?" Curtis's indignation, usually fueled by nothing more significant than cold beer, was blazing. "A job like that will run a man into the ground. Six days a week? When the hell will I have time for any recreation?" He knocked back half a glass of draft beer and motioned to the barmaid for another. "Son, I'd just as soon live in Moscow and eat potato soup all day as become a pheasant worker for the power company."

Nookey pushed back his cap, bent over the bar, and examined his fingers. "Daddy, I work on Saturdays sometimes."

Curtis glared at him, burgundy pools forming below his eyeballs. "Then you got the brain of a armadillo. What you think you're gonna do, get rich? This is Louisiana, son. Ain't nobody can get rich in this state through hard work." He threw a dollar bill at the barmaid when she brought his beer. She was an old, dark woman with hair so coarse and black it looked tarred. Leaning on her side of the bar, she listened.

"Sometimes I think you drink a little heavy, Daddy," Nookey said, rubbing the thin blond stubble on his narrow face and looking down sorrowfully. He picked up his half-full glass, wiggled it, put it down.

Curtis swilled his beer until his eyes watered, taking down half a mug. "You want to kill yourself working, go ahead. You'll wear your fingers off down at the weenie plant all your life for what? So you can buy some trashy piece of red dirt with a used trailer on it while some real estate fool gets most all your money and a lawyer gets the rest. You think *they* work hard? You think just because they went to parties and chased women at a college for four years that they sweat and worry every day that the sun comes up? Hell no, son. They don't have a education. They got a license to steal." A snarl crept into his voice. He took a swig and looked at a cheerful beer poster where two girl skiers posed before an out-of-focus mountain. Curtis was confused and rueful. Something was wrong with him, but he had no idea what it was. "If I never drank a beer or smoked a cigarette and then worked eighty hours a week for the almighty auxiliary power station, I wouldn't do better than a tar-paper house and a raggedy-ass Dodge."

"Aw, Daddy. Come on, now."

Curtis didn't hear his son. He was looking at the poster. "What the hell's them girls up to anyway?" he shouted. "Hey, one of 'em's a lawyer and the other is a politician spending our tax money at two hundred dollars a night out in Colorado." He waved a fist at the images, as though he could shame them for both their waste and his worries.

Nookey let out a long sigh. "I think it's time we hit the road."

The barmaid picked up his glass. "You want to know about a job?" she asked. "Mr. Cantrell is opening up the old sawmill in the woods back of Albany. His foreman was in here this morning. Said they're hiring."

Curtis's eyes widened. "That's the old Cantrell mill. I never worked there, but I worked one just like it."

"Rode the log carriage like in the old days," Nookey moaned, shaking his head glumly. In two minutes they were on the highway, the truck weaving between the white lines with the floating, mystical action of a street sweeper. Curtis was so drunk that Nookey tried to take the wheel from him. The old man responded by cuffing him twice across the bridge of his nose. When the truck stopped for a traffic light in Byron, Nookey jumped out. "Go on and drive in a ditch if you want to. I believe Momma was right when she took off." He stood on the white line at the edge of the blacktop, seeming ready to cry. He waited for his father to say something, but Curtis didn't look at him, just reached over and pulled the door shut, popping the clutch so hard that the Dodge shuddered like a horse and clods of dirt fell from under the fenders.

He pulled into the muddy lot of the Cantrell sawmill, dizzy and confident, seeing a great future ahead, full of money enough for the electric bill, cases of beer, and cartons of Lucky Strikes. That's what money was for—weekends, free time, lots of smoke, and great big barmaids.

The mill was an obsolete complex of huge wooden sheds with tin roofs bloody with rust. Curtis parked in front of the office and looked to his left across the swampy yard. The building where the main saw was stood fifty feet tall, the carriage running twenty-five feet above ground level. There was a decided lack of activity even though the boiler shed, about two hundred feet to the rear of the main saw building, gave off shimmering white streams of sawdust smoke from its three crooked stacks.

Inside the office he spoke to a man slouching behind a cluttered, greasy desk. "You want a job?" the man asked. Curtis nodded. "You got to see Mr. Cantrell. What can you do?"

"How come there ain't no sawing going on?" Curtis slurred only two words, but the room spun slowly, like a ferry leaving shore. Inside his head something hissed and popped like bacon frying.

"We're just starting up again. This plant's been closed down for eight years, and it was wore-out when it closed." He smiled as though his comment was funny. "What is it you said you do?"

"I can run the carriage," Curtis said, absently.

"We need a carriage man to run that old-time system until we get a new one set up, but we can't try you out today."

"You got steam up."

"Yeah, I know. But we tore out the safety bumper at the end of the carriage run because all the timbers were buggy. Say, here's Cantrell now."

A large, ruddy man came through the door of an interior office. He wore a tailored white shirt, a narrow silk tie, and a yellow hard hat. He gave Curtis a stony, appraising look. "What do you want?" he snapped.

"My name's Curtis Lado. I'm looking for work." He put his hand to his chin and stroked the stubble there. Suddenly, he felt rusty and worn-out.

Mr. Cantrell's face looked chiseled out of flint. He leaned forward and sniffed audibly. "I don't hire old drunks," he said, pushing past and into another office, rattling open a blueprint as he walked. Curtis felt as though someone had shoved him off a bar stool. He walked sideways toward the parking lot door, unable to control his movements. The door stuck in its frame and he took several moments to open it, feeling the eyes of those in the office on his back. He stumbled on the splintered steps. Out in the soggy mill yard, he leaned on his truck and stared at the building that housed the huge saw and log carriage. It looked like the one he'd worked in many years ago when he was young and sharp, a man with friends and a good job earned by his youth and raw strength only. Letting go of the truck, he set out tentatively, navigating the slop of the mill yard, climbing the long stairs that led to the big saw.

Inside, two men were welding. They glanced at him but continued to concentrate on their work. All around him, steam pipes hissed and dripped condensation. The main saw apparatus was dismantled, but the carriage was gleaming under a brush coat of linseed oil. A crew had rolled a three-foot-diameter log onto it for testing. He walked over to the carriage and stumbled, falling into the controller's seat. Tall levers stood before him and he placed his hands on them and laughed. He nudged one and the carriage trembled. Curtis smiled and felt he could control it, remembering the magical thrust of the steam-activated rod that payed out of a long cylinder and shoved the iron carriage against the saw and then pulled it away effortlessly, as though it were a puff of air. He squeezed the lever, confident that all a man needed in life was what he was born with—common sense and confidence. He gave a lever a mighty thrust.

The best view of what happened next was from the mill yard. A geyser of steam shot from a pipe in the saw shed's roof, and there was a sound like someone dynamiting a stump. The carriage and a huge oak log splintered through a wall and support beam, flying out into the mill yard and crashing down onto a late-model Cadillac, the only decent automobile for miles around. Planks, bolts, and hunks of iron rained down onto the sawmill, and an angry roar of steam rose from the punctured building. Curtis was seated on the carriage, his hands clenched white on the control levers. He stared with sober attention at the flattened Cadillac under him and tried to put his mind in motion again, but he could not think of what to do, whether to shout or run or cry, and as he studied the shiny catastrophe under him, it seemed that his mind would never start, that perhaps it had never worked at all.

Mr. Cantrell walked out into the mill yard and stood next to his car, tapping a crushed fender with the clipboard he carried. He looked up at the figure seated on the carriage, who had come through a wall of timber uninjured. "Curtis Lado. Is that what you said your name is? Well, I guess you got a little property somewhere, maybe a car, maybe your granddaddy's watch? By the time my company lawyer gets through with you, the only thing you'll have is your skin, and we'll put that in jail, and when you get out of jail, whenever you make a nickel, I'll have four cents of it for the rest of your life." He turned his back and began yelling for a crew to go to Hammond for a crane and jacks.

Curtis climbed down and walked across to his truck, his face on fire under the derisive looks he drew from the workers hurrying about the mill yard. He was embarrassed into soberness. Going home occurred to him at once. He would hole up there like a man waiting for a hurricane.

Jamming the key into the old Dodge's ignition, he turned it, but there was only a pained grunt in response. He tried the switch again, and again, until the engine would do nothing more than utter a series of snickering clicks. Out in the yard, men watched him while they worked. Cantrell put his hands on his hips and stared, then began writing on his clipboard, his eyes now on the truck's license. Through the window of the office, Curtis could see a man on the phone, staring back at him. Deep in his chest, his heart fluttered like an engine running out of gas. He lay down out of sight on the front seat, reached up, and turned on the radio.

An announcer was speaking in a smooth, educated voice, saying that writers living in France during the seventeenth century thought Louisiana was a wasteland. There were only evil men, pestilence, and wild Indians, and no one who lived there had any hope for a bright future. Curtis closed his eyes and tried to understand the commentary, which was about an opera, but the radio voice might as well have been using the language of owls. "A French writer," the announcer continued, "once introduced a section of his work by stating that it was set 'in the deserts of Louisiana.' " Curtis rolled onto his side and, for as long as he was able, listened to the words carefully, but they were being spoken in a tongue he had not been taught. A cloud of steam rolled past the windshield, and an orchestra filled the cab of the rusting pickup with a somber, incomprehensible music.

Floyd's Girl

T-Jean

Airborne, T-Jean's big sedan flew across the main highway, landing on a shell road like a crop duster coming down wrong. He had to find his cousin Floyd before the little girl was lost. The car hydroplaned over dips filled with rainwater, blasting muddy showers over the hood. T-Jean was afraid of the brimming roadside canals, so he watched instead the white frame house up ahead in the big field, and in a minute he swirled onto the farm road that was also the driveway, his tires spraying shells into the rice ponds. He braked, leapt from the car before it fully stopped, and charged up across the gallery and through the screen, almost knocking down Tante Sidonie.

"Floyd, where he's at?" T-Jean asked, his breath coming in little gasps.

Tante Sidonie adjusted her bifocals to look at him. "You T-shirt is wet as a dishrag," she said.

"Where's Floyd? The Texas man got his lil' girl."

She had to think for one second who the Texas man was. When she remembered, she yelled, "All the way to the tree line." She followed him out the door, her hands on his back, pushing.

T-Jean gunned his big Ford and drove straight back until the shell drive turned to mud and rainwater. When the car settled down to its frame, he was by the old tractor shed, and he headed for it, his boots blasting the sloppy mud. Without breaking stride he ran up onto the only machine left, a heavy International M, retired because it was too old to pull and ate gas by the drum. One yank on the starter ring and the worn engine rolled twice and fired, T-Jean slamming it into second gear and taking out the rotten back wall of the shed, the big rubber cleats throwing boards in the air behind and then biting ground as the machine found high gear and waddled up on top of the mud track toward the tree line, where Floyd's big air-conditioned John Deere was stopped in the water. T-Jean stood on the seat and yelled Floyd's name over the roaring tractor, his voice cracking with effort, but he was too far away. Floyd was a short, blue-jeaned island off at the edge of two thousand acres of swamped rice field. It was five minutes before T-Jean got there.

Floyd

"What's wrong with you?" Floyd asked. The wildness in T-Jean's gray eyes was contagious, and Floyd wanted to stay calm. Since he'd turned thirty, he'd tried to cool down. He had a ten-year-old daughter to raise.

"The man from Texas, he came when you mama's at the store and got Lizette."

Every feature of Floyd's face shifted, a movement of flesh terrible to watch. "You mean my wife's new boyfriend?"

"Yeah, man. Grandmère saw him. She sent me. She's waitin' by the house."

"How long?"

"Not twenty minutes."

"Ninety west?"

"His favorite way to Texas."

Floyd cupped his elbows in his palms, curled his upper lip, and sniffed his mustache, the whole parish road system lighting up in his mind, an aerial view of black lines against a green watery screen. He batted the other man on the knee, wheeled, and leapt up on his hulking green tractor, starting up and rolling the balloon tires north out of the field and into a trash woods of briers and saplings taller than his machine, exploding through in a scream of machinery and a rattling black column of diesel smoke. Trees snapped under his tires like breaking bones. A mile through all this was Mrs. Boudreaux's little white house, closer to the main road than Tante Sidonie's, if he indeed could come out of the woods in her backyard. Floyd adjusted his cap and pushed the pedals of the frantic machine with his thin legs, trying to think, trying to stay calm. He didn't know where his wife lived. She was still his wife, because once the priest married you, you were married forever, in spite of a spiritless divorce court and a Protestant judge and a Texas lounge bum in snakeskin boots.

Floyd pictured his daughter, Lizette, her moon face and dark hair. The girl was scared of her mother, who had beaten her with a damn chinaball branch for playing with her makeup. But she was smart, smarter than Floyd, the kind of smartness that sometimes got you in trouble with people. He hoped that she would not sass the Texas man. Not him.

Mrs. Boudreaux

"Chick-chick-chick-chick, *venez ici. Mangez ça.*" Mrs. Boudreaux scolded her white hens in the voice she long ago used to discipline her six children at breakfast. She broadcast the chicken scratch over the dirt of her backyard, then turned for the steps of her small cypress house, which shone white with rainwater. A terrific noise in the woods startled her chickens, and they raced ahead of her under the house. She turned to watch Tante Sidonie's big green machine mash three willow trees down into her yard; then she saw Floyd climb down from the cab and step over her one rosebush. He was sadlooking, she thought, like his grandpère with the big mustache. When Floyd was a baby and she held him in her lap, he was like a tough little muscle made hard by God for a hard life ahead. He was not a mean man, but determined enough to always do a thing right when it counted. It was rough, raising a young daughter with no help, having a wife who ran off with a *cou rouge.* She clucked her tongue at him when he came over to her; he was a pretty man, little, like she liked them, and dark from work.

"Hey, Misres Boudreaux, is T-man still in the service?"

She hitched her chicken-scratch bowl up under her bosom.

"What you need his car for, you?" Why else would he come here through the woods like that? she thought.

"The Texas man, he came stole Lizette just now. I got to catch him. T-Jean's grandmère is waiting to tell me."

She looked past him toward the rattling tractor, remembering the Texas man. A fear crept up through Mrs. Boudreaux's stomach as she saw the dark-haired Lizette ruined by outlanders, dragged off to the dry plains of Texas she imagined from cowboy movies. She wondered if her mother would take her to Mass or to the Stations of the Cross during Lent. She knew Texans had some kind of God, but they didn't take him too seriously, didn't celebrate him with feast days and days of penance, didn't even kneel down in their churches on Sunday.

"My old Dodge can't go fast, but you can use T-man's car if you can crank it," she told him.

She watched Floyd run over to a plastic-covered hump next to the barn and pull bricks and tire rims off so he could get to T-man's primer-painted Z. The key was in the car and it started immediately, sounding hot and mad as a bee in a bird's beak. In ten seconds, he was on the blacktop road, and Mrs. Boudreaux imagined her house as a white speck shrinking in his rearview mirror. He disappeared onto Sugarmill Highway, and she heard the exhaust storm as he accelerated toward his house three miles away, where she imagined that T-Jean's grandmère was standing in the tall grass by the mailbox, leaning against her walker, her faded cotton dress swinging at her ankles.

T-Jean's Grandmère

Potato salad. I'm going make me some potato salad and then something with gravy to pour over that and then some sweet peas. I got a deer roast in the icebox. I could put some garlic in that and make a roux. She was always planning meals. Three a day, if not for her husband, then for her children who lived in the neighborhood. Her grandbaby, T-Jean, asked her to stand by the road and tell Floyd something. What was it? Why was she standing out in the mist? Then she remembered Lizette. What would that poor baby eat for supper?

Can she get turtle sauce piquante in Lubbock? And T-Jean's grandmère thought of the gumbos Lizette would be missing, the okra soul, the crawfish body. How could she live without the things that belong on the tongue like Communion on Sunday? Living without her food would be like losing God, her unique meal.

She heard the approaching blast of a car and the cry of brakes as Floyd stopped next to her, driving something that looked like a dull gray space capsule on wheels. He asked her what color the Texas man's car was, and she remembered why she was there. She began to talk in her creaky voice: *"Ey, Floyd, bébé, comment ça va?* Ah, it's a big man what come up you driveway wearing a John Wayne hat, a skinny man straight as a railroad, with big tall boots. An' Lizette, she was crying she wanted to take a suitcase, but he pulled her in the car like this." Here she cranked up an arm, a bony right angle. "This is what her arm was like."

"Mais, what kind of car was he driving?" Floyd banged the backs of his hands on the steering wheel.

"Oh, yah. It was a green Chevrolet truck. A old one. At least I think it was that. Me, I don't know one from the other. I ought to have a *garde de soleil* on my head in this weather." Floyd revved the engine, getting ready to tear off, but she reached over the rail of her walker and put a hand on the window ledge. "How you gonna ketchum?" Her face darkened as she leaned down to Floyd's window. He told her quickly, all the while staring down the blacktop. "Ah," she said. "You should take the farm roads and pass up Eunice and catch him at Poteau. Look," she told him, "take this. I pulled it off the dashboard of my Plimmet."

He took a plastic statue of St. Christopher from her spotted hands. "Grandmère, the Pope said St. Christopher wasn't for real." He glanced at the magnet on the bottom.

T-Jean's grandmère gave him a scoffing look. "If you believe in something, then it's real. The Pope's all right, but he spends too much time thinking about things instead of visiting people in grass huts like he ought."

Floyd stuck the statue on the dash. "There."

She made a poking motion with her knobby forefinger. "Turn him so he sees the road."

Floyd twirled the plastic. *"Comme ça?"*

"Mais oui. Hey, Floyd?"

"Quoi?"

"The Texas man."

"What?"

She smiled widely, wrinkles chasing around her face like ripples on a sun-bright pond. "Bus' his ass."

Floyd

The parish had just blacktopped the farm roads, so he drove hard, afraid to look at the speedometer, feeling for safety through his tires, sensing from the sway and swirl of rubber for the point at which the car would slip off the asphalt and pinwheel out into the green blur of a rice field. The image of his daughter, Mary Lizette Bergeron, her pale face and dark hair inherited from her Cancienne forebears on his side, appeared on the shimmering road ahead. He saw his daughter growing up on the windy prairie in a hard-bitten town full of sun-wrinkled geezers, tomato barbecue, Pearl beer, and country music. There was nothing wrong with West Texas, but there was something wrong with a child living there who doesn't belong, who will be haunted for the rest of her days by memories of the ample laps of aunts, daily thunderheads rolling above flat parishes of rice and cane, the musical rattle of French, her prayers, the head-turning squawk of her uncle's accordion, the scrape and complaint of her father's fiddle as he serenades the backyard on weekends. Vibrations of the soul lost for what? Because her mama wants her, too? Her mama, a LeBlanc gone bad, a woman who got up at ten o'clock and watched TV until time to cook supper. Who learned to drink beer and smoke dope, though both made her throw up the few things she ate. Who gave up French music and rock and roll for country. Who, two years ago, began to stay out all night like a cat with a hot butt, coming in after he left for work on Tante Sidonie's farm. Who disappeared like that same cat would, leaving him to rock on the porch in the evenings, wondering whether she was alive or dead, kidnapped for the nervously pretty brunette thing she was, dead in the woods, or, worse, cowboy dancing in some bar out west, laughing at him with all the *cous rouges* she thought she loved. Six months ago, she called and asked him for Lizette. He told her to come home. He heard her laugh so loud that he thought he might hang up the phone, open a window, and hear that keening laughter threading in from the west over the bending heads of the rice plants. Then she told him she would send the Texas man and that he'd never find Lizzette in a place as big as Texas.

Floyd's black eyes were shiny and small, his mustache as dark as a caterpillar. There was not one ounce of fat in his 145 pounds, though he was fed by Tante Sidonie, who had already loved her husband to death with her dark gumbo. Floyd drank beer and made noise with his friends on weekends, spent his extra money on his daughter, her clothes, her Catholic school, her music lessons. Everyone in the community of Grand Crapaud knew he had good sense and would do a thing as soon as it needed doing. They knew this because he never hit a man when he was down, the grass in his yard stayed cut, he washed his car, and there were no holes in the screens of his house.

T-Man's Z seared the asphalt on the straight road south of Highway 90, spinning between the rice fields that lay swollen with steamy mirrors of rainwater. After two panic stops at intersections, he reached the turnoff to the north, blistered along for two miles, and cut a smoky bow bend onto 90 west, heading toward Texas, looking for the truck. "What kind of man would drive a green truck?" he said aloud. He checked his watch and struggled with the math until he figured he should be close, unless, of course, the Texas man had taken another route to fool him. But he felt in his bones that the cowboy, who used to drive a cement truck on this route day in and day out, would try to escape him this way, this road.

He had gone but three miles, skimming the potholes at eighty-five, when he saw the truck, a three-quarter-ton model with steel mesh across the back of the cab. Through the window he could barely see the top of Lizette's head on one side of the cab and the Texas man's broken-brim hat on the other, not a real cowboy's hat, just a dance-hall hat. He passed them, blowing the horn and motioning them to the side of the road. In his rearview mirror, he saw the truck move onto the grassy shoulder, and Floyd smiled. It was easy, he thought. He got out and the Texas man got out. They came together, and Floyd realized that he was much smaller than his wife's new boyfriend. He looked down at his own white shrimper boots and then over at the reptile splendor of the Texas man's footgear.

"You must be the coon-ass," the cowboy said. He had a nasty way of holding his head tilted off to the side, with his mouth belled out a bit to the left, like he was used to drooling on himself.

"I want my daughter back," Floyd told him, looking past at the pale, wise face of Lizette in the truck. She leaned out the window on her side.

"Daddy, I want to go home," she said. "This man talks funny."

"She's a-going to where she belongs, with her mama," the cowboy said.

"No, she's not," Floyd said, starting for the truck. The Texas man grabbed him, punched him in the mouth, and Floyd went down. He came up swinging, striking the other man in the jaw, but after a flurry of counterpunches and two sharp kicks from a set of pointed boots, Floyd found himself on his back in the roadside mud, staring at a new set of storm clouds coming up from the Gulf, listening to the green truck screeching off into the flat distance. He sat up, feeling his head spin, and thought it best to rest a while before trying to drive. A car slowed down and a farmer asked him if he needed help, but he waved him off. Then another car came along and pulled off onto the shoulder. It was a twenty-year-old Dodge driven by Mrs. Boudreaux. In the front seat was T-Jean's grandmère, who pushed open the door with her tiny hands. He got in and sat next to them.

"You caught 'em and he beat you up," the older lady said, running a cool hand over a lump on his forehead.

"*Mais,* that about sums it up."

Mrs. Boudreaux, who still had on her stretch jeans from the chicken yard, leaned over to look at him closely. "You got to catch 'em, Floyd."

"I'll start in a minute." His head spun like a pirogue caught in an eddy.

"Yah," T-Jean's grandmère began, "you got a bump on the googoon that's gonna make you wreck for sure. Me and Alida will drive after him." She tried to see over the dash to check the traffic.

"No, no. I've got to drive fast."

Mrs. Boudreaux clucked her tongue thoughtfully. "It'll take an airplane to catch him now." She and Floyd looked at each other instantly.

"Nonc René," they said in unison.

Nonc

René Badeaux sat on his front porch steps, patching a hole in a diatonic accordion with Super Glue and a piece of oilcloth torn from an old table covering. He pulled the bellows, and the instrument inhaled a squawk. *"Merde,"* he said. He tried to play "Allons à Lafayette," but on the fourth note the little patch blew off and floated toward the road like a waxy leaf. Then a C button stuck. He shook his head, thinking that he should have played a waltz until the glue dried. Looking up at a plane taking off from his strip, he remembered that the black fellow he had hired last week as a pilot was going thirty miles north to spray some worms. He waited until the drone of the engine had gone over the tree line, and then he popped the C button loose and laid the bellows of the old Monarch against his great belly and played, spraying the reedy music around the yard like nutrient for the atmosphere, breaking into whiny song. *"Mon coeur est tout casse,"* he sang, himself a wind box of lyrics playing for his own amazement.

Floyd was sitting next to him on the step before he saw him. That was one thing about Floyd—he was a quiet man, saying only what needed to be said, not yammering all sorts of bullshit when he came up. And then he said what needed to be said to his uncle. He told him about Lizette.

Nonc René had sung so many sentimental songs so badly over the years that he had become a tender man. Every woman he knew was an Evangeline bearing some great sorrow in life, and now he imagined his grand-niece dragged off to live among lizards and rock and only Mexican accordian music. How could she bear to stay there without the buzz of a fiddle and the clang of a triangle in her pretty head, the love songs sung through the nose?

"Please, Nonc," Floyd was saying, his little eyes shining with need in the late-afternoon light. "You know what I'm talkin' about. You know what to let me do. I can fly good."

"You could call the police," René teased.

"Louisiana police? Give me a break, Nonc."

René rubbed his gray stubble and rolled his eyes toward the plane shed. "Lollis took the good machine."

"Even a bad plane can beat a pickup truck," Floyd said with that smile that wasn't a smile, but a trick with those little dark eyes.

Nonc René was waiting for that smile that wasn't a smile. That's all. He wasn't hesitating for a minute. He remembered that Floyd was still famous in the region for installing an ancient DC-3 engine in a big biplane, and when he got that Pratt & Whitney Twin Wasp tandem radial engine in the sky, it corkscrewed his homemade canvas plane through a cloud like the engine was twirling the wings instead of the propeller, and straight down he came into a rice paddy. When Nonc René and his brothers got to the field, there was just a gasoline slick on top of the mud and nothing else. They dug Floyd out with their hands and boards torn from a fence. His clothes had been ripped off by the concussion of the crash. Three brothers at once had their fingers in his mouth, digging out a pound of mud so he could breathe. They pinched clay out of his nose, washed it from under his eyelids, cleared it from his ears with twigs. When they put him on the toilet that night at the hospital—mud and six grains of rice.

Now, in eight minutes, they were in the sky, Mrs. Boudreaux and

T-Jean's grandmère watching them through the windshield of the old Dodge. The biplane burbled off toward the west, following Highway 90 at two hundred feet.

Lizette

It had seemed the thing to do at first. The tall bony man with the long neck—she had never seen a neck like that, with a big bump in the middle—he came into the house without knocking, took her by the arm and said, "Let's us go see yore mama." She could smell the raw leather of his gaudy belt. He would not let her pack a stitch, and when she protested, he jerked her along the way you pull an animal out of a hole, and her arm still hurt. She asked him where he was taking her and he said, "God's country," which made her wonder if he was an Arab terrorist, though she didn't think Arabs had red hair and yellow freckles up their arms. She had ridden along hoping for the best, watching the fields full of blackbirds and puddles fly by the truck's windows. Then her father had stopped them and she had screamed when she saw the tall man knock him down and kick him, and she kept on screaming when the Texas man got in the truck. He hit her then, a bone-hard backhand to the mouth, a striking-out that she had never felt before, and her teeth went into her lip and stuck. But the pain and the blood didn't bother her, just the flying scent of his hand, the pasty tinge of cigarettes, which made her think of her mother, lying on the sofa smoking one after another, staring past her at the television, always the television. She had looked back at her father as the truck tore off toward Texas, wondering when he would get up. They drove by little wood-and-tin towns, rice elevators connected by bent and rusted railroads, and she felt an empty-hearted flutter when she saw the sign that said Texas was a few miles ahead. She knew then they would pass out of the land of her blood and into some strange, inevitable place, into what must happen sooner or later. She looked over at the man in the checkered shirt, glanced at his pearl buttons, bent over and spat blood on the floor mat, looked between her knees at the blood on

the floor and thought of her mother again, closed her eyes and said
a Hail Mary, opened her eyes and said a second Hail Mary, but
stopped after "blessed art thou among women" when she saw a
crop duster fly across the road under the phone wires about a mile
ahead. The plane looped and rolled over, coming back under the
wires again, flying in front of an eighteen-wheeler, drifting over the
field to the south and looping again, as though the pilot and his passenger were practicing for the air circus. She saw a barrel roll, another loop, a pass over the truck, and then the plane disappeared,
swallowed up by a field of tall coastal Bermuda. She looked out of
all the windows, but the plane was gone. She settled down to watching the straight strip of narrow highway threading through open
fields now, fields with rows freshly plowed for cotton or soybeans,
some experiment the rice and cane farmers were constantly trying,
those dogged Labats or Thibodeauxs, who had owned the land for
more than two hundred years.

When Lizette looked west again, she saw a movement out of a low
cloud and the same plane came down over the road a mile away, flying toward the green truck, coming lower and lower until its wheels
were touching the highway behind a sedan that sped up as though
it were a bug being chased by a hawk. When the sedan blew past,
the Texas man slammed on the brakes because the plane was taxi-
ing now, taking up both lanes and the narrow shoulders, which
sloped down into twelve-foot canals topped off with the morning's
rain. Lizette began to bounce on the seat, but only a few times. Her
face was rimmed with a brassy border of pain. She watched the cowboy take off his hat and place it on the seat next to her. Turning his
flinty face toward hers, he told her not to move an inch. He got out,
and she was glad to be rid of the smell of him, whiskey and cigarettes
and some mildew-smelling aftershave.

Her daddy and uncle climbed down out of the plane, her small
daddy and her old and wobbly nonc René. She knew the Texas man
would beat both of them up and throw them in the canal, and she
began to cry all at once with a fierce suddenness that startled her.
Her father and uncle had to see her, and then it would be all right.

If they did not see her, they would be beaten to pieces, so she blew the horn. She became angry when they wouldn't look, and then, as she thought would happen, the freckled, long-legged foreign thing took a swing, knocking the soft René to the ground. Her father came on punching, but in only a minute the Texas man had him down and rolling on the ground. Nonc came back up in front of the truck and fell on them both, and all three fought, her relatives taking a beating.

Ensemble

A little traffic began to back up behind the idling plane and in the westbound lane, too. A five-ton truck pulled up behind the Texas man's vehicle, and two men in coveralls got out to watch the brawl. The rolling and grunting battle went on and off the blacktop. After a good five minutes, Nonc René fell away and breathed on his back like a fish, his huge belly heaving. Floyd yelled and sat down, holding his hand between his legs. The Texas man tried to get up out of the mud, went down on one knee, and rested a while. Lizette blew the horn and tried to get someone to look at her. Out of the corner of her eye she saw a puff of silver smoke by the driver's side door, and she heard a tapping. Looking down, she saw the top of T-Jean's grandmère's head. Opening the window, she reached down for the old woman's hand and bawled. The woman looked up from her walker.

"How did you bus' you mouth?" was all she asked.

"The Texas man did it," she whined.

T-Jean's grandmère lowered her head and worked her walker ahead of her like some sort of field machine, and when she got to where the Texas man was still down on one knee, she raised the aluminum frame and poked one of its small rubber feet an inch into his eye socket. The Texas man roared, stood up, and fell back into a muddy rut, where he wagged his head and cried aloud in pain.

"You don't come to Grand Crapaud and take no Bergeron child

to drag off to no place," she scolded, threatening him with the walker. She looked around at the fields, the thin highway. "This child belongs with her papa. She's got LeBlanc in her, and Cancienne way back, and before that, Thibodeaux." Her shapeless print dress swelled as she gathered the air to tell him more. She pointed her walker off at the horizon. "You see that tree line two miles over there? Look with you good eye."

The Texas man, one bleeding eye held shut with his left hand, obeyed.

"Them tree, they used to be right there, across that ditch. Thibodeaux boys cleared all that with axes. With *axes*. Live oak and cypress with *axes*. Two hundred acre." She swung around to look across the road. "Over there." She pointed into a rice field, in the middle of which an oil-well pump drifted up and down. Nonc René rolled up on one elbow with a groan and followed the line of her walker. "Before the Thibodeaux was more Thibodeaux living in a house made out of dirt." She stamped her walker into the mud and turned on the Texas man, giving him such a look that he held up his free hand. "What you got to say, you what come to steal a Bergeron baby?"

"Yeah, man, what you got to say for yourself?" asked one of the two men who had walked up from the five-ton truck. Lizette saw that they were twins dressed in identical gray coveralls, fellows with dark, oily curls, crooked noses.

Floyd picked up his head and laughed. "Victor. Vincent Larousse."

"Floyd, baby. *Quoi ça dit?*"

"Tex stole my lil' girl and then broke my hand with his head." Floyd stood up, still cradling his hand against his work jeans.

"Shut up, all you crazy Larousse," T-Jean's grandmère told them. "I got to hear what he's goin' to say to me." Her small head bobbed like a fishing cork.

The Texas man rocked back in the mud a bit, a rill of muddy water beading over his thighs. "I'm a-goin' get in my truck, head on down the road, and when it's time, I'm a-goin' come back and get that little gal for her mama." He looked over at Mrs. Boudreaux, who was leading Lizette along the shoulder of the road toward her Dodge.

T-Jean's grandmère slammed her walker into the mud again. Turning to the Larousse twins, she asked them if they were still bad boys over in Tiger Island. Vincent spat between his teeth at the Texas man, who flinched. He chucked his brother on the shoulder and they walked back to their utility truck, which had MOUTON'S SCRAPYARD painted on the doors in orange paint. Two cutting-torch rigs sat in the bed, and the twins put on goggles, ran the gauges up to eighty pounds oxygen, fifteen pounds acetylene, and walked backward to the front of the Texas man's truck, pulling gas line behind them, the torches hissing blue stars. When they cut the hood off the truck, the Texas man began yelling for the police.

Floyd looked at the little circle of farmers and truck drivers forming around the scene. "You gonna tell a policeman you stole a little girl that was given me by a judge? You gonna tell him you punched her?"

The Texas man, who was climbing out of the rut, settled back down again, watching the Larousses burn off his fenders, the torches spitting through the thin metal as though it were paper.

"My truck," he cried, still holding his eye.

"Hot damn," T-Jean's grandmère said. "Them boy is still bad, yeah."

The Larousses cut bumper braces, motor mounts, frame members, and transmission bolts as two volunteers from the crowd rolled large pieces of truck hissing into the big ditch, where they disappeared. After fifteen minutes' work, they cut the frame and rolled the cab and the bed into the canal like boulders. Soon, all that was left on the side of the road was a puddle of oil and a patch of singed grass. The twins rolled up their lines, zeroed their gauges, and walked back to the Texas man. The one who had spoken the first time, Vincent, smiled slowly. "*Mais,* anytime you come back to Louisiana, Floyd gonna phone us," he said, holding his palm up and pointing with his middle finger. "An' unless you drive to Grand Crapaud in a asbestos car, you gonna wind up with a bunch of little smokin' pieces shoved up you ass." Vincent gave him a little salute and followed Victor back to the truck, where they washed their hands with Go-Jo, pulled two Schlitzes from an ice chest, and climbed into the truck to wait.

T-Jean's grandmère gave the Texas man a long look, turned to walk off, then looked down at him again. "You, if you woulda went off with her, all you woulda got was her little body. In her head, she'd never be where you took her to. Every day she'd feel okra in her mouth."

Floyd began walking with her to Mrs. Boudreaux's car, and Nonc René limped over to the Texas man, handing him a parachute. "Come on," Nonc said softly, with the voice he used to call a chicken from the coop before dinner. "I'll take you somewhere."

"I got to get to a hospital," he moaned. "That old lady like to kilt me."

When everyone was loaded into the bobbing Dodge, Floyd pointed Mrs. Boudreaux's own St. Christopher statue forward and began to drive with his good hand. Several men turned the plane at a right angle to the road so it could roll over a culvert into the field, where Nonc René guided the balloon tires in the furrows. The machine splattered along until it gained the sky in a furious storm of flying mud.

Floyd drove his group west, not east to Grand Crapaud, and everyone in the car was silent. In a few minutes they pulled to the side of the road in front of the state-line marker, a rough-cast concrete slab shaped like Louisiana. In the backseat, T-Jean's grandmère laughed and clapped her hands once. Floyd turned off the engine and put his arm around Lizette, kissing the top of her head, right where her fragrant hair was parted.

"Why we stopped here?" she asked, looking at the flat fields around the car. After a few moments, a plane moaned over their heads at a hundred feet, crossing into Texas and curving rapidly upward to ten times that height. It did a barrel roll and Lizette giggled. "Is that Nonc and the *cou rouge?*"

"Yes, baby." They all watched through the front windshield as the plane ascended into Texas, kept watching that leaden sky until the little wings banked off to the southeast for homeland, beneath them a distant silken blossom drifting down and west on a heavy Gulf breeze.

Returnings

E laine thought that hard work might clear her head, might not let her thoughts turn to her son. She had been coaxing the tractor through the field for four hours, turning two hundred acres into corduroy. When the rusting International was dead center in the farm, it began to miss and sputter, giving up under the April sun, far from the tractor shed. Elaine reached around the steering wheel, pulling the choke out a bit, hoping the carburetor would pass the water that she knew was in the gasoline, remembering with a pang that she had not drained the little glass water trap under the fuel tank. She hoped that her husband had been wrong when he'd told her that middle-aged women couldn't farm. Yet she had forgotten to get the water out of the line on a tractor that had been sitting up three months, its gas tank sweating on the inside. She frowned at the coughing machine. They were supposed to buy a brand-new tractor that year, a 1967 model. But there was no longer any need.

The engine fluttered and died. She checked her watch and saw that it was eleven o'clock. Climbing down, she poured a drink of water from a thermos tied under the metal seat with a strand of twine. She turned to stare at her house nearly a mile away, satisfied at the even rows of brown dirt she had heaped up. Like most women, she liked to grow things.

She was a nurturer and felt that this quality, better than any man's mechanical ability, would help her bring life to the fields of her farm. She saw a likeness between caring for a home and children and raising millions of soybeans. In her blood was a drive for generation more powerful than muscle and bone. This drive would make her a farmer.

Elaine hoped that her husband would see the tractor stalled out and would bring her some tools. His back was hurting, and he had little to do but watch out the kitchen window or endure Lyndon Johnson talking on television about the war. A half hour after the engine died, she saw his green truck bobbing toward her very slowly across the unplowed portion of field.

"Either you're out of gas or the engine sucked up a charge of water," he said, handing her a small toolbox through the truck window. He was tanned, clean-shaven, and strong-looking, but he winced when he raised the box up to her hands.

"Stay in the truck," she said.

"I plan to. The ride out here's awful rough." He ran his hand through his dark, graying curls. "You know what to do?" He asked in a way that pleaded that she did.

"Yes. I've got plenty gas. It's water, I'm sure. You stay put." She fixed him with a worried stare and plucked at her checked cotton blouse, which clung to her back in the heat.

Her husband blinked and rested his forearms on top of the steering wheel. "I'm sorry that you've got to do this. I'll be better in a month or so."

She gave him a smile as she pulled a pair of slip-joint pliers from the box. "Joe told me how to do this. I suppose you taught him somewhere along the line."

His eyes scanned the farm. "It's amazing how much he did around here."

Elaine did not answer. There was nothing to say that they did not already feel in their blood about an eighteen-year-old son who was healthy one week, plowing and fixing things, and dead the next from encephalitis. They refused to reminisce, but they talked around their son at mealtime, as though he were at the table and they were ignoring him. When they touched in any way, the message of him was on their skin, and they knew their loss. Talking could not encompass what had gone from them.

They had brought up two girls, now married and raising families in other towns, good girls, who visited. But it was to have been Joe's farm.

She made a face as she pulled the bowl of the water trap off the fuel line, spilling cold gasoline into her hands. The smell would stay in the cracks of her skin for hours, like a bad memory. Working carefully in the sun, she heard the truck start and turn for the house. She took a part out of the carburetor, cleared it of water, and put everything together, opening the gas valve once more, only to discover a leak. Twenty minutes passed before she had the tractor ready to run. Wiping her hands, she heard at the periphery of her attention the steady chop of a helicopter in the distance, a common sound in this part of the parish because of an air-training facility across the line in Mississippi. She mounted the tractor, pulled out the choke, and, with a finger in the starter ring, paused to look toward a helicopter that was passing closer than usual. A gunship, armed and camouflaged, skirted the edge of her field. It hovered a moment, approached with a whopping roar, and finally settled down in a circular dust storm seventy yards from her. She held her straw hat over her brown hair, glad at least that the machine had lit in an unplowed section. Only one person sat in the glassed-in cabin, and he watched her carefully. The pilot's stare made her uneasy. She had imagined military folk to be generally on the move, having no time for meditation. Also, something was unorthodox about the pilot's size. He appeared too small; his headphones were like cantaloupe halves clapped to his ears. He was rather dark.

After a while he kicked open a door and jumped out, the huge blades dying in speed above him. Jogging across the field in loose combat fatigues, his pistol holster flying out from his side with each leap over the bumpy soil, he trailed a partially unfolded map. Elaine squinted and saw that he was Asian and very young, maybe twenty.

"Hello," he said, smiling mightily. "Can you be of assistance?"

She glanced at the helicopter, wondering briefly if he had somehow stolen it. "What's wrong? You have engine trouble, too?" she asked, pointing down at the tractor.

"No, no," he said, smiling so that his face seemed ready to split.

He seemed desperately afraid that she would fear him. "I need advice."

She could see behind his smile and climbed down to the ground next to him. He was the size of a boy, his features rounded and new. "Advice about what?"

"It is hard for me to ask," he said, backing away, tilting his head to the left, to the right, almost crying through his grin. "I am lost." He unfolded a map, placing it on the ground. "If you please could tell me where I am, I could get back to base. I am on my solo training flight and have hour to return."

She stooped and tried to study the map, but it contained no red-lined highways and town names like the filling station maps she was used to. It was lettered in a bizarre military code. She told him she could not make heads or tails of it. She was intelligent, and her father had sent her to college for two years, but she could not deal with a map that didn't have Poireauville or Leroux spelled out on it. "I know where the fort is over the line in Mississippi, but I couldn't tell you how to fly there. Why don't we just give them a call and have an instructor come out to fly you back?"

"No," he wailed, his smile collapsing at last. Elaine thought of the pinched faces she saw on the newscasts in the evenings, the small people running from thatched houses, pillars of smoke in the background, the rattle of weapons. "If I fail at pilot school, I get sent back to Vietnam as foot soldier." He turned to look longingly at his machine, as though already it had been taken from him.

She stood and leaned against her tractor. "Your instructor would give you another chance, wouldn't he?"

He shook his head vigorously. "My instructor wants to see me dead in a rice paddy. He is a big American with red hair. Every day he tells me, 'Le Ton, if you do not fly right, we send you home with a cheap rifle to fight VC.' "

She studied him a while, looked back to the farmhouse and then to the map. Her husband could not read it, she knew. Joe probably could have.

"Le Ton. Is that your name?"

"Yes. I am from farmland, too." He folded up his map slowly.

"You flew out of Fort Exter?" The more she looked at him, the younger he appeared, some mother's favorite, she guessed, noticing something in his eyes. Why else would he be trying so hard to stay alive?

"That is so. I fly by map and directions given by my instructor at base. No radio." His face darkened. "My instructor gives me bad directions."

"You have an hour left to get back?"

He nodded. "Thank you for trying to help me."

She wiped her palms on her jeans. "I'll tell you what, son. I can't judge anything from that map, but if you take me up in that machine of yours, I might be able to show you where the fort is, and then you could drop me back off here. I don't think it's more than thirty miles or so." She could hardly believe what she'd said. She might be doing something illegal or unpatriotic. He took to the idea instantly. "Ah, that would be good. I fly you a few miles outside of base and return here. Plenty time to get back to base." She hung her straw hat on the breather pipe of the tractor and stepped over the big unplowed clods of earth to the gunship, climbing in next to him as he flipped overhead switches, manipulated foot pedals, and lifted hand levers at his side. The craft surged and vibrated like a toolshed in a tornado. In a moment they were whanging through the sky.

"Go east," she yelled. Elaine watched for the water tower in Poireauville but could hardly keep her eyes off the running fields below her feet, the sugarcane, bayous, levees, and willow brakes that flew by as in a dream or a wide-screened movie at a world's fair. It was difficult to concentrate on any one landmark when the giant oaks and longleaf pines were sailing just a few feet below. Le Ton glanced at her for direction. The water tower she saw in the distance had to be Poireauville's, and she pointed toward it, but when the craft came within two miles of the round silver tank, she felt disoriented and panicky. It was too small to be Poireauville's, too freshly painted. Le Ton flew a wide circle around it and she wished that all little towns still painted their names on the tanks as they had when she was a child.

"Which way?" he asked.

She scanned the ground. There were too many trees. Poireauville was a cut-over hamlet and did not support such a welter of sycamores. Perhaps they had veered a few miles northeast and were over Rodeaux. Looking to her left, she spotted a set of smokestacks and suddenly wished her husband was with her. An area man could look at a factory's stack from three miles away and tell the type of mill, the name of the owner, and the ages of his children. But she was lost.

She spotted a rusty thread of railroad and pointed down to it. "That's the Missouri Pacific branch line. Follow it." Her son had loved railroads and had shown her maps of the region's lines enough times that she had a vague notion of where the local tracks went. Before he was old enough to drive, she would take him on long rides so he could take pictures of stations and engines. She remembered telling him that he should photograph people, not only objects. People are what have to be remembered. She looked down at an abandoned crossroads grocery, its windows boarded up. Places are nothing.

Le Ton swirled above the railroad for six miles, looking down and then checking his compass. "Lady, we fly north? You are sure of the railroad?" He had lost his smile completely. His face shone with a nervous sweat. It worried her that he was more frightened than she was. Looking down, she thought that perhaps this was the old north track instead of the branch that led east. Everywhere were oaks and occasionally a flat field of sugarcane she did not recognize. She saw a barn she had never seen before, a large white home, and two rows of tenant houses. She felt like a child lost in a thousand acres of razor-leafed cane.

"Go that way," she yelled, pointing to her right. Studying the ground, she saw a cornfield slip under her and a tenant house that seemed to be empty, its iron roof bloody with rust. She was looking for a laundry line full of drying clothes, which would tell the presence of a woman. A full laundry line behind a house where the truck was gone would be a lucky find. She did not want to risk landing in the yard of a stiff-necked sharecropper who would call the sheriff before he heard her out.

A weathered cypress house passed below, and she asked Le Ton for field glasses, which he produced from a rack under his seat. She focused on the backyard. A string of laundry danced on the line, but there were many cumbersome checkered shirts, and in the front yard, two trucks.

A mile and a half across the field was a poorer house, the chimney broken at the top, the roof swaybacked. She motioned to it when she saw on its clothesline the wink of towels and sheets. She thought back to the days when she still hung out the wash, the clean damp smell of the pillowcases, and the breezy mornings her son chased his sisters through the laundry, the bright cotton licking their faces.

Le Ton was shouting, "The house is behind. Keep going?"

Looking back with the glasses, she saw no car and no electric meter on the wires leading along the side of the house. "Put down in the field across the road from that shack." There was no need to soil the laundry.

The helicopter descended slowly into a pasture as several bony, fly-bitten cows lurched away into a grove of wild plum trees. As the craft touched down, she looked across the gravel road to a porch where a stout black woman sat in a rocker and shaded her eyes.

Le Ton stopped the engine. "Why do we stop here?" He looked around at the sickly fields and the paintless tenant shack.

"I've got to ask directions from somebody who won't call a newspaper." She jumped to the ground and he followed her to the road, where she instructed him to wait.

Once on the porch she sidestepped a gap in the flooring.

"Don't bust a leg," the black woman sang, touching the kerchief that bound her hair. "My man supposed to fix that when he can find a right board."

"How you doing? I'm Elaine Campbell from down in Burkhalter community. Do you know where that is?"

The other woman stood, adjusted her apron, and stared at the floor. "No, ma'am," she said. "Don't you?"

"Well, of course I know where it is when I'm there. But this boy and I seem to be lost."

The black woman looked across the road at Le Ton, who stood

like a frail post against the slack barbed wire. "How come you ain't got on your uniform?"

"I'm not in the army. He is. He got lost over my place in Burkhalter and I was trying to show him the way to Fort Exter when we got lost again."

"I don't know where Burkhalter is."

"It's not far from Poireauville."

"Law." She sat down. "That's twenty miles off with the crow. The roads don't hardly run thataway." She peered across the gravel lane again. "They left that little Chinaman run that big machine?"

Elaine turned, looked at Le Ton, and grinned. "He's on a training mission. If they find out at the fort that he got lost, they'll send him back to Vietnam as a foot soldier. I'm just trying to help him out."

"Vietnam," the other woman repeated. "I heard that word a lot. My onliest boy been sent over there. I got three girls, but only one boy. He use to be at Exter, too. Name's Vergil Bankston." She smiled as she said the name. "My name's Mary Bankston."

Elaine sat in a straight-back chair and motioned for Le Ton to cross the road.

As he walked up to the porch, Mary Bankston examined him, then let out a gentle, high-pitched whine. "If he ain't just a baby, though. Is all Vietnam peoples easy lost like you?"

Le Ton smiled defensively, considering the question. He sat on the porch floor between the women, facing them, and folded his legs. "I am very stupid to Americans. Most trainees are farm people. We know how to plow with ox, how to use hoe." He made a little hoeing movement with his arms. "It is very hard to learn vectors and compression ratios, how to make big, fast helicopters run right." He looked from one woman's face to the other. "My cousin, Tak Dok, came to fly Corsair airplanes. In training flight, his cockpit shield blows off and he radios back what happens. Man in the tower says land at once. Tak Dok brings his plane down in the field of corn and lands without much damage. Instructors send him back to be foot soldier because they mean for him to come back to his airfield to land at once." He looked over his shoulder toward his craft. "Last month,

Tak Dok is killed. My young cousin was a good pilot but could not always understand your way with words."

Mary Bankston passed a long mother's look to Elaine, the expression a woman owns at night when she sits up listening to a child cough and rattle, knowing there is nothing she can do but act out of her best feelings. "I got a pot of hot water on the stove. I can drip coffee in a minute." She smiled at Le Ton. "Got a tea bag somewhere, too."

"We don't have a whole lot of time," Elaine said, looking down on Le Ton's camouflage cap. She pulled it off a moment to look at the thick, close-cropped hair and the young brassy skin at the roots. Everything about him was small and young, laden with possibilities. "Do you have any idea how far we are from the Mississippi line?"

"You wants to go to Exter, don't you?"

"Yes."

"Then tell him to fly straight east to that brand-new interstate about thirty miles, then take a right and follow it down to that big green sign what say Fort Exter."

Elaine placed her left palm on her forehead. "I should have remembered that. I've never been on it, but I knew it was there."

"Sure enough," Mary Bankston said. "Even a farmer Chinaman can find a four-lane highway. I been on it twice to go see Vergil."

Elaine returned Le Ton's cap. "Didn't you pass over that interstate to get into this region?"

He thought about this for a moment, and then with the expression of an old man wise to betrayal, he answered her. "Instructor says fly over Gulf and then come inland."

"Let's go, then." Mary Bankston offered to let them have two fried-apple pies for their trip, but they declined.

"He ain't never going to get no bigger if he don't eat," she yelled after them as they crossed the fence.

Elaine called back. "Don't tell anybody about us, especially your son."

She nodded from her paintless porch. "Who gonna believe me?"

Le Ton started the engine and the big gunship whirled off into the sky. She looked below and saw the old railroad they had followed earlier. "Why aren't you heading east? You could let me off on a highway outside of base, and I could figure a way to get home."

"That would not be right," he said. "You have been too helpful. I should not put you out in the middle of a wilderness." He glanced back to the tenant house, where Mary Bankston was probably watching him as she would a young child crossing the street. "I also have been on the big highway the black lady speaks of. I did not know it ran north-south. It is not on the map the instructor gives me."

With the field glasses, she found the correct water tower, a larger structure to the south emblazoned with SENIORS '66, a spray-paint legend her son had helped create one moonless night. She remembered how Sammy, the local deputy, had caught him, bringing him to the house, revealing what her son had done, working a wink into his speech while Joe stood behind him in the front door, repentant and fearful.

She had never told her husband. He wouldn't have punished their son severely, but Elaine let her instinct to protect him overpower her need to discipline him. She had been so glad that he had been brought home safe. Now as the painted words swam in the field glasses, she couldn't say whether she would ever tell her husband. She forced her eyes away, over to the highway, and in a minute found the blacktop that crawled to her farm. She had no idea that the place appeared so drowsy, the roofs tired with rust, the crystal green ponds oval like the sleepy eyes of children. Le Ton circled to the rear of the farm to avoid buzzing the house and set down where he had earlier.

"I hope your tractor starts now," he said, ducking his head, forcing a smile.

She reached over and grabbed his neck, kissing him on the cheek. "Call Ralph Campbell in Poireauville and tell me how you did," she said.

He was surprised, but he nodded, understanding her order. After seeing her jump down and clear the blades, he gave a broad wave, then mounted the sky.

She watched until the craft disappeared over a distant neighboring farmhouse, the home of John Thompson, whose blond daughter had loved her son. She listened to the clamor of the machine pounding into the eastern sky.

When she turned, she noticed her husband's truck lurching out toward her. Quickly, she reached under the tank and turned off the gasoline valve. He arrived, getting out this time, holding his back and walking over like someone much older. She held her breath, then asked the question. "What brings you out here?"

"I been sleeping," he said, rubbing his smooth jaw. "Something woke me up. I just looked out and saw you still hadn't started the tractor." He gave her a questioning look. "Why didn't you walk in and get me?"

"How's your back?"

He straightened up slowly, as if to test himself. "Feels better this afternoon."

"That's good. No, I've taken everything apart and blown out the water. It just won't start."

He walked up to the controls, pulled the starter ring twice, and listened. He reached up under the tank. "You forgot to reopen the gas line," he said.

She kicked at a clod of dirt. "I can't believe I forgot that."

"Women farmers," he said, smiling that cool, wrinkled smile of his.

"I suppose you've never done the same."

He thought a bit. "One morning I tried and tried to start this thing. I ran down a battery before Joe—he was about nine then—came out to the shed and turned on the gas for me. He said, 'Daddy, what would you ever do without me?'"

She walked over and stood next to him, the skin on her arms prickling. The empty quiet of the field was oppressive, and she pulled the starter ring. The tractor chuckled alive, but as soon as it did, he reached over and pushed the kill switch, the quiet settling on them like a memory. "We've got to get away for a while," he said, his voice so shaky it scared her. "Leave the tractor here. Let's get cleaned up and drive into town." He glanced up into the sky. "Let's drive two towns over and get a fancy meal. You need it. You never get off this place." He pounded the dull red tractor once with a fist.

She looked at the eastern horizon, then put her arm easily around his back and hugged him, her freckled cheek pressing against the fresh khaki of his shirt. Slipping a hand up to the hot skin of his neck, she felt his blood coursing away, knowing it to be her blood as well. They stood together in the half-plowed field, in the middle of all they had lost. He took her hand and led her to the passenger door of the truck, opening it for her as though they were on a date.

An hour later she was clipping small gold circles to her earlobes, and her husband was shaving. In the den the telephone began its slow rattle, and she bolted past the bathroom door for it. At first she was afraid to pick it up.

"Yes?" she answered, then said, "I see. Yes." Her expression remained neutral. "I understand you perfectly. Sure. And thank you for calling." She replaced the receiver and put a hand over a smile.

They got into the shimmering sedan and drove out onto the unlined road, heading through the hot afternoon toward town. In a month the land around her would bear cornstalks growing like children. She cast a long admiring gaze at the field she'd been plowing, at the straightness of her rows where they glimmered under the sun, rails of dirt running east under a safe and empty sky.

Deputy Sid's Gift

I'm going to tell you about the last time I went to confession. I met this priest at the nursing home where I work spoon-feeding the parish's old folks. He noticed I had a finger off, and so he knew I was oil field and wanted to know why I was working indoors. This priest was a blond guy with eyes you could see through and didn't look like nobody inside of two hundred miles of Grand Crapaud, Louisiana. He didn't know that when sweet crude slid under twelve dollars a barrel, most oil companies went belly-up like a stinking redfish, and guys like me had to move out or do something else. So I told him I took a night class in scrubbing these old babies, and he said I had a good heart and bull like that and invited me to come visit at the rectory if I ever needed to.

One day I needed to, yeah. Everybody's got something they got to talk about sometime in their life. I went to the old brick church on LeBlanc Street on a Saturday morning and found him by himself in his little kitchen in the old cypress priest house, and we sat down by the table with a big pot of coffee.

So I told him what had been going through my head, how I used to have a 1962 Chevrolet pickup truck, a rusty spare I kept parked out by the road just to haul off trash. It was ratty and I was ashamed to drive it unless I was going to the dump. One day after Christmas my wife, Monette, told me to get rid of the tree and the holiday junk, so I went to crank the truck. Well, in a minute I'm standing by the road with a key in my hand, looking at a long patch of pale weeds where the truck used to be. I'm saying to myself that the truck coulda been gone a hour or a week. It's just a thing you don't look at unless you need it.

So I called Claude down at his little four-by-four city jail and he said he'd look for it the next day, that he had more expensive stuff to worry about. Ain't that a hell of a note. Then I called the sheriff's office down at the parish seat, and when I told them the truck's over thirty years old, they acted like I'm asking them to look for a stole newspaper or something. It was my truck and I wanted it back.

The priest, he just nodded along and poured us our first cup of coffee from a big aluminum dripolator. When he finished, he put the pot in a shallow pan of water on the gas stove behind his chair and stared down at his shoe, like he was hearing my confession, which I guess he was. He even had his little purple confession rag hanging on his neck.

I told the priest how the cops searched a lil' bit, and how I looked, but that old truck just disappeared like rain on a hot street. Monette, she was glad to get it out the yard, but I needed something for hauling, you know? So after not too long I found a good old '78 Ford for a thousand dollars and bought that and put it right where the other one was.

One day my little girl Lizette and me, we was at the nursing home together because of some student-visit-the-parent-at-work deal at her school. She was letting the old folks hug her little shoulders and pat her dark hair. You know how they are. They see a child and go nuts to get at them, like the youngness is going to wear off on their old bodies. At the end of my shift, one of the visitors who was there to see his dried-up wife—I think he was a Canulette, kind of a café au lait dude from out by Prairie Amère—his truck won't crank, so me and Lizette decided to bring him home. Me in my smocky little fruit uniform and Lizette with her checkerboard school suit went off in my shiny thirdhand Buick, old man Canulette sitting between us like a fence post. We rolled down the highway and turned off into the rice fields and went way back into the tree line toward Coconut Bayou. We passing through that poor folks' section on the other side of Tonga Bend when Lizette stuck her head out the window to make her pigtails go straight in the wind. Next thing I knew, she yelled, daddy, there's your truck, back in the woods. I turned the car around in that little gravel road and sure enough—you couldn't hardly see it unless you had young eyes—there was my old Chevy parked up under a grove of live oaks maybe 150 yards away.

We walked up on it, and judging from the thistles that had growed up past the bumper, it'd been there three months. I held back and asked Monsieur Canulette if anybody lived around there, and he looked at the truck and said the first word since town: Bezue. He said here and there in the woods a Bezue lived and they all had something wrong in they heads. I told him I'd put me a Bezue in jail if he stole my truck, but he just looked at me with those silver eyes of his in a way that gave me *les frissons.* I brought the old man to his little farm and then came back to Tonga Bend Store to call the deputy, who took most of a hour to get out there.

They sent Sid Touchard, that black devil, and he showed up with his shaggy curls full of pomade falling down his collar, the tape deck in his cruiser playing zydeco. He got out with a clipboard, like he knows how to write, and put on his cowboy hat. He asked me if I was the Bobby Simoneaux what called, and even Lizette looked behind her in the woods for maybe another Bobby Simoneaux, but I just nodded. He looked at the truck and the leaves and branches on it and asked me do I still want it. *Mais,* yeah, I told him. Then Sid walked up and put his hand on the door handle like it was something dirty, which I guess it was, and pulled. What we saw was a lot of trash paper, blankets, and old clothes. I looked close and Lizette stepped back and put her little hands on her mouth. The air was nothing but mildew and armpit, and by the steering wheel was a nappy old head.

He's living in it, Deputy Sid said. His eyebrows went up when he said that. Even he was surprised, and he works the poor folks of the parish. He asked again do I still want it. Hell yeah, I said. He spit. He's a tall man, yeah, and it takes a long time for his spit to hit the ground. Then he reached in and woke the man, who sat up and stared at us. He was black—back-in-the-country black. He wasn't no old man, but he had these deep wrinkles the old folks call the sorrow grooves, and he looked like he was made out of Naugahyde. His eyeballs was black olives floating in hot sauce, and when Sid tried to get out of him what he was doing in the truck, he took a deep breath and looked over the rusty hood toward the road.

Finally he said, I'm Fernest. Fernest Bezue. My mamma, she lives down that way. He pointed, and I could see he been drunk maybe six years in a row. The old cotton jacket he had on was eat up with battery acid and his feet was bare knobs. Sid give me that look like he got on bifocals, but he ain't. Hell no, I told him. I want my truck. He stole it and you got to put him in jail. So Sid said to him, you stole this truck? And Fernest kept looking at the road like it was something he wasn't allowed to see, and then he said he found it here. When he said that, I got hot.

Deputy Sid tugged Fernest out into the sunlight, slow, like he was a old cow he was pulling out a tangle of fence. He put him in the cruiser and told me and Lizette to get in the front seat. He said where Fernest's mamma lived, my Buick can't go. So we rolled down the gravel a mile, turned off on a shell road where the chinaball and sticker bushes about dragged the paint off that beat-up cruiser. Lizette, she sat on my lap, looking at Deputy Sid's candy bar wrappers on the floor, a satsuma on the seat, and a rosary around the rearview. The road gave out at a pile of catbrier and we turned left into a hard-bottom coulee full of rainwater next to Coconut Bayou. The water come up to the hubcaps and Lizette wiggled and told Deputy Sid we on a ferryboat for sure, yeah.

There's this little shotgun shack up on brick piers with the tar paper rotting off it, stovepipe stub sticking out the side wall, no steps to the door, cypress knees coming up in the yard, egg cartons and water jugs floating around on the breeze. Deputy Sid leaned on the horn for maybe fifteen seconds until the front door opened and a woman look like a licorice stick stood there dressed in some old limp dress. He rolled down the window and asked if it's her son in the backseat. She stooped slow, squinted a long time. That Fernest, she said to the water. She sure wasn't talking to us. Sid stepped out on a walk board and told me to follow. I jacked up my legs, slid over all the junk, and brought out that satsuma with me. Can't leave this with Lizette, I told him. She loves these things. Sid took it from me, tossed it to her, and she caught that with one hand.

While he talked to the woman I looked in the house. All this while, my shoes was filling up with water. The first room had nothing but a mattress and a kerosene lamp on the floor and some bowls next to it. The walls was covered with newspaper to keep the wind out. In the second and last room, the floor had fell in. The whole place was swayback because the termites had eat out the joists and side beams. It didn't take no genius to tell that the roof rafters wasn't gonna last another year. A wild animal would take to a hole in the ground before he lived in a place like that.

Deputy Sid asked the woman did she know about the truck, and she said he was living in it. He turned to me and said, look around. You want me to put him in jail?

Hell yeah, I told him, and Sid looked at me hard with those oxblood eyes he got, trying to figure a road into my head. He told me if I file charges and put him in jail, that'd cost the parish. My tax money was gonna pay to feed him and put clothes on him. He said let him stay with his mamma. The old woman stooped down again, and Fernest stared at her like maybe she was a tractor or a cloud. I looked around again and saw that putting him in jail would be a promotion in life, yeah.

Sid took off the bracelets and walked him to the house. The old lady said he could stay. Then we left, that cruiser bottoming out and fishtailing from the yard, its mud grips digging down to the claypan. Back at my truck I threw all his stuff in a pile, old coats with cigarette holes burnt through, medicine bottles from the free clinic in town, dirty drawers I handled with a stick, fried chicken skin and bones, a little radio with leaking batteries. I put my key in but the engine didn't make a sound. When I opened up the hood, all I saw was a pile of a thousand sticks and three long otter-looking animals that took off for the woods. The sheriff's tow truck brought the thing back to my house and that was that. My wife took one look at it and one smell of it and told me it had to be gone. I already had one truck.

A rainy spell set in and the truck sank down in the backyard for a couple weeks with the crawfish chimneys coming up around it till I got a nice day and scrubbed it inside and out. Down at the home we got five new poor helpless folks from the government without nobody dying to make room for 'em, so another week passed before I could get to the hardware and buy me a nice orange FOR SALE sign.

Now this was when the priest kind of leaned back against the window frame and made a faraway smile and looked out to the rose garden Father Scheuter put in before they transferred him to Nevada. Priests try not to look you in the eye when you telling stuff. Scared maybe you won't tell it straight, or tell it all. So I told him straight that the second night that old truck was parked back out on the street wearing that sign, it got stole. I called up Deputy Sid direct this time and told him what happened. He said, you want me to look for that truck again? I told him hell yeah. He said, don't you got a truck already? I think that pomade Sid been smearing on his head all these years done soaked in his brain, and I told him that. He said, you got a nice brick house, a wife, three kids, and two cars. He said, you might quit at that. He said he didn't feel like burning fifty dollars gas looking for a forty-dollar truck. I told him I would talk to the sheriff, and he said okay, he'd look.

I wound up at the home helping out for music day, when Mr. Lodrigue brings his Silvertone guitar and amp to play songs the old folks recognize. Man, they love that rusty stuff like "As Time Goes By," "The Shrimp Boats Is A-Coming," and such 78 rpm tunes they can tap their feet to. I get a kick out of them people—one foot in the grave and still trying to boogie. And Mr. Lodrigue, who has wavery silver hair and kind of smoky gray eyes, he looks like Frank Sinatra to them old gals.

I got through with music day and went out to where my car was at behind the home, and there, big as a hoss, was Sid sitting on the hood of his muddy police car. I walked up and saw his arms was crossed. He said, I found it. I asked him where it was, and he said, where it was before. I said, you mean Fernest Bezue got it back in Prairie Amère? Man, that made me hot. Here I let him go free and he comes back on me like that. I cursed and spit twice. Deputy Sid looked at me like I was the thief. I asked him why didn't he haul him in, and he looked away. Finally, he said, he's alcoholic. That got me hotter. Like *I* could go down to Generous Gaudet's used-car lot drunk and steal me a car and somebody would let *me* off. Deputy Sid nodded, but he said, Simoneaux, you play with those old people like they your own *grandpère* and *grandmère*. You don't know what they done wrong in they time. I sat down next to him when he said that. The hood metal popped in and shook loose a thought in my head that kind of got me worried. It was about the folks in the home. Maybe I was nice to the old people because I was paid for that. Nobody was paying me to be nice to a drunk Bezue from Prairie Amère. I spit on the sidewalk and wondered if Deputy Sid's as dumb as he looks. Then I thought about Fernest Bezue out under the oaks, staring at the road. So I said, okay, get the tow truck to pull it in, and he says, no, I can't make a report because they'll pick him up.

What you think about that? I got to go get my own stole truck, yeah. That's my tax dollars at work.

The pot on the range gave a little jump like a steam bubble got caught under its bottom, and the priest turned and got us another cup. He was frowning a little now, like his behind's hurting in that hard-bottom chair, but he didn't say anything, still didn't look.

I went on about how I wanted to do the right thing, how me and Monette got out on the gravel past Prairie Amère, trying to beat a big thunderstorm coming up from the Gulf. When we got to where the truck was, the wind was twisting those live oaks like they was rubber. Monette stayed in the Buick and I walked up to the old red truck, and in the bed was Fernest, sitting down with a gallon of T&T port between his legs, just enjoying the breeze. You stole my truck again, I told him. He said he had to have a place to get away. He said it like he was living in a vacation home down on Holly Beach. He was staring up into the black cloud bank, waiting for lightning. That's how people like him live, I guess, waiting to get knocked down and wondering why it happens to them. I looked at his round head and that dusty nap he had for hair and started to walk off. But he had what was mine and he didn't work for it, and I figured it would do him more harm than good to just give him something for nothing. I said if he could get two hundred dollars he could have the truck. I didn't know where that come from, but I said it. He said if he had two hundred dollars he wouldn't be sitting in the woods with a five-dollar gallon of wine. I wondered for a minute where he wanted to go, but just for a minute, because I didn't want to get in his head. So I looked in the cab where he'd hot-wired the ignition, and I sparked up that engine. I pulled out his blankets and some paper bags of food and threw them in a pile. Then I jumped into the bed and put down the tailgate. I had to handle him like the real helpless ones at the home, he was that drunk, and even in that wind he smelled sour, like a wet towel bunched up in the trunk. I put the truck in gear and left him in the middle of that clearing under them oaks, him that wouldn't pay or work. When I rolled up on the road ahead of Monette in the Buick, the rain come like a water main broke in the sky. I looked back at Fernest Bezue and he was standing next to his pile of stuff, one finger in that jug by his leg and his head up like he was taking a shower. Then a big bolt come down across the road and the rain blew sideways like busted glass, and I headed back for town.

All that night I rolled like a log in the bed. I thought the weather would blow over, but the storm set on Grand Crapaud like a flat iron and dropped big welding rods of lightning almost till dawn. On the way to work I got tempted to drive back to Prairie Amère, but I didn't, and all that day I was forgetting to change bed linen and was slopping food on the old babies when I fed 'em. It took me a week to relax, to get so I could clean the truck some more without seeing Fernest looking up at the sky, waiting. I got it ready and put it on the lawn, but this time I took the battery and left it in the carport. Nobody looked at it for about a week. One morning Lizette, she kissed me bye and went out to wait for the bus. A minute later I heard the screen door open and Lizette said the old truck was trying to run. She said it was making running noise. So I went out and looked through the glass. Fernest Bezue was in there snoring on his back like a sawmill. When Lizette found out it was a big drunk man she yelled and ran for the house. She was scared, yeah, and I didn't like that. I opened the driver door and it took me five minutes to convince him I wasn't Mr. Prudhomme, a cane farmer he used to work for ten years back. When he sat up, his left eye capsized, then come back slow, and it was weak, like a lamp flame at sunup. He stared out the windshield at a place I couldn't see.

I told Fernest that I ought to pull him out and turn the hose on him for scaring my little girl like he did. He mumbled something I didn't catch, and I told him to get the hell away. But he just sat there in the middle of that old sprung bench seat like he half-expected me to get in and drive him somewhere to eat. Finally he told me the house had fell in and his mamma went off somewhere and didn't tell him. Man, I let him have it. Told him to stop that drink and get a job. He said that his drinking was a disease, and I told him yeah, it was a *lazy* disease. He said if he could help it, he would. That his daddy was the same way and died in a wreck. I told him he was in a slow wreck right now. I looked back at my house and them wilting camelias Monette planted under the windows. Then I told him if he could stay dry for a week I'd see if I could get him a mopping job at the rest home. He could save up and buy my truck. Then he put his head down and laughed. I can't stop, man, he said to me. That pissed me off so bad I went in and called the cops. After a while Claude come up in the town's cruiser, took one look at Fernest, then looked over where I'm standing by my Japan plum tree. How they made a gun belt skinny enough for that man, I don't know. He asked me, *mais,* what you 'spec us to do with him? Claude is real country, can't hardly talk American. He said Fernest can't do nothing to that truck he can arrest him for. If he steal it again the mayor gonna give him the town beutimfication award. I said arrest him, and I could see in Claude's eyes that nobody was on the night shift to keep a watch on Fernest down at that one-cell jail. Do something, I told him. He's scaring Lizette sleeping out here.

What Claude did is put him in the squad car, stop by Bug's café and buy him a ham sandwich, and drop him off at the town limits, by the abandoned rice mill buildings. They told me that when I called the station later on.

This was when the priest got up and stretched. He pointed to my cup and I shook my head. He fixed himself one more with lots of

cream, got a glass of water from the tap, and sat down again, looking at me just once, real quick.

That made me feel like I could keep going, so I told him how that
night and a couple nights more I couldn't sleep without dreaming
something about that no-good drunk. I mean, lots of people need
help. My one-legged uncle needs his grass cut, and I'd do it, but he
says he don't want me to mess with it. Says I got better things to do
with my time. Other people deserve my help, and that Fernest didn't
deserve nothing, yet when I went to sleep, there he was in my head.
When I read a newspaper, there he was in a group picture, until I
focused real good. But after a while he started to fade again, you
know, like before. I settled into business at the home, putting ointment on the bald men's heads, putting Band-Aids on the old ladies'
bunions so they can wear shoes, though there's no place for them to
walk to.

Then one morning here she come, in with three poor folks the
government paid us to take, Fernest's mamma, all dried up like beef
jerky. She had herself a stroke out on Mr. Prudhomme's farm, where
she was staying for free in a trailer, and one side of her wouldn't work.
I stayed away from her for three days, until it was time for Mr. Lodrigue, the music man, when everybody gets together in the big
room. I was just walking by to get Mr. Boudreaux his teeth he left
in the pocket of his bathrobe when her good arm stuck out and
grabbed my fruity little uniform. I didn't want to look in her eye, but
I did. She slid out her tongue and wet her lips. The mailbox is the
onliest thing standing, she told me. The house fall in. I told her it's
a shame and I wanted to walk away, but she got hold of my little
smock and balled it in her fist.

She told me his government check come in the mailbox, then he
walk five miles for the wine. She told me he was gonna die of the wine
and couldn't I help. I looked at her and I felt cold as a lizard. I asked
her why me. She said, you the one. I told her he was past all help.
He had the drinking disease and that was that. I pulled away and
went got old man Boudreaux's choppers, and when I come back I
saw her across the room, pointing at me with the one finger what
would still point. You the one, that finger said. I laughed and told

myself right then and there I wasn't going to help no black drunk truck thief that couldn't be helped.

The priest, he made to swat a mosquito on his arm, but he changed his mind and blew it away with his breath. I didn't know if he was still listening good. Who knows if a priest pays a lot of attention. I think you supposed to be talking to God, and the man in the collar is just like a telephone operator. Anyway, I kept on.

I told him how after work I used the phone out in the parking lot to call Deputy Sid to help me find Fernest. Yeah, I was ashamed of myself. I didn't know what I was going to do if Sid found him for me, but I had to do something to get the old lady's pointing finger out my head. I went home, and about a hour before sundown Deputy Sid pulled up in my front yard and I went out to him, carrying Lizette, who had a cold and was all leechy like a kid gets when she's feeling bad. Sid had him a long day. His pomade hair hung down like a thirsty azalea. He said we got to go out to Prairie Amère, and so I put my little girl down, got in the old truck, and followed him out.

We went through the pine belt and past the rice fields those Thibodeaux boys own, and by them poor houses in Tonga Bend, then we broke out into Prairie Amère, which is mostly grass and weed flowers with a live oak every now and then, but no crops. The old farmers say everything you plant there comes up with a bitter taste. All of a sudden the cruiser pulled off into the clover on the side of the road, so I rolled up behind. There ain't a thing around, and I walked up and Deputy Sid said empty land is a sad thing. He stretched and I could hear his gun belt creaking. I asked why we stopped and he pointed. Maybe a hundred yards in the field, eat up by weeds, was a little barn, the kind where a dozen cows could get in out the sun. We jumped the ditch and scratched through the buttonbush and bull tongue. Deputy Sid stopped once and sneezed. He said I told him to find Fernest and he did. It wasn't easy, but he did. He asked what did I want with him, and I said his mamma wanted me to check, but that wasn't it, no. It was the people at the home what made me do it. I was being paid to be nice to them. I wanted to do something without being paid. I didn't give a damn about some black truck thief, but I wanted to help him. I couldn't tell Deputy Sid this.

We got to the tin overhang on the barn, and we wasn't able to see much inside. The sun was about down. We stepped in and waited for our eyes to get used to the place. I could smell that peppery-sweet cypress. A building can be a hundred years old—if it's made of cypress, you going to smell that. Along the side wall was a wooden feed rack three feet off the ground, and sleeping in there was Fernest, his face turned to that fine-grain wall. Deputy Sid let out a little noise in his throat like a woman would make. He said Fernest was trying to sleep above the ground so the ants couldn't get to him. He said one time two years before, Fernest passed out on the ground and woke up in blazes with a million fire ants all over him like red pepper in a open wound. He stayed swole up for three weeks with hills of running pus all over him, and when his fever broke, he was half blind and mostly deaf in one ear.

I went over to the feed trough and shook him. He smelled strong and it took five minutes before he opened his eyes, and even in the dark you could see them glowing sick. I asked him was he all right and he asked me if I was his mamma, so I waited a minute for his head to get straight. Deputy Sid came close and picked up a empty bottle and sniffed it. I reached through the slats and bumped Fernest's arm and asked him why he drank so damn much when he knew it would kill him. He looked up at me like I was stupid. He said the booze was like air to him. Like water. I told him maybe I could get him in the home with his mamma, and he stared up at the tin roof and shook his head. I asked Sid if maybe his mamma could get him picked up and put in the crazy house, and Sid told me no, he's not crazy, he's just drunk all the time. The state thinks there's a difference. Fernest sat up in the trough, hay all stuck in his hair, and he started coughing deep and wet, like some of the old folks do at the home late in the evening. Night shift is scary because them babies sail away in the dark. Anyway, Fernest's face got all uneven, and he asked me what I wanted. That stopped me. I opened my dumb mouth just to see what would come out, and I told him that Deputy

Sid bought my truck and was giving it to him so he could stay in it sometime. I held up the key and gave it to him. He nodded like he expected this, like people wake him up all the time and give him cars. I looked at Sid and I could see a gold star on a tooth, but he stayed quiet. Then I told Fernest I knew he couldn't drive it, and I was going take the insurance off anyway, but he could use it to sleep out of the weather like he done before. He looked at Sid and reached out and gave him some kind of boogaloo handshake. In a minute I had the truck up in the grass by the barn, and I pulled the battery out just in case, and Deputy Sid brought me and the battery toward home. We pulled away from all that flat, empty land, and after about five miles Sid asked why I told Fernest *he* gave him the car. I looked at a tornado-wrecked trailer on the side the road and said I didn't want nothing for what I did. The cruiser rattled past the poor folks in Tonga Bend, and Sid tuned in a scratchy zydeco station. Clinton Rideau and the Ebony Crawfish started pumping out "Sunshine Can't Ruin My Storm," but I didn't feel like tapping my foot.

I went home and expected to sleep, but I didn't. I thought I did something great, but by two A.M., I knew all I did was give away a trashy truck with the floor pans rusting out and all the window glass cracked. I gave up the truck mostly to make myself feel good, not to help Fernest Bezue. And that's what I told the priest I come there to tell him.

The priest looked at me in the eyes then, and I could see something coming, like a big truck or a train. Then he leaned in and I could smell the soap on him. He told me there's only one thing worse than what I did. I looked at the linoleum and asked, what's that? And he said, not doing it.

I like to fell out the chair.

About a month later Fernest's mamma died in the night, and I called up Deputy Sid at dawn. He went out to look but he couldn't find Fernest nowhere. Sid brought his big black self to my house, and I saw him bouncing up my drive like he got music in his veins instead of blood. He got on a new khaki uniform tight as a drumhead, knife creases all over. He told me the liquor store past Coconut Bayou said they ain't seen him. The mailbox at the old place been eat down by termites. None of the farmers seen him. I said it's a shame we can't tell him about his mamma, and Deputy Sid looked at me sidewise and kissed his lips like he's hiding a smile. I told him to come inside, and Monette fixed us all a cup of coffee, and we sat down in the kitchen and cussed the government.

Summer come and the weather turned hot as the doorknob to hell. The old babies at the home couldn't roll around outside, so we had to keep 'em happy in the big room by playing cards and like that. I had to play canasta with six ladies who couldn't remember the rules between plays, so I would spend three hours a day explaining rules to a game we'd never finish.

I guess it was two months after Fernest's mamma passed. I got home and sat in my easy chair by the air condition when Lizette come by and give me a little kiss and said Deputy Sid wanted me on the phone. So I went in the kitchen, and he told me he's in his cruiser out at Mr. Thibaut's place in the north end of the parish, west of Mamou. He found Fernest.

I couldn't say nothing for half a minute. I asked him was he drunk, and he said no, he was way past that, and I said when, and he said he died about yesterday in the truck. I got a picture of Fernest Bezue driving that wreck on the back roads, squinting through the cracked windshield, picking his spot for the night. I told Deputy Sid I was sorry and he said, don't feel like that. He said, we couldn't do nothing for him but we did it anyway.

About the Author

Tim Gautreaux was born and raised in south Louisiana. His fiction has appeared in *The Atlantic Monthly, Harper's, GQ, Story, Best American Short Stories, New Stories from the South*, and elsewhere. The recipient of an NEA fellowship and a National Magazine Award, he has taught creative writing for many years at Southeastern Louisiana University.